Rodeo Heart

Copyright © 2025 by N

All rights reserved.
No part of this publication may be reproduced, distributed, or transmitted in any form or by any means, including photocopying, recording, or other electronic or mechanical methods, without the prior written permission of the publisher,

For permission requests, contact
natalietaylorauthor@gmail.com

The story, all names, characters, and incidents portrayed in this production are fictitious. No identification with actual persons (living or deceased), places, buildings, and products is intended or should be inferred.

Book cover by Natalie Taylor
Illustrations by Natalie Taylor

First edition 2025

Rodeo Hearts

Natalie Taylor

Content note

Disclaimer: This novel contains sexually explicit content. This means it is not suitable for under 18-year-olds.

If you still wish to read Rodeo Hearts without these scenes, I have decided to list the following below.

Chapter 15

Chapter 17

Chapter 25

Chapter 36

Bronc

noun

uk/brɒŋk/ us/brɑːŋk/

A wild or partly wild horse of the western US.

Rodeo Hearts

To my Nanna
The brightest star in the sky.
I love you.

Chapter 1

Blair Reynolds

The sound of the city is like a hum in the background of my life. Traffic. Laptops. Phones. Emails. Pings of messages. People striding in every direction, as if they know exactly where they are, and where they are going.

New York is a city of millions, always alive, never asleep. The streets are never empty – packed with people, energy, and movement at every turn. It's impossible to step outside and not be surrounded by the lively pulse of the city.

However, I have never felt more alone. Sitting in my spotless office, I look over the bustling city. The streetlamps act like stars, blinking against the sky, although it might seem pretty to some, I'm not pleased with my view.

The office lights glare off the glass, throwing sharp reflections of myself back at me. My ponytail is pulled tight, every strand in place – a perfect image, but it feels foreign, like I'm watching someone else in this glass cage. My clothes are perfectly pressed, and my stilettos gleam, reflecting the room's harsh lights.

Rodeo Hearts

Until Tomorrow.

Tomorrow, I will be setting foot back on the ranch as the official owner. After my grandfather passed, he left the ranch in my possession.

The text from mom is crystal-clear. They need me. As the only grandchild, it's my responsibility to get the place back up and on its feet.

My mom absence is deliberate, she wants nothing to do with Copper Creek. If I don't show up at that ranch tomorrow, I know for a fact the ranch will be sold off without my approval and demolished. My grandfathers legacy will be six feet under, along with him.

I didn't want anything to do with Copper Creek. My plan is simple: fix it enough to sell it, then walk away. Though, a wave of guilt washes over me at the thought of abandoning something my grandfather once cherished. The idea of selling the land without his approval makes my stomach churn. He would never have entrusted me with the ranch if he knew I intended to part with it.

The thought of his disapproval lingers in my mind, leaving a bitter taste in my mouth as my thumbs hover over the screen, nothing seems like the correct response.

Memories of my grandfather flood me – him teaching me to ride, to clean stables, the thrill of racing across the fields. Now, they feel distant, like fading photographs, as if his world no longer exists in mine. The nostalgia is bittersweet, tainted with guilt.

From the outside I seem put together. Po[cut] strong, boss women. However, on the inside[cut] empty and disconnected, as if the city keeps r[cut] and I'm stuck in place, watching from the o[cut] The faint buzz of my phone disrupts me fro[cut] thoughts, spinning in my chair, I grab the [cut] black screen and read the text that is from my[cut]

Mom: *I have taken care of everything, all yo[cut] to do is sign the paper, see you next w[cut] Wyoming.*

I release a ragged breath. It has almost k[cut] decade since I last set foot on Copper Creek [cut] Memories of my grandfather and my dad [cut] flooding back into my brain, as if the dam [cut] them back just demolished.

My grandfather, James Reynolds, talked [cut] Copper Creek like it was his first love. He [cut] stubborn and determined man, doing all th[cut] himself. Leaving before the sun rose and [cut] home till it was dark out. When his son – C[cut] Reynolds, my father – married my mothe[cut] moved in a small house on the land of the ra[cut] Growing up, I never saw the problems that sin[cut] behind closed doors. But when my father di[cut] car accident when I was fifteen, everything fe[cut] My mom and grandfather had a vicious fight[cut] didn't take long before she packed up our thir[cut] turned her back on Copper Creek – leavir[cut] behind, never to return.

I'm still staring at my screen when my mom's assistant, Sadie Brown, comes barrelling into my office. Although Sadie works alongside my mother, she is also my best friend and my only friend since moving to New York years ago.

Her fiery red hair is neatly pinned into a tight bun as she strides over, carrying a stack of heavy, bulky folders. With a sharp motion, she slams them onto my desk, causing it to shake and pens to scatter across the floor.

"Oops." She chuckles, reaching down to pick up the pen that had fallen at her feet. As she straightens, her smile fades into a frown when she notices my face. That's when I realise the tears that are streaming down my cheeks, smearing my makeup. I swipe at my eyes, coating black eyeliner across my hands. I focus on the open files, but Sadie's gaze weighs heavily on me. She silently takes a seat in the leather chair across from me, the squeak of the leather echoing in the quiet room as her uniform shifts "Are you okay?"

No.

"Yeah." My voice shakes an octave higher. I shuffle my files around on my desk, my hands are shaking, and my calm exterior is slipping. The more I sit at my desk, the more panic comes flying in.

How the hell am I going to do this? I haven't seen the ranch in almost a decade, and I've never worked a day on one in my life.

As if sensing I'm teetering on the edge of a mental spiral, Sadie places both of her pale hands gently over mine, which are trembling. My gaze snaps up

Sadie squeals, leaping from her chair and throwing her arms around me. She pulls me into a tight, comforting hug, laughter spilling from us like we'd just won the lottery. "You've been stuck in this office for too long, Blair. You deserve something more."

She pulls back, releasing me from her embrace, and grabs the bulky folders off my desk. As she sets them aside, she places a small envelope on the table, my name scribbled hastily across the front.

She starts to turn toward the door, then pauses and calls over her shoulder, "That was sitting at reception when I came in this morning. I didn't have a chance to give it to you earlier." She hesitates at the door, glancing back one last time.

"Oh, I almost forgot," she turns and faces me with a smirk plastered on her face, "Don't forget the cowboy rule." She winks.

"What cowboy rule?" I ask, raising an eyebrow.

"Take the hat, ride the cowboy."

I gasp, watching her retreating form, her laughter echoing down the hall as she heads toward the elevator. Damn Sadie and her undying love for country boys.

As I shove the remainder of my files in my desk drawers, the white envelope remains untouched. Grabbing it with shaking hands, I open the letter from the person I least expected.

Blair,

I know you're probably not expecting much when you get here, but I'll tell you this much: this place isn't what it used to be. Your grandfather had his ways, but he also had a vision for this land that's hard to walk away from. Whatever your plans are, you're going to need to decide fast – either fix it or sell it off. I'm not here to push you either way, but I've been holding this ranch together for years, and I'm not going to let it fall without *a fight, even if that means dragging you into it.*

Cole.

What the hell am I getting myself into.

Chapter 2

Cole Walker

I wipe the sweat from my brow and rest against the thick wooden fencepost I've just driven into the earth, the weight of the day pressing down on my shoulders.

As sun sets on the horizon, it shines a warm copper glow onto the ranch. The view is stunning here. Fields stretching as far as I can see, making it seem endless. The cattle spread out, grazing in the field. The small whispers of wind against the sea of green grass. The view was unforgiving. It gets under your skin like dirt under your nails, making you feel as if you are something bigger than yourself.

From the outside, Copper Creek looks like it might crumble with the next storm. The house sags under the weight of neglect, it's nails barely holding on. The fences slump weathered and crooked. The cattle are too thin, the horses restless, untamed, just like the land itself.

But if you look closer, if you dig into the heart of this place, you'll understand why I stay – why I can't walk away, even when everything seems broken. It's not just land to me. It's my blood, my father's sweat, and the echoes of a past that refuse to fade.

My father – Jesse Walker – worked alongside James Reynolds for almost three decades. James

mentored my father, teaching and showing him why he loves Copper Creek so much. Then, when I turned thirteen, my father taught me everything I know about maintaining this ranch. From the simple jobs to the most challenging, my father mentored me, as James Reynolds mentored my father. That's why it feels like home. The smell of the air reminds me of my father, warm with hints of pine and cedar.
I think of him then, the strong and knowledgeable man with wise words which echo in my mind.
"The land would speak if you listened."
I never truly knew what it meant, until now. I hear the cries of the wind. The groaning of the old stables. The scuttle of the dirt, blowing dust onto the grass. The ranch is speaking, I can hear the protests to not give up. To continue to work hard. That this will all be worth it in the end.
That's why I won't let this ranch get out of my tight grasp. This ranch has deep rooted history that goes back decades. You would need to be a damn idiot to let this go.
That's why I sent Blair that letter.
I knew Blair Reynolds since a teenager. She was a bright kid, with dreams that were too big for this small ranch. I never understood the reason why she left. Yet, the rumours spread like a match on dry hay. I never listened or paid much attention to them. All I needed to know was that Blair and her mother abandoned the ranch when we needed them most. I picked up their slack, working long hours and putting my blood, sweat and tears into Copper Creek, trying to keep the legacy afloat.

Though, when Blair arrives, she is going to see Copper Creek is drowning in some dark water I don't think she is ready to swim in.

A bitter taste fills my mouth. The thought of Blair trying to sell off the legacy of this ranch makes my insides burn. I have worked *too* hard and *too* damn long for this place to be shipped off and destroyed. The weight of the years, and the work my father and I put into this place for Blair's grandfather must not be wasted.

It's not just about the cattle and the horses. It's the determination. The responsibility. The commitment. The effort, and the love that has been seeded through the soil on this land.

I am going to make one thing clear when Blair Reynolds arrives at Copper Creek. This land isn't just a place, and not just hers. This land is mine. And if Blair thinks she's just going to waltz in and take it from me, she's got another thing coming. I'll fight for it with everything I've got.

Driving my truck into my local small town, Misty Pines, I can't seem to shake the thoughts of Blair Reynolds. I never paid much attention to her when we were teenagers, but now the urge to look her up, find her, is too strong to ignore. What does she look like now? Does she still wear those flowy skirts and cowboy boots? Or has she completely changed? Does she even remember me?

My jaw clenches. I have never thought of Blair Reynolds once in the past nine years, so why the hell is she in my head so damn much? I crank up the radio in my truck, the old classic country songs blasts through the speakers, yet the thoughts of Blair don't disappear until I arrive at my towns local bar, *The Tipsy*. Parking my truck to the closest space to the door, I hop out and make my way into the busy bar.

It's a Friday night, so as expected it's fucking *packed*. Throngs of people line the bar, with cowboy hats and boots. It's easy to tell who here are tourists, and who is a legitimate rancher. Some of the women are wearing tacky pink hats with feathers on the top, and the men, wear some sort of ridiculous tassel tunic, as if they are in the 1800s. I scan the bar, looking for a particular group.

The Tipsy is a weathered, wood-panelled bar on the outskirts of Misty Pines. The warm, amber glow of the lights creates a cozy atmosphere, while the old jukebox hums country classics in the corner, blending with the clink of glasses and the sounds of laughter. It's a place that feels like a second home to me, a retreat from the ranch where I can just relax and unwind.

Although it's busy, my height adds an advantage, allowing me to scout over people's heads, spotting the group of guys tucked in the corner.

I make my way through the crowd, trying to squeeze past a group of young women. One of them deliberately leans back into me, as if she tripped and fell. With a dramatic gasp, she spins around, tossing her fake ice-blonde hair right into her friend's glass of wine, leaving her with an annoyed, sour expression.

"Well, well, well," she hums, "Look who it is, Cole Walker." She smirks.

Don't get me wrong, I don't mind a little female attention now and then, but not from her. Isabelle Bishop is one girl you don't want to mess with. She has been chasing after every rancher in Misty Pines, marking them off as if it was her own shopping list. Though, she has yet to make her 'mark' on me. She can't stand the fact I don't want her. She thinks she will crack me any day now, however it will never happen. With a small nod of my head, I do my best to give the nicest greeting possible.

"Isabelle." I offer a tight nod, trying to keep my irritation in check. She bursts into laughter, as if I'd just cracked the world's best joke. Her high-pitched cackle grates on my nerves, making my ears ring.

"What brings you here on a Friday night? Looking for some fun?" She bites her lip, causing her cherry red lip stick to smudge all over her teeth. I try my hardest not to cringe.

"No, I'm here for a boy's night." I nod my head over to the group of guys tucked tightly in the corner, all laughing and sharing drinks, like a family.

"Oh." Isabelle smirk drops for a beat but then quickly recovers, pushing her chest out so it grazes my forearm. It doesn't appeal to me in the slightest.

"Well, if you ever get sick of your boy's night and want to have some fun, you know where to find me." She winks.

"Sure thing." I say with a nod and march my way over to my table as fast as I can. I think I can hear her calling my name again, but it doesn't matter, I respectfully want nothing to do with the girl.

Trying to avoid any unwanted attention. I keep my head down and my hat low, until finally I get to my table and slide into the booth, crushing my best friend, who is also my big brother, Milo. I lean back in my chair and release a heavy breath.

I'm exhausted. I feel the weight of this week catching up on me. My boots are well worn to the point there are holes in them. My hands are callused and look dirty, no matter how hard I scrub, the soil never disappears. My muscle ache. It's getting hard to keep up with the ranch, Milo helps when he can, but he is too busy, out of town every weekend, riding bulls and chasing the high.

I study my friends at the table. Milo is necking back his whiskey like it's water. My other friend, Travis Maxwell, sits quietly watching NFL highlights on the flatscreen mounted on the wall. And Eli Sullivan, sits straight back, a glass half full of whiskey, with a small grin plastered on his dark face.

As normal as we all appear, there's an undeniable tension in the air – one that even Eli can't seem to shake. Since the news of Blair's arrival, the unease lingers, simmering beneath the surface of our group. We are all sitting in uncomfortable silence. I quickly order a beer, hoping it will settle me down and make me forget about the women who is about to shift my world on its axis.

In the corner of my periphery, I see my brother Milo give a look at Eli. Trying to signal him to speak first. Eli shakes his head, moving his hand underneath his chin, as if he just beheaded himself. I roll my eyes; *these guys are fucking idiots.* Finally, Milo plucks the courage to speak first.

"So, do you think she will show up in some pricey city girl outfit? Or do you think she is ready to get stuck in and get her hands dirty." A playful smirk falls upon Milo's lips.

My jaw clenches, my mind instantly goes back to the infamous Blair Reynolds. She is the granddaughter, the only heir. Her coming back is complicated. She isn't just the kind that left the ranch almost a decade ago, she is the *sole* heir to the ranch. She doesn't know one thing about the place she is inheriting, the ranch is nothing like it was when she was a kid. She will think it's better to sell Copper Creek off. The place is rundown, and the debt is mounting up, the percentage of her selling the place is becoming higher and higher. The thought gnaws at me, a bitter ache settling deep in my gut.

"You going to say something, Walker? Or are you going to stare at my face the whole night?" Eli speaks with his deep voice. As if sensing I am starting to lose my mind, he frowns and says, "You look like a man that's got a lot on in his mind."

I bring my cool beer to my lips, giving me a chance to think of what to say. Placing it back on the worn wooden table, I start to peel the label off the bottle, when I say, "I'm just think about Copper Creek. How much is going change when *she* arrives."

My brother snorts a laugh and leans back in his chair, his eyes sparkling, "I say, you seem more worried about the girl's arrival than the ranch." He lifts a brow. Milo's words hit me like a bucking bull, knocking the wind out of me. I hadn't thought about it that way, but now, I can't shake the feeling that maybe I care more about Blair's return than I care to admit.

My brother stares at me, as if he just exposed my deepest secrets. I straighten in my chair and say, "Blair isn't just a city girl... she is like family. Her grandfather meant something to me, if it weren't for him, I wouldn't know one thing about handling a ranch," I continue to rip the bottle label, exposing the inside of the glass, like I'm exposing my thoughts to my closet's friends, "I promised James Reynolds and dad I would keep this place going."

"You think Blair would be okay that? With you running the place? Keeping it going? The girl has never set foot on the ranch in a decade?" Eli grimaces.

My jaw hardens "I don't give a shit about what Blair thinks, it's up to her if she wants to sell it off or keep it. That ranch has been in their family for generations, but it has been a long fucking time since they even cared about it."

"Well, if she does end up selling it, you can always come and work for me on Redwood, we could always do with an extra hand." Eli sighs.

"Thanks bud."

"You never know Cole; She might surprise you. She is family, right? She might know a lot more about that land than you think." Travis finally speaks up.
Maybe my friends are right, maybe I'm not giving Blair enough credit. Maybe she is a different person than the light I painted her in. Except that doesn't change the fact that the ranch is tumbling down a steep slope. Just because Blair is family, doesn't stop the fact that the land is starting to fade, and the ranch is dying.
Milo coughs, "Let's not get ahead of ourselves brother. The city girl might be tougher than we think. Or she might decide the place is too much for her and sell it off to the highest bidder."
"That's the last thing I want to happen." I mutter down to my boots.
"Whatever happens Cole, we are all here for you." Eli speaks softly.
The door to The Tipsy swings open, the bell above it jingling in its old, familiar tune. The evening light pours in, casting long shadows over the bar, but my eyes are already locked on the figure in the doorway – the one person I never wanted to see.
It was *her*. Blair Reynolds.
Clad in smart business attire, Blair looks out of place. Although as her eyes snap of mine, it's clear she isn't here to be pampered, she is here for negotiations.
"Well, well, I guess now is the time to find out what this city girl is really like?" Milo nudges my shoulder, wide eyed.

Blair steps forward, her heels clicking against the floor, her gaze still set upon me. As she gets to our table, she eyes all four of us and says, "Cole Walker?"

Setting my beer on the table, I stare up at her, "That's me."

"Blair Reynolds," She holds out her small, slim hand. A hand that has never seen a day of work on a ranch. There is nothing to deny now; the next chapter of the ranch is going to begin. Whether I like it or not. "I'm the one who inherited this mess."

I take her hand in mine. The contrast is stark. My hands are tan and rough, looking filthy in comparison to her soft, delicate, manicured ones. Yet they fit perfectly, almost too perfect.

I grip her hand firmly, feeling her soft skin against the calloused roughness of mine. This isn't going to be easy. But I'm not about to let her take this from me without a fight. I stand, my six-foot-two frame towering over her, my voice low and steady. "Let's talk."

And so, it began.

Chapter 3

Blair

When I stepped off the plane into Wyoming, I never realised how much I'm not used to this. The quiet. The vast open spaces. The lack of noise.
It feels like I'm in a movie. As if I'm *Hannah Montana*, living a double life. Switch the microphone for a briefcase, and now, you got a similar picture.
The world seems different in Misty Pines. It's slowed paced, as if the planet took an exhale and a new breath of air is being taken in.
However, my grip on the steering wheel doesn't loosen, as I smell the scents of the earth underneath me, thick and damp. The small breeze of the air blows through the crack in my window, I can feel the weight of the world slamming down on my shoulders, with every gust of wind, the heavier I feel.
The road underneath my tires shift, I glance up from my windscreen to spot the soft illuminated glow of *The Tipsy*. It's the only bar in town – so I have been told – the run-down wooden structure doesn't look like much; still, it is clear to the locals it means everything.
I take a left into the parking lot and kill the engine. I didn't plan to come here tonight but when I read that letter from Cole, I realised how much the ranch meant to him.

As the heir to the ranch, it's my decision on what to do with it. Selling it is the best option for me, yet all I can feel is uncertainty. I have never owned a ranch, I have never worked on a ranch, I don't care enough about the ranch. Yet, the future for Copper Creek rests shakily in the palm of my hands. If Cole really wants to keep the place up and running, he is going to need to do *a lot* of convincing.
Releasing a heavy sigh, I look through my windscreen. The bar is packed, throngs of people walk in and out the door in western style outfits. The neon sign of '*BEER*' pressed up against the window flickers. There is no going back now, if I plan to sell Copper Creek, then I need to try and get the locals to like me, starting with Cole Walker.

Pushing the front door open, The Tipsy is much different to the sleek polished bars and fancy cocktails in New York. The air smells of sweat, beer, and leather, and the wooden floors creak under every step. This place is worn, but there's something about it – something real – that feels like it's been lived in for decades.
The walls are painted a rich, deep blue, adorned with a collection of old black-and-white photographs. Each frame tells a story – of cowboys, bull riders, and sprawling ranches. Though the images have faded over time, they remain vivid enough to capture the essence of each moment, preserving their history in silent detail.

The low murmurs of conversation hit my ears, as I continue to scan the room. I spot a group of cowboys tucked tightly in the corner, each of them staring wide eyed at me. As I examine over each face, my eyes snap to a familiar pair of brown ones. *Cole Walker.*

I make my way over. My heels click loudly against the wooden floor, no doubt drawing attention from others. Though, I don't care.

Getting on Cole's good side is my priority at this moment. If I want to sell the Copper Creek and leave this town forever, I need to be in his good books. He is my ticket to never seeing this place again.

Standing as confident and as tall as I can, I speak out over the group of men, "Cole Walker?"

The man with familiar dark eyes, places his empty beer bottle on the table, "That's me."

"Blair Reynolds," I hold out my hand, trying hard to not make it shake with the bundle of nerves in my stomach. "I'm the one who inherited this mess."

I'm making my intentions clear. I am the last person who wanted this place.

When Cole places his rough large hand in mine, I feel like I have been electrocuted. I feel waves of energy flow in my fingertips and straight into my heart, making the steady beat, pick up the pace.

It's hard to deny that Cole Walker is an attractive man. His dark eyes look soulless, staring intensely, curiously, into my blue ones. His dark hair looks black in the dimly lit bar, small curls peak out beneath his hat, looking soft but untamed. His strong jaw is

lined with a dark five o'clock shadow and his broad shoulders strain against his dark flannel shirt.
He stands, towering over my five, eight frame, "Let's talk." His body brushes past mine, but before we have left the table, the man who was sitting next to Cole speaks up.
"Well, well, it was about time you finally showed up." He smirks, with the same dark eyes and dark hair, it's easy to tell that this man is Cole's brother.
"Milo." Cole's voice is deep, warning his brother to watch what he says. "Don't start."
Milo leans back in his chair, his smirk wide as he teases, "You sure kept us waiting after your granddaddy passed, darlin'."
His directness throughs me off, with a tight-lipped smile I reply with, "Sorry to disappoint, I didn't mean to make you wait that long." My mind races, trying to stay focused as Cole Walker's presence presses behind me. My heels click too loudly on the worn wood, and every glance feels like a weight on my chest. I'm out of place here – too polished, too city-girl, in a world that feels foreign.
The bar quiets for a heartbeat. Conversations pause, eyes shifting to me like I'm the next big spectacle. The weight of their stares presses me down, and I feel a knot tighten in my stomach. Cole's gaze is the hardest to bear – intense, unwavering, as if he's already judging me.
A deep chuckle, sounds behind me, I turn around to look at Cole, he is smiling, but it doesn't quiet meet the eyes, "I'm sure we can find something to keep

you entertained, *sweets*." His voice drops low, heavy with a challenge that lingers in the air.

His dark eyes lock onto mine, and for a moment, I feel like he's seeing right through me. It's not just the lost city girl – there's something else in his gaze. A challenge. Or maybe it's just the nerves twisting in my gut.

The scrape of glass on a wooden table disrupts my thoughts, looking to my right, Milo slides over a full bottle of beer, and says "You might need that, some liquid courage." He smirks.

I don't grab the bottle, I'm not planning to stay here long, "Thanks, but no thanks, I'm just here to see what's left of the family legacy." I voice.

I feel Cole's eyes burn into the side of my face, turning back to him, his eyes narrow, like he isn't convinced about my intensions for the ranch. "You might find more to what you expect." His tone softens ever so slightly.

I give my head a hesitant, small nod. Am I to believe what this guy says? The ranch has been neglected for years, no thanks to me and my mother. Was it even salvageable? What does Cole see that makes the land worth saving?

Tension filled the air. It felt thick and muggy. Like fog that was so thick, you couldn't see your own hand. There is a pull too, something I cannot place.

"Let's talk about the ranch then." My voice sounds confident, I'm ready to face this challenge. Cole takes a step forward, the scent of wood and soap, fill my nose. His face is dark when he says,

"You are going to have to do a lot more than just talk, Blair, Copper Creek... it needs a *lot* of work."

"I'm up for the challenge," I say, forcing my voice steady. "I've worked hard before. I can handle this." But inside, uncertainty gnaws at me. Can I really bring this place back to life? Can *I*?

"You better be ready," Cole's voice is quiet, it's hard to hear over the loud country music. "You might be staying a lot longer than you planned."

I inhale a deep breath, I'm not just here to settle an estate. I'm here to claim my future. Whatever that might be.

After my conversation with Cole, I head out The Tipsy towards my car. I'm so drained. After the flight to Wyoming, the five-hour drive to Misty Pines, and the conversation with Cole Walker and his rowdy cowboys, finding a pillow that I can rest my head on sounds heavenly.

The parking lot is cloaked in darkness, the rows of vehicles stretching out before me. I know I parked near the back, so I head in that direction, my eyes scanning for my car. Despite the town being remote and quiet, a sense of unease creeps over me. My grip on my bag tightens, and I quicken my pace.

My heart begins to pound in my chest at the sudden sound of heavy thuds of boots echoing behind me, their rhythm matching my frantic steps. His breath, deep and laboured, fills the silence, and I can't help but quicken my pace. The sound of my heels clicking against the pavement blends with the steady approach of those boots, the noise amplifying the unease creeping down my spine.

I spot the familiar outline of my car, parked beneath a dim streetlight.

Just a little farther. If I can reach it faster…

I push myself into a full sprint, my heart racing. But then, one of my heels flies off my left foot, throwing me off balance. Just as I'm about to crash face-first into the dark concrete, a large hand grabs my arm and yanks me upright. My back collides with his chest, and for a moment, everything stills.

My first instinct is to punch the guy in the face. So that's what I do. I yank my arm out of his tight grasp and with my other, clock him in the face. My fist meets his flesh, his face snaps to the side with a satisfying crunch.

Though, when my brain finally catches up with my instincts, and I freeze. *Holy shit*, I just punched Cole Walker in the face. The man I *need* to convince to let me sell the ranch.

"What the FUCK, Blair!" Cole roars, clutching his jaw. Blood trickles down his chin as his eyes burn with a mixture of surprise and anger.

"I'm – I'm so sorry!" My words trip over each other, my face flushed with embarrassment. "I didn't know it was you! I thought – I thought you were some creep from the bar, and when I heard those footsteps, I panicked and—"

"Jesus Christ." Cole spits blood onto the ground, shaking his head, his hand still cupped over his jaw. "You've got one hell of a left hook, sweets."
Cole releases my arms, his eyes lingering for a moment as he looks me over. He smirks at the sight of me teetering awkwardly on one heel in the gravel, and for the first time, I feel like the joke's on me. He walks away without a word, and I expect him to leave – then, to my surprise, he picks up my discarded shoe.

His hands are warm as he kneels in front of me, the air thick between us as he slides the heel back onto my foot, his touch sending a strange shiver up my spine.

With a small cough Cole rises and stares deeply at my face. Crossing my hands over my chest I say, "Why the *hell* were you chasing me in a dimly lit parking lot?"

Cole huffs out a breath and places his hands on his hips. "I thought... I thought you might not have anywhere to stay for the night."

Huh? Is Cole Walker actually concerned about where I'm going to sleep tonight? The thought that maybe, just maybe, that cold exterior of his is just a façade.

As if reading my thoughts Cole's warmth turns icy, his jaw hardens, and his brows pull down. "The Misty Pine Festival's coming up, so all the hotels are going to be packed. Honestly, you're better off staying at the ranch with me – at least for a few days. You say you want to help with the work, so... what's the harm?"

His voice softens for a moment, a flicker of something unreadable passing through his dark eyes.

As much as I hate to admit, Cole is right. I can't afford to drive back and forth from the ranch every day and night and if hotels are being booked up, I guess I have no other option.

"Fine, I'll stay at the ranch." The words leave my mouth with more distaste than I intend, and the thought of rooming with Cole sends a strange chill down my spine.

Cole smirks, his eyes narrowing. "Great. Pack up. I'll give you a ride over... though, I'm not sure how I feel about having a city girl under my roof."

"But, what about my car?"

"I'll get Milo to bring it down tomorrow, hurry up sweets."

"Don't call me that."

"Whatever you say... *sweets*." He gives me a boyish smile letting me get a glimpse of his pearly white teeth.

This is going to be a *long* couple of weeks.

Chapter 4

Cole

"I can drive myself perfectly fine to the ranch, I don't need you to babysit me." Blair stands in front my truck, with her arms crossed and her chin tilted up. She looks a lot less like the helpless city girl I imagined her to be. It baffles me how different she is now, compared to when she was a teen. The shy girl I once knew, had now turned into a hellbent women. "You think I'm babysitting you?" I raise an eyebrow, and a smirk plays on my lips. Before she even replies, I open my truck door and tilt my head, "Get in the truck." After a beat of silence, she reluctantly slides in the passenger seat. I slam the door, round the truck, and jump in, twisting the key until the engine roars to life. The sound cuts through the quiet like a punch to the gut.

I don't like Blair. She walks onto my land, my territory, like she owns the place, and starts making decisions about its future as if I don't have a say. It's infuriating. The nerve of her, thinking she can waltz in and call the shots.

Putting the truck in reverse, I drive out my space, and down the road towards Copper Creek. The engine revs as the wheels kick up dirt. I see Blair grab the handle above her head, her knuckles turning white from how hard her grip is. As we make our way out of town the air becomes thick with silence – uncomfortable, suffocating silence.

In my periphery, I can see Blair glancing at me from time to time. Although the drive is short, it feels like we have been in this truck for hours. She glances at me again, her dark ocean eyes heating the side of my face. My jaw clenches and my voice breaks the silence.

"So, what is your plan?" My voice feels gruff. "You plan to sell the ranch off to the highest bidder? Or do you plan to keep it? Make something out of it?" I sound desperate. I want to know what this girl has planned up her sleeve.

I feel her stiffen beside me, I glance over finding her gaze locked on the road ahead of me, thinking of the answer to all our questions, "I'm not sure yet." Blair says tightly. "But I'm not here to discuss it with you, I couldn't care less about what you have to say."

I grimace, she's right. She can do whatever the fuck she wants to Copper Creek. She doesn't need my approval. The power she has is scary. I stare out to the long dirt road illuminated by my headlights, the darkness outside seems endless.

"I don't need your help. I can figure everything out."

I chuckle darkly, "That city attitude of yours? It's not going to cut it here, Blair." I keep my tone low, more measured. "Things don't get fixed overnight. Maybe it's time to listen to the folks who know how to make it work out here."

I can see her becoming frustrated. Her hands are curled in tight fists, the heavy groove in her forehead and the sneer plastered on her lips. Yet, when I look in her eyes, all I see is guilt.

As we near the ranch, the dark outline of the porch comes into view. The ranch stands in front of Blair like a reminder of everything she hasn't done, and everything she will face.

She glances her eyes towards me, I snap my gaze back towards the house. My jaw tightens, I'm not going to make this easy for her.

But she isn't going to make this easy either.

The distance between us was eminent. Anything I say rubs her the wrong way; I couldn't blame her for it. I had this way to get under her skin, make her feel more lost as she does right now.

I glance back towards her; her gaze is now shifted towards the house. Though, she isn't quite *looking* at it. She may be staring straight ahead, but her lips are pressed together in a tight line and her eyes are narrowed. Maybe she is wondering how fast she could get back to her fancy office. I couldn't guilt her for it, this place is a far cry from anything she has known.

"Well, we are here." Even though she doesn't care, I didn't know much else to say. It wasn't a great greeting.

Unbuckling her seat belt, Blair hops out the truck. She pulls open the back door and retrieves her suitcase. Stepping out the truck myself, we make our way over to the house. The only thing that can be heard is our footsteps crunching against the gravel and the ringing of the crickets. The night is cool, and for the first time, I see Blair shiver.

The porch light casts a soft, yellow glow over Blair, her shadow flickering behind her. One side of her face is bathed in warm light, the other half swallowed by darkness as she faces me. I glance at her from the corner of my eye, the soft porch light casting shadows on her face. Her chestnut hair catches the faint glow, and for a split second, her blue eyes lock with mine. I have to look away, the weight of her stare lingering longer than I'd like.

Though, it doesn't stop me from thinking about the light dusting of freckles that trails across her skin, down her neck, and no doubt onto her chest. Her lips, soft and pink, seem to draw me in, adding to her undeniable beauty. And her –

No. Stop.

This girl wants to sell off something you worked so hard to maintain. Don't let it slip through your finger.

The more we stand in the porch staring at each other, the more Blair becomes annoyed. Her arms are crossed, and her face becomes stormy. I'm wasting her time. *Perfect.*

To lighten her mood I say, "Don't get too attached, the place isn't exactly up to your fancy office standards." However, my joke becomes more bitter than I attended.

"I'm not here to play your game Cole, I'm here to look at the place, hurry it up." She snaps.

"Right... here we go." I open the door; it creaks on its hinges – another thing that isn't perfect – and step inside. The house looms ahead, dark, and heavy with the weight of time. Blair hesitates behind me, her footsteps still. I can almost feel the battle playing out in her mind – turn around, head back to her comfortable office, her cushy chair. Or stay, confront the history she's tied to and make the hard choices. I almost want her to walk away.

Option one seems the best choice in my opinion, I would never need to see her again and continue to live my days fixing up this ranch.

However, to my surprise she takes one big step into the house, dragging her suitcase behind her. I lead her deeper into the house, as if I'm dragging her further and further into the mess. When we get to a set of stairs, I start to make my way up, but Blair doesn't follow.

"You have to go up," I nod my head towards the stairs "The bedrooms and bathroom is up there." I point vaguely up the stairs. She didn't move.

"I'm not staying here, Cole." She snaps. Blair crosses her arms, her jaw clenched. Every inch of her posture is a barrier, as if the air around her has thickened into something unapproachable. There's no mistaking it – she's already building walls, and I can feel the cold from here.

"Fine. Suit yourself." I scoff. "But I recommend that you rest up, you have a big day tomorrow. Decisions to make. *Work* to do."

She stares at me for a beat, her blue eyes flashing with frustration and fury. I have almost made her snap, the walls she built threaten to crumple, as she fights the urged to challenge me harder. Finally, she mutters "I'll be upstairs."

She brushes past me; the smell of tangerines and lemons fill my nostrils. Continuing to climb the stairs, I watch her defeated form. She leaves me with dust and the tension of the night in the air.

This wasn't how I pictured my night to go. I was never meant to feel this way. To feel the need to help Blair or make her feel comfortable in a place she can't remember. There is something about Blair that gets me, I think about pushing past her barriers, to see who she truly is. Maybe it was the glimpse I caught when she stepped into a place she already saw as a lost cause, or maybe it was the thought of the ranch burning to nothing, simply because she couldn't be bothered to care.

Life isn't easy at Copper Creek. It's hard work and determination. It's putting blood, sweat and tears. It's about making mistakes. Blair needs to learn and face that, just like the rest of us.

Still standing on the stairs, I lean back against the railing and listen. The silence is deafening. I can hear the house creaking and groaning from the combined weight of Blair and me.

The silence doesn't feel like a win or a loss – it feels like something more. This isn't just about the legacy anymore. Maybe it's about *her*. The way she challenges me, and the way I'm drawn to her despite it all. There's something about her – something I can't quite put my finger on. But I know this for sure: Blair Reynolds is a game I can't afford to play.

Chapter 5

Blair

The sounds of the birds chirping and the distant creeks from the house, jolt me awake. Although the curtains are closed, the ascending sun casts a warm glow throughout the room, highlighting the heavy dust particles floating in the air.
The unfamiliar surroundings cause a swell of panic in my chest.
This isn't my life, this isn't room. It's a dream.
I roll over in the bed, the lumpy mattress digging into my back, the clumpy pillow doesn't support my head, my neck is stiff. It's nothing like my deluxe life at home. The scratchy blankets on top of me swallows me in discomfort, a reminder of how out of place I am. I can smell the dust lingering in the air, the smell of the wooden floor. The stillness of the house is something I'm not used to. The quiet makes me feel isolated.
It's only now I realise where I truly am. That this is not a dream, this is reality. The sleep has worn off from my eyes and now I can get a good glimpse of what my life is going to start looking like.
The faded wallpaper, the old furniture and the creaky floor are all going to be a constant part of my life for now on. Nothing about this house feels like a legacy. I feel like I'm holding up the weight of this building in

my own two hands. I can see my arms are buckling, shaking under the force, then it all comes crashing down on top of me.

Should I just pack up my shit and go? Or should I stay for my grandfather's sake, to try and see what he really saw in this disaster?

Throwing the itchy blankets off me and stepping out my bed, I creep over to the window and peel back the curtain. The view is somehow beautiful. The fields feel vast and endless, the sun breaking through the green hills in the background and the trees shake from the little summers breeze. It's gorgeous in a rough, wild way. I can feel the land pulling me in, like a magnet. This place is serene, nothing to what I'm used to in the city. The stillness is so different, I feel like the world has stopped, or maybe just me.

I take a step back from the window and turn back towards my room. It's clear that this ranch is debt ridden and has been neglected for years. I think of the tasks I must do, the job I need to commit to, they all seem impossible. It's only so long that I can pretend to know what I'm doing. The weight on my chest becomes heavier and heavier with each breath I inhale.

I shake the thought from my head and get dressed. I had to put my life on hold for this place, I had to walk away from my relationships and my job. If I don't manage to revive Copper Creek, I have my old life I can get back to.

But what about Cole?

A wash of guilt splashes over me, part of me wants to say fuck him, he has been nothing but an arrogant ass since my arrival. Yet another part of me feels guilty for letting him slave away, day after day, whilst I have been living my life happily, not caring about a place he loves so much.

I pull on a pair of jeans, mind still racing. When grandfather left me the ranch in his will, it was an unexpected responsibility. I don't want this life; I don't even know if I will be capable enough to fix the mess he left behind.

My thoughts are disrupted by the faint sounds of Cole's truck engine outside, I head down the stairs, the steps groaning under my weight. The darkness that swallowed house last night has completely disappeared. It's now transformed into a big open plan home; the kitchen looks out into the fields of lush green grass. The wooden countertops are remarkably clean considering the dust lingering in all corners of the house. Brass handles line each drawer, and the cupboard are painted a beautiful shade of dark sapphire blue. The living room has worn leather couches, a small coffee table sits proudly in the centre, with a pile of books stacked messily on top. Surprisingly, there is no TV.

The engine roars closer towards the house. Moving towards the living room window, I peek outside to find Cole pulling up towards the drive. I see his door open, his boots hitting the dirt, and his cowboy hat that peaks above the large door.

Something stirs inside me when I look at Cole from afar, I don't know if it's irritation, wonder, or maybe something deeper. I still don't know where I stand with Cole, or why I feel this pull towards him. It could be because Cole is a hard worker – like me. Or perhaps that he isn't the same boy I used to remember as a teenager. I have distant memories of Cole Walker when I was a teen, not once have I ever considered him rude or cold when he'd vaguely talk to me, so what has changed?

Whatever it is, thinking of Cole makes me want to be ready. The last thing I want is to show how unprepared I am as I feel.

Striding out onto the porch, I squint my eyes against the sun. As the it beginnings to rise, I feel the air become hot and thick. The view from the outside of the house is a lot different from looking out of windows.

Being outside makes it feel more real, it makes me feel uneasy, the vast open spaces and empty fields is nothing to what I'm used to at home.

The heels of my shoes crunch against the dirt as I step off the porch, trying to take in my surroundings in even more. The land looks like it's in despair, nothing to what I felt looking out the window. I have never been a rancher. It will take a miracle for me to fix the place, make it look buyable. Debt is piling up. The legacy is dying a slow painful death.

My mind drifts back to Cole. He has been managing simply fine in this disaster, every day, week, and years. He must understand how to manage everything, how to play the part to get it done. Yet, trusting him – and his way of life – isn't going to be easy.

My eyes pull away from the view of the empty land and fall upon Cole. His movements are smooth and fluid, as he makes his way over to the porch. The bright glare from the sun reflects around his body, creating a silhouette for my vision. It's hard not to admire him. Cole fits in at Copper Creek, I do not – I'm the puzzle piece that doesn't fit, no matter how hard you try. Though, I'm not letting that entertain me. I'm not here to get distracted by a man who is out of my depth.

"Morning." He speaks in a deep voice.

"Good morning."

"Sleep well?" He smirks, like he knows how uncomfortable and lumpy my bed was. *Prick.*

"Yeah, brilliantly." I say tightly, his smirk grows more deeper, like he knows I'm bullshitting.

"Hmm," He throws a thumb over his shoulder in a vague direction, "Milo brought your car over, as promised."

"Oh, where is he… so I can thank him?" I ask, looking past Cole, to see my car parked neatly at the side of the dirt road – out of the way.

"Down at the stables… look I got a lot of work to do today, mend fences, feed cattle, making sure everything is in order…"

He places his large hands on his hips, he speaks in a matter-of-fact tone, his gaze looks at me up and down. He is sizing me up. Seeing if I am up for the job. If I will make it through the day or not. He is still rambling about all the shit he has got to do when I cut him off.

"Give me a job, and I will do it." If Cole is so insistent that I must help on Copper Creek, then it is only fitting he gives me a role to do. I'm not here for idle chatter or to play games, and I'm sick of people thinking I'm just a useless city girl. I'm here to prove myself and them, that I can step out my comfort zone, work hard and achieve something that isn't city life related.

"Train the horses." He smirks. He knows he gave me an impossible challenge. It's almost laughable. A city girl, who hasn't seen a horse in almost a decade, now must try and train wild ones, to prove herself to a rancher. What a joke.

"You have got to be kidding? That is extremely dangerous!" I cry, no way this is happening.

Cole sighs and says, "Look Blair, you have two options, take the reins and ride, or walk away. It's your choice."

My temper rises and I feel the apples of my cheeks start to heat. "What's going to happen if I don't step up, Cole?!" I snap.

My question hangs in the air, heavy and unspoken. We both know what will happen if I don't step up.

"Look Blair, if you want to save this place, you need to roll your sleeves up, there is no easy way out of it." He sighs, "This place isn't like the city, this isn't a job you can quit and find a new one the next day. It's a ranch that need hard work, to see improvement."

I feel my chest tighten, as I realise how deep the hole, I have dug myself in. I can't afford to walk away;

it's not that simple. My family's legacy is walking on a thin tight rope buckling to snap.
Cole stares intensely at my face, I stare back. The air feels severe. Swirls of my emotions float within the oxygen, anger, annoyance, frustration and oddly, respect. Cole's sincerity and straightforwardness bring me clarity on what I need to do.
I can't let him witness me struggle. So, I push my shoulders back and make my way down to the barn, to see the horses. My first decision on this ranch has been made.
I'm staying.

As I walk into the rundown wooden barn, I'm surprised to see Milo. Dressed in dark jeans, a blue shirt, brown boots, and a classic cowboy hat, he doesn't look too bad. Still, I don't feel the same pull toward him that I do with his younger brother.
"Hey," I call out, making Milo look up from his work in the stables. He dumps a large load of horse manure into his wheelbarrow and flashes me a proud grin.
"Hey there, city girl!" he says, clearly pleased with his latest nickname for me. *Great. Another one.*
I make my way over to where he is working, passing all the horses on the way. Waves of nostalgia wash over me as I go deeper into the barn. The memories of when I was a teen come flooding in. My grandfather and I would always work together in the stables. Brushing manes, scraping hooves and filling feeds. In a way, I'm kind of glad Cole decided to put

me on horse duty, the familiarity add a small comfort blanket over myself.

Although the barn looks rundown from the outside, the interior still holds a certain beauty, just as I vaguely remember. Large wooden timbers stretch along the walls and ceiling, giving the space a sense of grandeur. Two wide doors, one at each end, stand open – one leading to a small sandy rink and the other to a path that winds out toward the fields. I cast a quick glance to my left and right, reading the names of each horse on the stalls.

McFly.

Misty.

Apples.

Biscuit.

Ranger.

And **Bluebell**.

I rush over to the stable and glance above the door. There she is – *Bluebell*, a snow-white, silver mare, calmly chewing on hay. She was always my favourite to ride with my grandfather. A gentle soul, and a beautiful horse. Her tail is still as white as I remember, and her eyes, as dark as coal, still hold that familiar warmth. She never let anyone else ride her. I wonder if that's changed over the years.

I'm so lost in thought that I don't notice Milo until he's standing beside me, peering into the stall, watching both Bluebell and me. He smiles and asks, "Old friend?"

A small grin plays on my lips, "Something like that."

He chuckles, "You know, she hates when we ride her, she screeches and kicks, trying to buck us off. It will be interesting to see her with you riding with her."
Huh, looks like Bluebell still refuses to let anyone else ride her – except for me. That's my girl.
I turn back to Milo and say, "I'm here to train the horses."
His eyebrows raise in surprise. "Says who? You?" He looks me up and down, clearly sceptical. "A city girl and horses don't exactly… mix."
"Your brother," I reply with a shrug.
"Really?" He clicks his tongue, rubbing his chin thoughtfully. "So, my brother actually wants you to prove yourself, huh?"
"Yep. No question about it."
Milo smiles, shaking his head. "Alright then. You've got some experience with horses, I'm guessing?"
"Of course," I say with a hint of pride. "I grew up around them."
"Okay," he says, his expression softening a bit. "We'll start with Bluebell. She's been out of practice, needs to get used to riding again." He glances over at the stall. "I'll get her ready for you. You grab a helmet, just in case."
I roll my eyes. "Seriously? Bluebell knows me better than anyone. She won't hurt me."
Milo smirks. "Maybe not, but she might not remember you, city girl. You've been gone a long while."

A wave of guilt floats back over me. Another reminder that I have deserted this place becomes more and more prominent.

I had completely pushed Bluebell to the back of my mind when I left Copper Creek – abandoned her, just like I did with the ranch. The thought that she might not even remember me sends a sharp pang of guilt through me. It's a fear I didn't want to face.

As I fasten the buckle under my chin, securing the helmet, the familiar sound of Bluebell's hooves fills the barn, growing louder with each step. Milo has already attached her harness and saddled her up with a rich brown leather saddle that looks worn but well-loved.

He leads her out of the barn and into the sandy rink, and I follow closely behind. The heavy gate slams shut behind us, the sound echoing in the quiet. Bluebell's ears flick up, and she pauses for a moment, listening carefully, as if trying to sense who's joined her in the rink. She's always been keenly aware of her surroundings.

"She's all yours," Milo says, holding out the reins. Hesitant, I take a slow step forward, my fingers brushing the warm leather straps as I grasp them. His gaze lingers on me for a moment before he continues, "I'll be watching from outside the rink, just in case anything happens." He points back toward the gate we just came through. "Good luck, city girl."

With that, he turns to leave, but before he takes a step, I call out, "Thanks for driving my car over from The Tipsy. I owe you one."

I see Milo's back tense, muscles shifting under his shirt as he halts. He turns around, a flicker of confusion crossing his face. "No worries," he replies, his voice low.
His eyes linger on the buckle of my helmet, assessing it one last time. Then, much to my surprise, Milo steps closer and reaches for the strap. Without a word, he tightens it until it presses against my chin. I instinctively take a small step back, my back brushing against Bluebell's side, the horse shifting under me as if sensing the tension.
Milo's proximity is undeniable. There's no mistaking he's an attractive man – those tattoos peeking out from under his shirt, the subtle dimples that appear when he smiles, and those dark eyes that seem to study me a little too intently. And yet, there's no pull. No spark. Not like with his brother. With Milo, something feels off, like a static hum in the air – something that doesn't quite connect.
He lets go of the buckle, nods once, and turns away, heading back toward the gate. I watch him go, feeling that same emptiness settle in my chest. It's strange.
The sun is blazing in the Wyoming heat, I better get started on Bluebell before the day slips away.

Chapter 6

Cole

I'm supposed to be wedging fence posts in the ground but instead I find myself walking in the direction of the stables. I know I gave Blair an impossible and dangerous task. Yet, when the small, sandy rink comes into my vision, I'm surprised to spot my brother and Blair standing with Bluebell.

I watch from a distance as my brother steps closer to Blair, his hands tightening the buckle on her helmet. A bitter taste rises in my throat, the urge to march into the rink and push him away from her is almost overwhelming. But then Blair takes a small, deliberate step back into Bluebell, her body subtly shifting as if she's seeking space. A strange comfort washes over me, knowing she doesn't seem too keen on my brother's attention. The thought makes something in my chest settle, though I can't quite shake the uneasy tension lingering beneath it all.

Milo makes his way out the rink, climbing on the gate and taking a seat, supervising over Blair. I join him.

"You think she will be able to find the courage to get on?" Milo asks as I get myself seated on top of the gate next to him, overlooking the rink and Blair.

I don't respond. Instead, I watch Blair as she rounds to the front of Bluebell, until she is standing in front of her. Holding out her palm of her hand, raises it in front of Bluebell and waits till the horse places her nose in her waiting palm. Bluebells ears perk up and her tail swishes back and forth, then hesitantly she takes a small sniff of Blair's hand. Bluebell shifts on her feet, unsure about the city girl.

Blair spends a few more minutes of getting first greeting out the way, until she rounds Bluebell and mounts her. She looks unsure about what she is doing, her movement are off and her hands tremor in nerves. From where I am perched on the gate, Blair looks out of place, like a city girl in cowboy boots, but I can see a glint of determination in her sky-blue eyes.

Her shaky hand tightens onto the reins, it's only for a moment that I think she will back out, I know how difficult it is to get onto a saddle for the first time, especially if you haven't been around animals in a decade. It's like learning to ride a bike after so many years.

She gutsier than I give her credit for. Taking a deep breath, Blair gives a small gentle kick of the heel. It's obvious that she is nervous, but the determination inside her doesn't seem to frizzle out.

Guiding Bluebell forward, she wobbles unsteadily. The seat isn't steady and the horse shifts on its feet, sensing the nervousness radiating of Blair. I hop off the gate and into to rink, starting to make my way over to Blair to give her some advice. It's only then, Blair pulls firmly on the reins and manages to get Bluebell under her control.

I stop in my tracks impressed, "Didn't expect that." I mutter under my breath.

Blair starts a rhythm, her posture improving with every step. She drifts confidently over the sandy rink; a small smile plays on her lips. I feel the tension decompress and unravel in my chest as I watch her ride, a fleeting moment of admiration passes over me. Blair's not perfect at riding, but she is learning. Milo cuts through my thoughts. "Maybe the city girl has got more ranch in her than we think."

A soft smile plays on my lips as I continue to watch Blair guide Bluebell around the arena. I feel her confidence growing from here. Although, what amazes me the most is how *good* she looks out there – the elegance, her attention, the sheer awkwardness of it all. The assurance radiating off her is showing brightly, showing me of how strong she is under her exterior.

Stay focused, Walker. We aren't here to get distracted.

I cross my arms, my gaze is still trailing Blair as she moves across the small arena, her face full of utter concentration. The image of Blair trying to remaster something foreign triggers a thought of my own family, especially my father.

Noticing my shift in expression, Milo raises a brow and says, "She's looking better." Nodding in the direction of Blair, "Seem's that she is a quick learner."

I don't answer. I watch as Blair guides Bluebell around the bend of the small arena, her posture becoming increasingly confident. I can see Blair is trying to prove herself, just like I did when I first started working on Copper Creek many years ago.

My thoughts slip away from Blair and land upon my father once again. I think about how worse he is getting. About the sickness that can't be cured. Sensing I'm in my head, Milo cuts through my thoughts, "What's on your mind? You seem to be in your head."
I sigh, shifting my weight back and lean against the fence. Looking at the ground, I say, "It's dad. You know how bad it is getting."
Milo's face softens, lifting the hat off his head, Milo rubs the back of his neck, a slight nervous habit he has picked up since he was little. "Yeah... I realised the last time I saw him. Started yelling at me when I tried to help him with his boots. The nurse came in and explained who I was. The confusion on his face was... heartbreaking."
I'm eyes snap towards Milo's as I say, "He used to be such a sharp, bright man, so *present* in everything that he done. Now he is like a star fading out the sky. I hate seeing him like this."
Milo nods his head delicately. As we look into each other's eyes, the quiet understanding of the weight of our fathers decline falls onto our shoulder. "I heard from the nurses that he forgets entire conversation now."
"Yeah," I agree, "It's like losing him whilst he is still here, it really fucks with your head."
Silence falls between us, yet the ranch still beats to life. The sounds of Bluebell's hooves thudding against the ground. The distant mooing of cattle in the far away fields. The rustling of leaves against the wind and the faint chirping of the birds.

"Do you ever think how *he* would manage this if he was still…" Milo sentence trails off as he glances around the ranch. The empty house, the rundown barn, the thin cattle, they all seem like a shell of what my father left behind.

I exhale a shaky sigh and smile, "Yeah. Dad would be tough on her. Wouldn't let her get away of being scared, but he would respect her for trying." I release a small chuckle, "Probably tell her that she isn't in the city now and is in his grounds."

Milo laughs too, "Dad always had a way to make you feel you could do anything… even if it felt impossible."

I watch as Blair slows Bluebell, a pleased smile spreading across her face. Sweat glistens down her golden, tanned arms, clinging to her skin in the heat. Her cheeks are flushed, but there's something different in her eyes now – something that wasn't there before she climbed onto the horse an hour ago. Determination? Focus? Willpower? Whatever it is, it's undeniable, and it makes her seem… untouchable.

"You think she'll stay?" Milo's voice is quieter now, almost thoughtful, like he's considering the weight of the question.

I hesitate, the uncertainty creeping up in me. "I don't know. I don't think she's figured it out yet. But there's this fire inside her… I'm not sure if I'm imagining it, but I think she's going to stick around longer than we expected."

Milo nods slowly, his gaze distant. "Maybe. But it won't be easy for her – not with all her ties in the city and the family legacy she's carrying." His words hang in the air, heavy with unspoken truths.

"She's stronger than she looks, Milo," I say, feeling an unexpected surge of protectiveness rise in me. I don't know where it came from, but it's there, deep in my chest, something I didn't expect to feel for someone like her. Maybe it's the way she holds herself, the quiet strength I've seen flash through her even when she doesn't realize it. Or maybe it's the way she doesn't back down, not even when everything's stacked against her. It's hard to ignore that fire inside her.

Milo claps a hand on my shoulder, "Guess you are going to stick here long enough to find out."

I watch as Blair dismounts the horse and gently stroke Bluebell's silvery mane.

They stand for a minute, lost in the silence of the ranch until they make their way back over to us. Although the conversation of our father sits heavy in the air, there is something else now too – something new, something uncertain. I straighten as Blair comes closer. There's still a long way to go, but as I watch Blair struggle to navigate and find her footing on the ranch, something shifts inside me. Maybe, just maybe, I begin to see that this place could use a change. A real one. And that change? It starts with Blair.

The sun is starting to set when I return to the stable. Milo has finished work for the day, so it's just Blair I find still in the training rink with Bluebell.

I watch from afar as she pulls on the reins and looks out toward the small expanse of the arena, considering the challenge ahead. I cross my arms. I already know what she is thinking, she is pushing the limits today. I know she is a fighter; I learnt that she doesn't back down from a challenge, but a part of me wonders if she will sit this one out.

Without warning, Blair kicks off into a gallop, her posture looks stiff, but she doesn't falter. She is riding faster than she has even gone, my heart beats fast, concerned for her safety. I can see the nervousness on her face, she is gripping the reins tightly, but she doesn't slow down, the horse's hooves thud violently against the ground.

I'm overwhelmed by a rush of emotions – pride swelling in my chest as I watch her confidence take root in this small corner of the ranch, and a knot of fear twisting in my stomach, wondering what might go wrong. She moves across the sand effortlessly, her chestnut brown hair whipping beneath her helmet, a blur of strength and grace. There's something about seeing Blair like this – independent, fierce – that catches me off guard, making my heart skip a beat. It's a quiet ache I can't quite place.

I'm still watching Blair race across the arena when I notice it – the small smile on her lips fades, replaced by a subtle frown. Her brows furrow, and her grip on the reins tightens until her knuckles are white. Something's wrong.

Bluebell's breathing grows heavy and erratic, her head jerking left and right. My stomach tightens, a sense of dread creeping up my spine. And then, it happens. In what feels like slow motion, Bluebell bucks, throwing Blair off balance. She's launched from the saddle, her body twisting midair before hitting the ground with a sickening thud.
The sight feels like a punch to the gut, my breath caught in my chest. Every part of me freezes, helpless, as the world slows around the impact.
One second, I'm standing on the sidelines; the next, I'm kneeling beside Blair on the ground.
She groans on the ground, rolling onto her side, and before she can even sit up, I'm at her side, carefully pulling her to her feet. My hands are steady, but my heart is racing a million miles an hour. I scan her body quickly, checking for any signs of injury, the tension in my chest tightening with each second.
"You alright?" My voice comes out rougher than I intended, like the words are being dragged from the depths of me. I'm not sure if I'm asking her or telling myself.
Her face flushes with embarrassment as she looks down, brushing the sand off her clothes. "I'm fine. Just got a little too cocky, that's all."
My jaw tightens, the words slipping out before I can stop them. "You shouldn't have pushed it. You're not ready for–"
"I'll be fine," she cuts me off, her voice steady, but there's a fire behind it. "I'm not a delicate flower, Cole. I'm here to learn."

She is right, I can't wrap her in bubble wrap and expect her to learn how to get the job done. I need to let her make her own choices. "Alright, but next time take it slower?" I say gently.

Although I'm not meant to like Blair, the pull I feel towards her is getting harder to ignore.

She stands taller, but the vulnerability in her eyes shatters the carefully built walls of her exterior. For the first time, I see it – Blair is scared.

The tension between us fades, quiet and unspoken. No words are needed. We both understand, in that brief, heavy silence, that Blair is stronger than we ever gave her credit for. My role here isn't just to help her; it's to believe in her.

The sun sets, casting a warm, golden hue over her skin, and for a moment, she seems to radiate with it. There's no sarcasm, no tension in our gaze – just a quiet understanding, unspoken but clear, as the day slips away.

Chapter 7

Blair

I wince as I make my way down the stairs, the twinge of pain prickles on my lower back with each step I take.

I saw the bruises starting to form when I was in the shower. I was too determined to ride by myself, too determined to prove myself that I could handle what this ranch throws at me, but with every small step I take, the pain in my back intensifies, giving me a reminder that I am truly out of my element in Copper Creek.

The fall was embarrassing. When I flew off Bluebell's back and landed on the sand, it felt like I failed before I even started. I felt like I was never meant to inherit my grandfather's legacy. When Cole appeared in my stary vison, a flood of humiliation came over me, it felt as if he witnessed first-hand how much I am going to destroy the place before I even had a good grasp on it. With each step I take down the stairs, it feels as though I'm sinking further, like the descent mirrors how much I'm spiralling downward.

When my two feet land firmly on the wooden floorboards, I'm instantly hit with the smell of spices and burning wood. Looking towards the kitchen, I find Cole with his back to me.

He seems to be grilling some kind of meat, the loud pops and sizzles reaching me from across the room. He's wearing a faded blue plaid shirt, sleeves rolled up to reveal his sun-kissed forearms. The collar is crooked, a sign of a long day's work. His boots are scuffed and caked in dirt, and his jeans are well-worn from years of use. He's the perfect picture of a rancher – confident, at ease in his element – something I can't quite relate to.

"You planning to sit down, or stand there all night?" Cole's voice comes from over his shoulder, booming over the loud crackles of cooking meat.

He's entirely in his element, cool and calm as always, with no trace of stress or concern in his voice.

"Yeah," I grimace, another sharp pain shooting down my spine. "Just about there." I force a tight smile, hoping Cole doesn't notice the way I'm trying to mask the discomfort. I can't let him see any weakness, especially not now. Not when everything feels like it's on the line. I swallow the pain, pretending it's nothing more than a fleeting inconvenience, even though every fibre of my body is telling me otherwise.

Cole glances over his shoulder, his eyebrows pulled together, a deep crease lines his forehead, "You sure you're, okay?" There is a hint of concern in his usual stoic expression. It was fleeting, but definitely there.

I don't want to admit to him that I'm not fine, that my pride was bruised as much as my body is. I have fallen in front of him. I tried so hard to hold onto the reins and look capable, yet I ended up like a fool on the ground. Before I could even pick myself up Cole was there to do the work for me, another reason to add to my list on why I'm not cut out on managing Copper Creek.

"I'm fine," I say with more confidence than I have felt since arriving here, "Just a little sore, that's all."

By the look in Cole's face, I can tell he isn't entirely convinced, but he didn't press the matter, instead he nods his head towards the set table and says, "Sit down. Dinner is almost ready."

As I make my way to the table, I can feel Cole's gaze fixed on me. I lower myself carefully into the wooden chair, biting my lip to suppress a groan as pain shoots through my back. His eyes linger on me longer than usual, as if he's waiting, making sure I'm settled before he can turn back to cooking. But when our gazes meet, he quickly shifts his focus back to the stove, as if nothing happened.

Sounds of the sizzling meat fills the silence between us. Watching Cole work so easily, watching him move around the kitchen with ease, makes me feel oddly out of place. I'm not used to being served, especially by someone who seems too comfortable in their life. I was always the one doing all the work, leading the meetings, filling out the paperwork, telling people what to do. Yet, in this small kitchen it appears that that Cole is the one in charge. The one who has everything under control.

"So, how bad was it?" He asks whilst flipping whatever is in the pan.

I laugh softly; my face starts to heat with embarrassment. "That bad that it will hurt tomorrow."

I shrug my shoulders, even though his back is facing me, "I guess I need to get more practice in."

"I can give you pointers if you want," Cole says, his tone teasing, though there's something more beneath it. Amusement? Or something else entirely? It's hard to tell.

"I don't need any pointers," I snap harder than I intended to, "I just wasn't prepared for the fall, that's all."

"Hmm. Some advice then." Cole eyes flick briefly over his shoulder, his dark eyes are soft, the teasing being replaced with empathy. "Falls can happen, what matters is getting back up and trying again." He speaks this line like he has rehearsed it, like it was something he had to learn himself.

I lean back in my chair. I have heard that phrase a million times before, but somehow when Cole says it, it doesn't feel like a children's rhyme, it feels... real.

Maybe his life is riddled with flaws – both literally and figuratively – and maybe he's had to pick himself up over and over again. Perhaps that's what sets Cole apart from the people I know in the city. In the city, no one has to *fight* to keep something alive. No one has to struggle to keep a dream – no matter how foolish – flickering.

The sound of plates clinking broke my cloud of thoughts. Cole places a plate of a steak, cooked perfectly, vegetables and mash potatoes in front of me. It's only then my stomach rumbles and my mouth fills with salvia do I realise how hungry I am after a day of riding Bluebell.

"Thank you." I mumble. I'm unsure if I'm thanking him for the food or the comfort for earlier.

"No problem." Cole sits down in front of me, the silence is deafening, the sounds of the scrapes of our knives and forks against the plates, and the occasional sips of our water are the only things that can be heard. However, we eat in comfort, not effected by the stillness in the air.

When I look up from my plate, I catch Cole staring at me. This happens multiple times – his calm gaze is watching me steadily – I try my best to ignore the heat subtly rising in my cheeks. It's hard to figure Cole out. One moment he is giving me grieve and teasing me about falling off a horse, the next he is providing me support.

"You know," I say, "I don't think I am cut out for this ranching life."

His unreadable eyes don't leave mine as he says, "It's harder than it looks, I'll give you that."

"I thought I could do it... I thought if I push through, if I learned, I might accomplish... I don't know *something?* This isn't as easy as I thought it would be."

Cole places his knife and fork down, "Nothing worth it is going to be easy, Blair. If something is worth doing, you have to work hard to achieve it."

The words off his lips floated in the air, maybe Cole's words aren't just about the ranch. Maybe he is talking about life.

"When did you get so wise?" I tease, a smirk tugging at my lips. "You're not exactly the moody teen I remember." I try to lighten the mood. Cole laughs, shaking his head, and my heart skips a beat. He spears a piece of steak with his fork, pops it into his mouth, and then says,

"When did you become so…" He waves his fork in the air, trying to find the word. I raise a brow waiting for his reply.

"So…" I'm not letting him get away that easy. His eyes flick down to his plate then back to me when he says,

"Stubborn."

"Huh?"

"You like to do things your way." He shrugs; a teasing smirk plays on his lips. "You like control. You pride yourself with independence when I offer help. And when confronted with tasks? You're determined and persistent. What happened to shy teen, Blair? You aren't exactly the girl *I* remember."

I tilt my head to the side, my gaze locked on his. A teasing smile of my own plays on my lips as I say, "I don't know, maybe living in a city all those years changes a person…or maybe I just grew up."

Cole leans back in his chair; his distractingly strong arms are now pinned against his chest. The playful look on his face has now softened when he utters, "Yeah I can see that," he pauses, his eyes fall down my body, grazing my chest, until they rise back to my face, with a boyish smirk he says, "But I think I like the old Blair better. She was a lot easier to tease."

I playfully roll my eyes and release a dramatic sigh, "Well, I'm sorry to disappoint you. I guess I'm just a *grown-up* now."

A small laugh escapes his lips as he picks up the remainer of his steak on his plate. His eyes never leave my face, it is as if he is studying me. "Nah, you are still the same girl under all that," – he waves his fork in my direction – "stubbornness. But a bit more… complicated now."

"Complicated?" Now it is my turn to laugh, "Now, was that is a compliment coming from you, Mr. I-know-everything-about-this-ranch-but-will-never-ask-for-help. If anyone is complicated, it is you, Cole."

"Guess that makes us a perfect match, doesn't it."

I blink at him, totally caught off guard by his intensity of his words. It wasn't what I expected him to say, but then again, it is Cole, I should know better to expect the usual.

"Is that so?" I raised a brow, half teasing, half intrigued. I shift back in my chair, adding more space between us. "Well, I don't know, you might have a point about me being stubborn, but I think you're just as set in your way as I am mine."

"Oh, I'm set, alright," he smirks. "But one thing I've learned is that change can actually be a good thing."

Something stirs in my chest as he says it – something in the way his eyes hold mine, the way his words seem to carry a weight that has nothing to do with the ranch. It feels like we're talking about more than just change here.

"Well, change isn't always seen as a good thing," I reply, my voice softer than I intended.
The air changes for a fleeting moment – just a fraction – but it's enough for me to notice the small spark hidden in Cole's dark eyes. It's then that I become conscious the small ounce of fear that lands in my stomach when I realise that despite my carefully built walls, there is something about Cole that makes me want to rip them down and let him in. The feeling is dangerous, like a beast getting ready to pounce.
"Guess we will see, *sweets.*" His voice sounds deep, more serious but hints of amusement still linger. And just like that we realise that there is more back-and-forth going on between us than we let on.

After my conversation with Cole last night, I woke up today feeling a little lighter and a lot more determined – or *'stubborn,'* as Cole would like to say – since arriving here.
'Change can actually be a good thing.'
Cole is right, which is why I have spent the morning trying to muck out stables, feed the horses and try to fix this damn gate. Emphasis on the *try*.
When I walked into the barn this morning everything that could have gone wrong, went possibly wrong.
As I was mucking out Biscuit's stables, I ended up slipping in horse shit and landed on my already sore back. Covered in horse poop and straw, I attempted to feed Bluebell some of her hay. Instead of eating

the hay, my braid became the victim of a very hungry horse. And now I'm sitting crossed legged on the ground with a hammer and a dream, trying to fix this stupid gate.

The sun is only starting to rise, painting the farm in light oranges and yellows. I woke up before Cole today, I was too eager to wait for my assigned job and just got to work myself. I know Cole intends on trying to ease my way into this ranching lifestyle, but I rather be thrown into the deep end. I'd rather tackle challenges that seem impossible, even if it means failing and learning from it, than settle for easy tasks that come with training wheels.

Although this is much harder than I anticipated. I never truly realised how much I *didn't* know.

"I can't believe that a wooden gate is getting the better of me." I mutter to myself as I dig for a screw in the toolbox I found lying in the corner of the barn.

My hands are covered in dirt, my nails are black for the mud I'm sitting in, yet my willpower doesn't seem to dim.

I finally pull out a small screw and place it against the wooden gate. I know it's pointless – it's rotten, falling apart – but still, I hold the nail between my thumb and forefinger, aligning it with the hammer. The sound of the hammer striking is sharp and loud, echoing through the quiet stable, undoubtedly giving Cole an unpleasant wake-up call.

I smirk at the thought of him being rudely awaken but the loud sounds of banging, that work is being done without him or his input. Yet, my thoughts are instantly interrupted as I slam the hammer down on my thumb, completely missing the nail.

"SHIT!" I scream and drop the hammer, the sound of metal clattering muffle the string of curse words that are flowing out of my mouth. I cradle my hand against my chest, I take a deep breath and count to ten, again, and again, till the pain has settled into throbbing. "I knew I shouldn't have tried to fix this stupid gate." I mutter, standing and giving it a frustrated kick. The gate rattles on impact.

Bluebell's head appears outside her stable, she screeches loudly, as if she is mocking my clumsiness.

"Oh, come on Blue." I raise my hands in the air, clearly frustrated, still staring at the gate. "It's not my fault this thing is a piece of shit!" I huff. Bluebell neighs again, as if she is telling me off, I roll my eyes. "Seriously, look at it – it's falling apart!"

She huffs, clearly not impressed my complaining. "Oh, don't give me the sass, Blue, after the shit morning I had – *quite literary* – the last thing I need from you, is attitude." Bluebell's head returns into her stable with an exaggerated huff, "Can't believe I am arguing with a horse."

"Me neither." I deep voice chuckles.

Startled, I whip around to find a smirking Cole leaning against a stable door, his muddy boots crossed at the ankles. He has been watching me the whole time, no doubt at getting a laugh at my expense.

His arms are crossed, as he casually watches me – just like he always does when he's quiet for too long.

"Great," I mutter, "Now I have got someone else to laugh at me too." It's embarrassing for him to see me like this. Covered in muck, hay in hair and talking to horses like I'm in some fairytale. I can feel my cheeks starting to warm in humiliation at the thought of him watching me kick the gate, he must think I'm ridiculous. He pushes off the stable door and steps closer to me,

"You were having a full-on conversation with her you know," he says, a wide grin plays on his lips, "I'm not sure if I should be impressed or concerned about you, sweets."

I give him a half-hearted glare, "Sorry, I didn't plan for you to show up and witness me losing my shit over a damn gate."

"It's not just about the gate, Blair. It's everything else. I can see it." He steps closer, until I can smell his soap and pine. His expression has softened, the teasing glint in his eyes becomes a more thoughtful one, but before I can look any further to explore, Cole takes a step back, his usual grin plastered on his face again. "You need help with that?"

I hesitate for a moment before I say, "Yeah, I could use the help."

"Don't worry, I won't laugh at you too much."

"Right." I roll my eyes. I watch him as he picks up the discarded hammer on the ground and walk over to the toolbox.

Something flutters in my chest, I don't know if it's to do with our conversation last night, or the fact that I can appreciate Cole becoming less guarded – the quiet understanding – the way he makes everything look effortless, but for once I don't mind asking for help.

Cole gets to work on the gate with that ease and a practice rhythm. I find myself watching him, the way his arms flex as he hits the nail on the head, his dark eyes focused, the large hands he splays against the wood, and the hat he has thrown on the ground, his devilish dark curls free. As distracting and dangerous Cole may seem, there is something comforting being around him, fixing this stupid gate together.

And for the first time today, I start to think that maybe – just maybe, I'll be okay.

Chapter 8

Cole

The dust sticks to my sweat as I survey the damage of the fence. The sun is starting to set on Copper Creek, casting a sprawling auburn glow over the ranch.
The warmth of the day starts to cool, kissing my skin in a delightful way. I am working on the west fence line, trying to mend the fallen away pieces before the last piece of sun slips away. Even though my muscles ache and I drip in sweat, I'm determined to get the work done.
I grunt as I lift the heavy wooden beam, steadying it against the posts. This section of the fence was one of the first I built when I took over the ranch. The weather has worn it down over the years, and now it's time for repairs.
As I reach for the hammer, a soft voice filters through the air, "You need help with that?"
I freeze my movements. I didn't need to look up to know who it was. Blair's voice had a way of cutting through the drone of Copper Creek, like rain on a dry afternoon.
I glance over my shoulder and spot Blair standing casually with her hands in her back pockets – and if I was being honest – despite the dirt and the odd piece of straw in her hair, she looks like she has

stepped out a country model magazine. Her boots were dusty from this morning and her hair was pulled back messily in a braid. A miniature sparkle shone brightly in her blue eyes, something about it made me feel *something*.
I release a long breath, trying to make the pull I have towards Blair disappear. I didn't need her help. Although, it would be hard to tell her no, especially when she is standing there looking so persistent.
Her hands has now ditched her back pockets and are now replaced on her hips. "I don't need your help, Blair, I have got it under control." I muttered. I watched her jaw tighten, clearly not wanting to back down.
She takes a few steps closer, the dry grass crunches underneath her boots, "I have fixed plenty of thing before, Cole. I know how to swing a hammer."
I chuckle – uncomfortable and amused – there was something in the way she said my name softly that makes my insides start to twist.
I place the wooden post into the grown and stand, wiping my soiled hands on my shirt. "I'm fine." My voice sounds less convincing than it should have, "You don't need to be working out here to the bone, and besides…" I chuckle, "I *definitely know* you can swing a hammer after the way you almost smashed your own fingers off this morning."
She gasps and lets out a loud laugh, I smile. With the sun painting her skin, she looks gorgeous out here, she looks carefree. She raises a brow and smiles, "Oh, come on Cole, I can handle it." She

takes another step closer, "I have seen you work; I can't let you do all the effort yourself, not for long."
Her word hung in the cool air, changing the atmosphere into something we haven't outright said aloud. There was an unspoken truth between us; this was more about fixing fences. This was about us learning how to trust each other, work side by side together.
The weight of the day feels heavy on my shoulders. The sun is quickly slipping away, the light is starting to fade. So reluctantly, I nod my head. "Alright, if you are going to help, you might as well grab that hammer."
A prideful grin splays on her lips as she walks over to the toolbox without any hesitation. As I watch her rummage around trying to find the correct tool, I couldn't help but notice the way the sun kissed her skin, making her silhouette seem to glow against the burning of the sun. It wasn't just the physical beauty of Blair, it was the way she moved, the confidence that has slowly started to grow since her arrival. It made everything inside me feel tingly.
"Here." I said, handing her a piece of the wooden beam. Her slim fingers brush my rough ones. It was a quick touch, a mere second of contact, yet the tingly feeling inside me erupted like small sparks.
"Careful, I don't want you to hurt yourself." I mutter; my voice low as I stare into her eyes. She meets my gaze; her soft eyes feel too intense to look at.
"I'm not so fragile, you know. You have to stop thinking of me like that."

"I wasn't –" I cut myself off, realising how foolish I sound. "You remind me of a horse sometimes. Hardheaded and strong."

Blair laughs lightly, "Well I'm not sure if I should take that as a compliment, but I'm glad you think I'm strong." She teases, then gets to work hammering the beam into place. I watch her for a long moment – how she hammers with precision, the steady focus in her eyes. I take a step closer.

"You know." I say softly, "I never thought I would meet someone like you, not out here anyways."

Blair pauses, looking up at me with the tilt of her head, "And what is that supposed to mean?"

I hesitate, unsure how to form the sentence, "I don't know… I didn't think anyone could handle this life. This place is nothing like the city. It's hard labour and loneliness."

She places the hammer down, and turns around, our faces are only mere inches apart, "Well, I can handle it a lot more than you think."

The air feels thick with tension between us. A familiar ache erupts from my chest. I was used to being alone, to trust no one but myself. Yet, when Blair is standing this close, with warmth and confidence, I realise it is getting harder to ignore.

Without thinking, my hand reaches up, brushing lightly against the side of her arm. Just a moment, enough for the warmth to transfer between us. Her eyes lock onto mine at the touch, and in that instant, everything else fades. The ranch, the work, even the setting sun – all of it disappears, leaving just the two of us in the quiet, electric space between us.

"I think I'm starting to realise that I might need you more than I thought." I speak softly, although my voice sounds gruff.

Her gaze softens, her breath caught in her chest. She doesn't pull away when she says, "I think I am starting to realise that too."

Chapter 9

Blair

My body still hums from the light touch of Cole's fingers a few hours ago. The sun has now set, and the sky is a blanket of constellation, which makes it seem endless above me.

I sit in the creaky rocking chair on the porch, letting the quiet of the night settle around me. The distant howl of coyotes and the soft rustle of leaves in the nighttime breeze are surprisingly comforting, a stark contrast to the noise I'm used to back home. The constant buzz of the city, the starless sky, the sharp scent of fumes – they all feel like fading memories now, slipping further away with each breath I take here.

You can't get used to this place, Blair. Remember, you are only here to try and sell the ranch.

I sigh, leaning back in the chair and pulling my legs up to my chest, my gaze drifting out toward the vast, endless sky. There's something oddly comforting about it – a quiet freedom that washes over me. It's as if I could spill every secret, every worry, and they'd be swallowed whole by the night. Lost between the stars, too small to be seen, too dark to ever be uncovered again.

My thoughts are broken by the familiar sound of boots on the weathered wooden porch. It's not the first time I've felt his presence, but tonight, there's something about him I can't quite place – something magnetic – that makes me acutely aware of him, even in the quiet of the night.

I hadn't expected him tonight. But there he was, stepping out onto the porch, the light flicking on and casting a soft glow that revealed both of us – me hidden in the shadows, him standing in plain view. My eyes instinctively follow him as he steps outside, his tall, broad-shouldered frame silhouetted against the dim light. There's a quiet intensity about him, controlled, unwavering, and the heat that seems to radiate off him is impossible to ignore. It makes my pulse quicken, just like that.

After that brief touch on my arm, I tried to tell myself it meant nothing. But deep down, I knew it wasn't just a touch – it felt like a spark, a jolt of something unexpected and raw. Like something inside me, something I hadn't realised was there, had suddenly been lit.

My heart began to race, each beat quickening, but I forced myself to keep it in check.

I couldn't afford to be obvious, to let myself become vulnerable. Not with Cole. We're on different sides of this ranch, each of us pulling in opposite directions. He wants one thing, I want another. And this… whatever this thing is between us; it's only a distraction. A dangerous one. It has to be let go before it grows into something neither of us can control. Whatever it is, it can't stay.

I clear my throat, feeling a sudden tightness in my chest as Cole glances my way. "Oh, hey!" I say, my voice coming out high-pitched and awkward. "I didn't know you were coming out here. I'll get out of your way." I reach down to grab my discarded shoes, but before I can pull them up, Cole's hand wraps around my wrist. The spark from before ignites into something much stronger, a fire that flares through me, unexpected and intense.

"Stay." He says as he throws a warm blanket over my lap, wrapping me up in his scent. "I could use the company, and I couldn't sleep." He drops into the chair beside me and pulls his arms behind his head, looking up at the sky.

This gave me a chance to look into Cole's eyes. They look softer tonight, as if he finally let me in, just a little bit. The thought made my chest tighten in a way I was unprepared for.

I take a deep breath and get my emotion in check, "I was just thinking," My voice is barely above a whisper, it feels inappropriate to speak loudly over the silent night. I force a half-smile, trying to mask the stirring that was happening near my heart. "The stars out here are brighter. They are lot different to the ones in the city – which is none." I let out a forced chuckle.

Cole nods, his gaze shifting from the sky to me. The silence stretches between us, as vast and unbroken as the sky above. The way he looks at me makes me feel both exposed and seen, as if he could reach into me and understand parts of myself, I haven't even figured out yet.

My thoughts started to tangle. *Why is he looking at me like that? Why does he make me feel this way?*

My mind continues to race, letting myself get caught in something that is dangerous. For years, I've built walls around myself – first in New York, protecting my independence, my career, my relationships. But now... now it feels like I'm building them to shield myself from him. From the pull he has on me. Yet, deep down, something inside me is questioning whether I even want these walls anymore. And that thought, that uncertainty, scares me more than I'm willing to admit.

"Do you ever think about what it means?" I blurt, starting to think about anything to pull me away from my thoughts.

"What?" His voice come off guarded. I shift in my seat, pulling my knees closer to my chest and wrap the blanket tighter around me, fighting off the cool night breeze.

I look up to the sky and murmur softly, "I don't know. I just... I look up to the sky sometimes, and I wonder if there is more to all off this. This life. I mean you spend your whole life working hard, doing what is expected of you. But then you look at something so... so big, and you wonder if it means anything more. Or maybe we are just really small and none of it matters. I don't know."

Cole stares intensely at my face whilst I look to the sky, considering about what I have just said. "I don't think it is about understanding at all." He speaks quietly. "Maybe it is finding the moments that make you think this all worth living for. Even if they don't all make sense in your head. Even if it is a spark in the dark that seems unexplainable."

I turn to him, my eyes meeting his in the dimly lit light. There is something in his stare that makes the air seem charged, like the night is holding its breath.

"Maybe that is the thing." I whisper, "You have got all the land, acres of space to do what you want with it. Yet, you are in the middle of it all. Unsure what to do, where to go." A soft smile plays on my lips, "I think you are like me Cole, you're looking for *something*, aren't you?"

He looks away into the lands of Copper Creek when he admits, "I've been looking for a long time, Blair. I think I have always known it, but I never had a clue where it was."

I don't say anything. I let the weight of his words hang in the air, letting them sink into soil. Then I bravely push my chair closer to him as I say, "You don't have to find it alone Cole. You know that right?"

My words hit him like an ice-cold bucket of water. He releases a ragged breath, his hand run through his dark hair. I give him a comforting smile, and try to meet his gaze, "We don't need to be ready for anything just yet. Sometimes it is about being here, being in the present."

Cole releases another pained breath slowly; the tension that was once riddled within his body starts to ease away as he lets my words settle in him. Maybe for the first time Cole realises he doesn't have to do this alone.

His callous hand reaches out and grab my hand. His thumb brushes against my knuckles, leaving a trail of goosebumps shooting up my arms. However, unlike today, we didn't feel the need to pull away. The touch was quiet like the night around us, filled with everything that didn't need to be said. As we sat side by side under the stars, I can't help but think that this could be the first time in Cole's life that he didn't need to work hard to achieve answers. That he simply doesn't need them all.

I wake up to the obnoxious sound of vibrations on my bedside table. The sun has just started to rise, small slithers of rays peak out between my curtains, offering a friendly hello.
I blindly reach over and grab my phone, not bothering to look at the caller ID. Sadie's voice immediately fills my ears, she is brimming with energy and excitement, even if she is two hours behind in time. The contrast is jarring, I can hardly get a word in as Sadie talks about the latest office gossip, trends and all the social scenes of the city.
My friend's life is starting to feel so far away from the ranch. Like I different planet. "Blair! You've got to come back here! It's so boring without you here. No one knows what to talk about in the coffee shop anymore. You had the best stories! Are you falling for any of those rugged ranchers yet?"
My stomach clenches at the mention of Cole. I have only woken up and the weight of today is already dragging me down. "Sadie, it's… it's different. I'm not sure what I am doing here. It's quiet, the air feels clean, it's totally out of my element on what my used

to, but I'm still trying to figure everything out." I whisper down the line, hoping Cole can't hear me through the thin walls.

"I get it, but you are still having fun, right? I mean you weren't exactly happy here, slaving away in that office, missing out on relationships… so why don't you enjoy yourself?" She coughs into her phone, switching to a southern accent, "Find some hot cowboy who knows how to treat a lady."

A faint smile tugs on my lips as I roll my eyes at the thought, yet my mind drifts to that particular cowboy I was talking to late last night. I imagine the thought of his rough hands drifting up my arms, down my back, rubbing my thighs, touching my breasts, and sliding into my wet– no. *NO!*

"Blair? Blair! *Helloooo*, you there?"

"YES!" I cough, "Yeah, I'm here."

"What are you thinking about?" I can imagine Sadie smirking down at her phone, definitely knowing *exactly* what I was thinking. "Look, Blair, if you want to go ride some–"

"Sadie enough!" I hiss down into my phone, paranoid that Cole will walk into my room any second.

"I'm kidding, I'm kidding!" she laughs into the phone until she says, "Blair, what's up with you? I feel like you have gone radio silent since you have been at the ranch."

"I know, I know." I sigh, sitting up against the headboard of my bed, "I guess… like I said I am still trying to figure everything out."

"What does that even mean Blair?" Sadie asks softly, "Is it due to with the ranch, or... *him?*
I freeze, a lump forms inside my throat. I haven't talked to Cole about anyone. I have been keeping it locked inside since my arrival at Copper Creek. Sadie knows something is brewing between us from miles away, does that mean he knows too? "I don't know Sadie. Everything feels so different here. I don't know if I can come back to the city when I finish this thing up. It feels like I'm becoming a totally different person than I was in the city, and I don't know if that is a good thing or bad thing."
"Well," She sighs, "I'll be here waiting when you figure it out. Just don't get lost in the quiet little world, okay? Come back to the city before you forget what's it's like to live outside a country song."
I know Sadie means well, yet she doesn't know what it is like to have this constant pull in a direction you never thought to go. The ranch, Cole, it's all getting harder to ignore as the days passed by.
I glance around my room, the sunlight dances against the wallpaper. I think back to the women I was when I arrived here a few days ago. Strong, independent, and driven, compared to who I'm becoming now, quiet, and reflective. I let Sadie words sink in. However, I feel like I'm at a crossroads, unsure which part of the path I should take. "Hey, Blair, I gotta run, catch up with you next week?"
"Sure." I say, yet I'm totally distracted by my thoughts.
"Love you, bye!"

"Love you too." She hangs up. I get changed for the day and head down the stairs to find Cole cooking breakfast.

"Morning." He glances in my direction, a devilish smirk on his face. Immediately my thoughts of him this morning come rushing back into my mind.

"Good Morning." I croak. *This is going to be a long day.*

"When you said you were going to give me a proper tour of the ranch, this definitely wasn't what I had in mind."

I stand a few feet away from Cole, watching as he effortlessly hoists himself onto the back of the largest horse I've ever seen. The stallion is a towering mass of muscle, dark and imposing – nothing like Bluebell. The difference is almost comical. Cole, for all his size, looks almost small atop the beast.

"If you think I'm getting on that thing, you've lost your mind," I say, shaking my head. "That horse is twice my size!"

Cole chuckles, his posture relaxed as he leans forward, crossing his arms over the horn of the saddle. "McFly? He wouldn't hurt a fly. Come on, sweets," he teases, the words slipping from his lips like a challenge, "Stop making this harder than it needs to be and get on the damn horse. I promise I won't let you fall."

With a reluctant sigh, I take a hesitant step forward, eyeing the massive creature warily. "If

Bluebell hadn't thrown me off, I'd be riding myself," I mutter, half under my breath.

Cole raises an eyebrow, the corners of his mouth twitching upward. "Is that so?"

"Well," I grin, "If Bluebell didn't have such an attitude, you might've let me ride on my own by now."

Cole shakes his head, a quiet laugh escaping his lips as he shifts on the saddle, making room for me. He holds out his arm, a silent invitation.

I hesitate, then place my foot in the stirrup, pushing myself up, until I'm sitting high on McFly. My hands tremble slightly as I squeeze my eyes shut. "Is it too late to admit I'm terrified of heights?" I mumble; my voice more uncertain than I'd like it to be.

Cole's warmth floods my senses as his chest brushes against my back. His strong arms encircle me with ease, steadying me as his hands grip the reins. His chest rumbles with laughter, the sound vibrating through my spine. It's low, rich, and surprisingly comforting. "Guess it's too late now," he teases, his voice a little too close to my ear. The warmth of his breath sends a shiver down my spine. "Open your eyes, Blair," Cole's voice is low and steady, wrapping around me like a calm reassurance. "Nothing is going to happen to you, I'm right here."

I slowly blink open my eyes, the sun's heat pressing down on us, but it's the extra warmth of Cole that has my senses humming. The air is thick with the scent of pine and fresh grass, the earth beneath us alive with sound. The rhythm of hooves on dirt, the distant rustle of birds in the trees, and the steady noise of

Milo working in the stables – it all swirls together, grounding me, somehow both peaceful and overwhelming.

Two large hands wrap around mine, guiding my fingers to the reins. The simple touch sends a jolt of heat through my body. "See? You're okay. I got you," Cole's deep voice hums in my ear, a quiet promise, but it feels like too much, like I'm suddenly too aware of everything, too aware of him.

We start moving, the soft clip-clop of McFly's hooves marking the rhythm as we walk along the trails that snake around the ranch's perimeter. Cole talks, his voice filling the quiet space between us as he lists off everything that needs fixing – the work that's piled up, the bills that never stop, the debts we owe, the repairs that keep coming. Each word he says builds a weight on my chest, the tasks stretching out endlessly before me. I can feel the tension tightening in my body, the overwhelming sense of impossibility that comes with it. How is it all supposed to get done? How are we supposed to fix everything?

Coles hands firmly squeeze mine, "Hey, what's wrong?"

I shake my head, "Nothing, it's not important."

"Bullshit, come on tell me." He stops McFly by a small stream, the sound of the cool water, unties some of the knots forming in my stomach.

Cole slides off McFly, his movements effortless, before reaching up to grab hold of my waist, guiding me down from the saddle. I try to ignore the way his hands seem to fit perfectly around my torso, or the way the space between us crackles with a tension that makes my heart race, as if we're a breath away from something much too dangerous.

I quickly step out of his grasp, the absence of his touch somehow leaving me cold. Without a word, I walk briskly toward the stream, the sound of rushing water pulling me away from the moment.

The silence stretches between us, thick with things unsaid, until finally, I break it. My voice is softer now, quieter, as if I'm trying to put distance between my words and the things I'm too afraid to confront.

"This ranch. It feels like there is always something wrong. There is always something to fix, to mend. It feels like we are solving a puzzle that seem impossible because every piece is wrong, there is always a piece missing." I stare at the water, and cross my arms, "I left my old life for this place, I thought... I thought it was going to be different. I thought I would be the saviour to the legacy," I sigh, "But clearly, that isn't the case if the place seems to keep falling apart around me. You were doing well before I arrived, you seemed to be managing great without me, maybe I bring bad luck, maybe I just—"

"Blair."

I glance over my shoulder to find Cole standing closely behind me. "Yeah?"

"Are you finished?"

"Oh! Sorry, I didn't mean to go on a rant, I just get in my head sometimes and—"

"Blair, stop talking for just one second."

"Sorry." I wince.

"Don't apologize. Blair, just you being *here* is doing so much for your grandfather's legacy. There is never a day on a ranch anywhere, where there isn't a job to do. Some challenges seem impossible, some of the puzzle pieces may seem they don't fit, but this isn't a puzzle piece, *fuck* I don't even know what it is, but I can tell you one thing for sure," He stands closer, so close our nose brush, "Since you arrived, Blair, it may have seemed that we were managing well without you. But truthfully, we weren't. We were starting to lose sight of what this place meant to your grandfather, my father, your father. However, when you arrived... well maybe you bought those extra missing pieces to make the part."

I stare at him, stunned, my mind racing as his words settle like an explosion in the air. It feels like the ground has shifted beneath me, and I'm left standing in the aftermath. "You really mean that?" I ask, my voice barely above a whisper, the weight of his statement pressing against my chest.

"Of course, Blair. I wouldn't lie to you."

A warm flush spreads across my cheeks, and I feel it before I can even try to hide it. Cole grins, clearly noticing. "Are you... blushing?"

I turn my back to him quickly, grabbing my boots and making a beeline for the water. "Of course not! It's just sunburn. You're losing it, *Buckaroo*."

But before I can even dip a toe into the water, his arms are around me, lifting me off my feet and spinning me with surprising strength. The cool river splashes over us both, drenching me from head to toe.

"What did you just call me?" He growls playfully in my ear, close to the sensitive skin, making me shriek. "Nothing! Nothing!" I laugh loudly as he continues to twirl us around. The water may only be ankle-deep, but we're both soaked to the bone, our clothes clinging to us as droplets of cool water trickle down our skin. I roll onto the grass, choosing to dry off in the warmth of the sun. Nudging Cole gently, I turn to him with a half-smile.

"You know," I say, a teasing edge to my voice, "you're not nearly as bad as I expected, *Buckaroo*."

He flashes a grin, his hands laced behind his head, damp hair falling messily around his face. Somehow, it makes him look younger, more carefree than usual.

"You're not half-bad yourself, *sweets*," he replies, his voice carrying an unexpected warmth.

I turn my head, grinning at him, then do something that catches me off guard. I lean in and press a soft kiss to his cheek, my lips lingering for a moment against his stubbled skin before I pull away. "Thank you," I murmur, my voice quiet, "for today. I really needed it."

Cole doesn't look at me, but I notice the subtle shift. The tips of his ears flush a deep red, his lips part slightly, and the faintest hint of a blush spreads across the apples of his cheeks.

I'm not sure why, but I feel like I've just thrown him completely off balance.

Chapter 10

Cole

I stand outside a building I know I should visit more often. The guilt gnaws at me, tightening my stomach in knots. Maybe it's the weight of the memories that linger – the days when health and strength were taken for granted, when things felt normal and whole. My father has been at Misty Pines Care Centre for five years now. In that time, I've watched him slip further away, his mind unravelling little by little until he's nothing more than a shadow of the man he used to be.

I run a hand through my hair, taking a deep breath. This place... it's always been hard for me. I can't afford to let anyone know how much it eats at me. Especially not Blair. If she knew, she'd probably see it as a weakness, a crack in the armour. She already thinks I'm some unfeeling hardass – always has. The last thing I need is for her to see the real toll it's taken on me.

I glance around, making sure no one's watching, then head toward the entrance. The last thing I want is for Blair to show up here unexpectedly, asking questions I don't have answers to. No one can see me like this. Not her. Not anyone.

I straighten my back and force my expression into something impassive before stepping through the door. I'm here for my father, not to feel sorry for myself. Not to let anyone see the cracks that are starting to show. I've spent so long hiding them. I'm not about to let Blair, of all people, get a glimpse.

My father was never an easy man to love. As much as I speak highly of him to others, our relationship was filled with its share of highs and lows throughout my childhood. With the weight of carrying on the legacy of the ranch after the Reynolds left, and the lessons he taught me about tending to the land and caring for it like family, I'm torn. Should I pity him for the man he's become? Should I be angry for how he overshadowed my teenage years, or is it sadness I feel – mourning the father he once was and what he's left behind?

"Cole Walker," A nurse speaks quietly behind her desk, her glasses cover half her face, "What a surprise, Jesse is just his room. I'm sure he will be happy to see you." She smiles.

The discomfort lingers as I think back to the last time I visited my dad. The forgetfulness, the anger, the distant look in his eyes – it all felt like a slow, brutal unravelling. Watching him slip away like that, piece by piece, was gut-wrenching. It's a kind of pain you never expect to feel – watching time steal away someone you love, until they're barely a shadow of who they once were.

As I walk through the halls of the care home, everything feels suffocating – the harsh lights, the sterile smell, the soft murmur of voices, and the sight of frail, aging bodies. Each step seems to heighten the weight in my chest, the reminder of time slipping away, of my father's slow decline. I try to push past the growing anxiety, but it clings to me, impossible to ignore. When I reach the door marked 'Jesse Walker,' my phone buzzes in my back pocket. I pull it out, and the name flashing across the screen stops me cold – it's a message from the last person I ever expected to hear from.

Unknown: *Hey Cole, thanks for the number! Quick question—how would you feel about the barn being painted pink? I promise, it'll really make the ranch pop.*

Me: *No.*

Sweets: *Aww, please, I think it would look so cute!*

I smile down at my phone at the thought of Blair painting my barn pink, I type back a reply.

Me: *Cute? I think it would make it the least intimidating barn in the country.*

Sweets: *Oh, come on, it would be so fun! Plus, it would make it stand out. You can't deny, it would be a conversation starter.*

Me: *Well, if it gets the people talking, maybe you've got a point. But I'm not sure my cows would be too thrilled to see a pink barn. They've got enough* trouble without having to deal with a new colour scheme.

Sweets: Cows are colourblind, Cole. So really it is you. You'll be the one having to look at it all day.

There is no way I'm actually considering painting the barn pink right now.

Me: I'll consider it, only if you do the painting yourself. Then we could talk.

Sweets: DEAL!! 😉

Me: You think you can handle it? I've got paint and brushes, just don't come crying to me when you have pink paint on your hands for days.

Sweets: Oh, I'm not afraid of a little paint, I've got a VERY persuasive way with colours. You'll see, it's going to be a masterpiece.

Me: A masterpiece, huh? Well, I can't say no to that. Just make sure you don't start painting the cows too. I've got enough of a circus to deal with without giving the neighbours something else to gossip about.

Sweets: That would be a sight, wouldn't it? Pink cows wandering around the pasture. But I'll leave them alone... for now – your cows are safe with me.

Me: *You better. I'll hold you to that.*

The light-hearted exchange with Blair fades, a distant echo now, as the weight of reality crashes back down on me. I stand frozen before the door labelled 'Jesse Walker,' my mind heavy with thoughts of the man behind it. I take a steadying breath and push the door open, my heart hammering in my chest.

The sight of him hits me like a physical blow. There, in the worn leather chair by the window, sits the shell of the man I used to know. His fragility is stark against the warmth of the room, and for a moment, I just watch him – lost in a quiet world that doesn't seem to belong to him anymore.

I clear my throat, the sound harsh in the silence, and knock gently against the doorframe. It reverberates off the bare walls, filling the empty space between us. "Dad?" The word hangs in the air, heavy and unfamiliar, as if it belongs to someone else.

He turns his head slowly, his eyes break away from the window and narrow at me, as if he is trying to place the shape of the person who is standing at his door. There is no acknowledgement in his face – just a blank stare – he doesn't even remember who I am.

A tight knot forms in my chest as a lump rises in my throat, the fear of my father not recognizing me creeping closer. He blinks a few times, his lips parting – though not in a smile, not in recognition. Just a quiet, empty question: "*Who are you?*"

I step inside slowly, my heart pounding in my chest as if it might escape. A small smile tugs at my lips, one I hope will reassure him that I'm not a stranger. "It's me, Dad. Your son. Cole." I don't know why I keep saying it. Maybe some part of me is still clinging to the fragile hope that one day, he'll remember – remember me the way I still remember him: strong, sharp, full of life. But those days are long gone, swallowed by time and illness. All I have left are fragments, fleeting glimpses of the man I once knew. My father's dark eyes scan my face, clouded with uncertainty, yet there's a faint glimmer of something – maybe recognition, maybe confusion. I'm grasping for any sign of the man I used to know. "Ah, Cole... you came by again?" His voice is soft, distant, like a memory struggling to surface.

I can't decide if I'm relieved that my name escaped his lips, or if the fleeting recognition only deepens the ache. It feels like both a blessing and a curse. I pull up a chair, settling beside him. Dad's gaze drifts back to the garden outside, his expression distant. His hair, once dark, is now streaked with grey, the change growing more noticeable with each visit. Wrinkles that weren't there yesterday carve deeper into his face. His hands – once strong enough to lift the world – are now thin, fragile, like the rest of him is slowly slipping away.

I shift in my seat, the words feeling heavier than I expect. "Hey... I got you something." I reach into my jacket pocket and pull out a small pack. It's nothing special – just his favourite salted peanuts. He used to eat them every night at the ranch, the ritual almost as familiar as breathing. Maybe, just maybe, they'd stir something inside him. A memory, a moment, something of the man I once knew.

I sit them on the small table beside him, but he doesn't reach for them, he doesn't even glance at them. He continues to look outside the window into the garden, as if he is waiting from something to happen. "How's the garden? Still growing strong?"

His gaze snaps to mine, it's like a dull knife, almost sharp. It's almost like the memory is trying to claw it's way to the surface. His voice is hoarse as he says, "The garden... the garden is good. The roses are blooming. They remind me of... *her*."

We never talk about my mother. She passed away when Milo was born, and it's a silence that's hung over us both, unspoken but understood. It's one of those things that's always been there – too painful, too much to dig into. I swallow the knot in my throat, trying to ignore the sharp sting that rises with the memory. I nod, forcing the moment past me. The mention of her – of her absence – feels like a sudden punch, and I wasn't prepared for it today. It's strange, though, how even after all these years, her presence lingers in the small, forgotten corners of my life. I never knew her, but in some ways, I've spent my whole life trying to fill the space she left behind.

For a second, I think about what she might have been like. Would she have smiled the same way I remember in old photographs? Would she have liked the ranch? And, most painfully, would she have ever understood the man my father is becoming – or the one he used to be? I push the thoughts down before

they take too much of me. But just for a fleeting moment, I can almost feel her presence with us, like a shadow we're both still trying to outrun.
In that tiny, fragile moment, though, I catch a glimpse of something. A fragment of the father I once knew. Maybe it's the way he said her name, or the way his eyes softened just a little. Whatever it is, I hold onto it. It's small, and it's fleeting, but it's enough to remind me that some part of the man I loved, the one who taught me to keep going, is still here. And for now, that has to be enough.

"Yeah," I crock, "She loved roses." The familiar silence stretches between us, something I have come accustomed to when visiting. I wish there was something I could say, something I could do to make it easier. But I'm at a lost. He shifts in his chair and looks at me, his voice is quiet, almost hesitant.

"I should've done better by you, son."

His words hit me like a physical blow, sharp and unexpected. I freeze, staring at the man who once taught me to bury my feelings, to never show weakness – and now, here he is, laying bare his regrets in a way I never thought possible. The weight of his confession settles in my chest, and for a moment, I don't know whether to feel sadness, anger, or something else entirely. Maybe all of them. I take a slow, steadying breath, fighting to keep the emotions from spilling out.

"We both should've done better, Dad," I finally say, my voice steady despite the turmoil inside me. It's the truth. We both failed each other, in different ways, at various times. But saying it out loud makes the bitterness sink deeper. Still, the words hang in the air between us, a reminder of everything left unsaid for so long.

His cloudy eyes look at me, although he starts to droop, as if the weight of his words was too much for him. The silence creeps back into the room. I sit with my Dad for another hour, just being present. That's all we can do. Just *be*.

Before I leave, I give my Dad a small squeeze on his frail shoulder. "I will try and be back next week. Remember your peanuts, okay?" He doesn't answer, I don't even know if he can hear me. Silence is the best answer I can get out of him these days. I step out the room, the door clicks shut softly behind me, for a moment I stand there, leaning against the hallway wall. I close my eyes and try shake off the emotion rising inside of me. It's no use, they won't go away anytime soon. My phone vibrates in my pocket, pulling it out I see it's another text from Blair.

Sweets: So, GREAT news!!! I found some brushes and paint. The barn will soon be the work of the art, just you wait!!!

I stare at the text. It serves me a reminder – a different world, one where I don't need to feel this heavy. I smile briefly at my screen, then make my way outside the care home, stepping back into a world that is waiting for me. A world that is a little brighter but just as complicated.

Rodeo Hearts

When I drove up to the ranch, I already had a feeling something was... off. Stepping out my truck I rub my eyes as if I am imagining things. But nope. It was definitely real and *there*.

The barn. My barn. A soft, pastel pink. I'm almost at a run as I make my way toward my now *girly* shed, my eyes narrowing at the sickening hue. The sharp, chemical scent of fresh paint clings to the air like a bad memory.

As I round the corner of the property, there she is – Blair, perched on a ladder like she owns the place, wearing loose, faded jeans and a paint-splattered T-shirt. My gaze lands on the familiar design of a bull printed on the back. And then it hits me– *Wait a minute...*

"Is that *MY* shirt?!"

Blair jumps, whipping her head around, clearly unaware of my approach. Her eyes widen in surprise as she scrambles to recover, a guilty little smile tugging at the corners of her lips.

"Oh. Hey, Cole." She smiles, turning back around to finish off the last wooden panels of the barn. I lean back against the wooden fence, watching her work with complete focus.

"Well, I have got to hand it to you, Blair. This was not what I had in mind when you said you wanted to help out on the ranch."

Peeking over her shoulder, her face splays a mischievous grin as she says, "Oh, come on. It'll make the place stand out. Imagine it against the sunset, it would look *so* cute!"

"I'm trying to imagine it right now, but all I see is a flamingo that has exploded all over my barn." I grumble, trying to sound as unimpressed as possible. Blair lets out a loud laugh, clearly enjoying my teasing.

"Aww, come on. Don't be so dramatic. You can't deny that it gives this place some... I don't know, personality." She dips her paintbrush into the tin of paint and starts brushing another coat onto the barn. I watch her face; she is so intent on the task.

"Personality, huh? Well, I would definitely give you that. It's absolutely got a personality that I was definitely... not expecting." She gives me a playful look over her shoulder and climbs down the ladder.

Dusting off her hands on her pants. She gives me a wink as she says, "I thought you might've been surprised when you saw my masterpiece. But it's only paint, right? Besides, I figured if anyone could pull this off, it would've been you." She smirks. She takes a step towards me, that playful look lighting up her eyes.

"You really think I was being serious when I considered painting the barn pink. What's next neon green cows?"

Blair laughs loud, moving even more closer, until she is standing right in front of me – an innocent expression on her face – I know better. She was enjoying every second of this.

"Maybe you will like it when it's done. I bet the cows will love it. And it would make killer photos on *Instagram*."

"Oh yeah? I'm sure it would look amazing on your *Instagram*. But let's not get ahead of ourselves, you are still going to have to convince me." She takes a step forward, her beasts graze against my chest. I can smell the fresh paint and the lingering hint of soap off her skin. Yet, it was her smile that was mesmerizing me the most. The way her eyes sparkled with playfulness, the way she places a hand over my thundering heart rate and pushes me back against the fence.

"Oh, I'll convince you with something." Before I could even think of a chance to respond, Blairs lips brush against mine placing a feather light kiss on my lips, making them tingle with want. But before I have the chance to deepen the kiss any further, she pulls away.

A breathless smirk plastered on her lips, as if it took her so much energy to not give into that pull that was between us. As Blair climbs back onto the ladder, I smile, for the first time today. Maybe now I was considering that the pink barn wasn't as half-bad as I made it out to be. In fact, it felt like it belonged here.

"Alright, I will admit, it's not as bad as I thought it would be. But don't expect me to let you paint anything else pink."

She hums playfully, "We will see about that, cowboy." She gets busy painting the barn as I watch her from afar. I think about the colour of the barn, or more so... the colour Blair was bringing back into this farm. My life.

Blair stands with a proud grin on her face and hands on her hips as she inspects her work. There were splatters of pink paint everywhere, and while the barn was starting to definitely look... *different*, there was something about it that felt... right. Despite my initial resistance, a part of me couldn't help but think that maybe it truly belonged this way.
"You finally made your point Blair; I call a truce."
She looks over at me with a soft smile and glint in her eyes. Grabbing the paint can, she dips her brush inside saying, "I don't think you are totally convinced yet." I raise my brow, totally knowing where this is going. *Oh no, she didn't.*
But before I could even have the time to react, Blair flicks her wrist occupying the brush, sending splatters of pink paint all over my face and clothes.
"What the hell!" As I try and rub off the excess paint on my face, my jaw hardens. I could see the look in her eye. There was no way I was going to let that one slide. Not after she made my barn look like a cotton cady factory. Without a word I lunge for a bucket of paint and throw the contents in her direction, though it misses, Blair squeals. Realising there is a war about to happen, she grabs another big brush, she yells teasingly, "You're *so* going to regret that."

She swipes the brush across my chest, causing gloopy paint to slide down my torso. I dart behind the ladder to give myself some cover, "Oh, I'm not the one regretting anything, sweetheart." I dart forward, and grab a fistful of paint, smearing it across her face. Blair gasps is pretend terror, a large smile spreads over her face.

"You are *so* dead!" Before I had a chance to react, Blair charges me down, climbing onto the lander and leaping into my arms. The unsuspected impact throws me off balance, causing me to fall to the ground with Blair. Paint splatters everywhere around us. I groan from the impact but start to belly laugh, Blair straddles on top of me, her fingers and palms covered in gloopy paint.

"You're going to be the death of me, Blair."

"You love it." She grins down at me mischievously, her chest rising fast and heavily trying to catch her breath. I feel the tension in the air change. I not sure if it is the paint fumes that are making me high, but I sense the playfulness to the air change to something hot and heavy. Blair, leans down, her face is mere inches from mine. Our faces were so close, I feel my heart racing like a stallion.

"You've got a hell of a way to make me regret things." I whisper as Blairs face softens. Her paint encased fingers, glide against the stubble lining my jaw. Without a word she leans in and firmly presses her lips against mine. This isn't like the feather light kiss we had a few hours ago. The kiss started slow; I feel her heat creep through me as our lips continued to explore. As my hands find her waist, I pull her closer, pulling us deeper into the tension. The taste of the paint mixed with something sweet I couldn't place, was making feel addicted. Like a drug I couldn't live without.

As we pull away, we smile softly at each other, our faces splattered in soft pink. "Now that was a kiss worth fighting for." She utters tenderly. I laugh and bring my hand up to her cheek, swiping away the paint with my thumb.

"I think I am starting to get used to this whole... pink thing." I smile. I watch Blairs eyes sparkle, as she leans in and brushes her lips over mine again.

"Good, because I think the barn could do with more of that in the future."

I grin, my hands still resting on her hips, I pull her closer and murmur in her ear, "As long as you are doing the painting, I could get used to that."

I watch as goosebumps erupt down her arms. Neither of us could ignore this now. Although the barn is pink, the real colour was between us, and that was undeniable.

Chapter 11

Blair

My phone vibrates loudly on the bedside table, dragging me from the peaceful quiet of sleep. The calm of the countryside is starting to settle into me, making the harsh buzz of the phone feel almost jarring. I reach for the screen, expecting another call from Sadie. But when I answer, the voice on the other end isn't hers – it's the one I've been dreading to hear.

"Blair! Finally! I've been trying to reach you all week. You're avoiding me, aren't you?" My mom's voice cuts through the line, sharp and expectant.

"Hey, Mom. Sorry about that," I mutter, rubbing the sleep from my eyes, already feeling the weight of her tone. "The reception's been terrible out here." I brace myself for the guilt-laden lecture I know is coming. "And no, I haven't been avoiding you. Just been... busy." I sigh, pinching the bridge of my nose, trying to starve off the inevitable.

"Busy doing *what,* exactly? Have you at least talked to *someone* about selling that ranch." My stomach tightens, a knot twisting painfully as the words land. The mention of selling the ranch hits like an icy blade, cold and merciless. I've heard it a thousand times before, yet it never gets easier. It's all she's talked about since we found out I'd inherited the place – fix it up, sell it, move back to the city. The life I walked away from.

It's like an alarm blaring in the back of my mind, always there, relentless, reminding me of the weight that's slowly crushing me. Keep it. Sell it. Either way, the decision looms over me, and it's only a matter of time before I have to choose.

"Mom, I have already told you, this is my choice. What if I could make this my home? Permanently. Like it used to be"

My mom scoffs, the sound laced with disbelief, as if the very thought is laughable. Her voice sharpens, the words cutting through the air like a blade.

"It's not your home anymore, Blair. Not after everything. Your father's gone, and the place is just... decaying, falling apart. There's nothing left to fix. You're not saving anything by staying out there. You need to sell it, move on, and stop holding onto something that isn't coming back."

Her words sting, each one sinking in deeper, reminding me of the things I've been trying to ignore. I've spent so long trying to do right by her, trying to make her proud, trying to please her. But the anger is building inside me now, simmering like a pot on the edge of boiling over. I draw in a deep breath, struggling to keep it contained, to keep my voice steady. The last thing I want is another fight with my mother, but maybe this – this pressure – is exactly why I left in the first place. The constant weight of expectation. The suffocating guilt.

My father's death hasn't been enough for her to see what truly matters to me, and that's exactly what I need to figure out. Whether I sell the ranch or not, I need to understand what *I* want. Not her, not anyone else. Just me.

"I'm not running away from anything, mom. I just need time to figure things out." I speak down into my phone quietly but also firm, "I'm not ready to sell, not just yet. I need this time to think about it, mom."

She scoffs again, and I can almost feel her eye roll through the phone, even from miles away. "Time? Don't be ridiculous, Blair. You've had an entire week to figure this out. The ranch is losing money every second you waste. By the time you finally decide, it'll be worth nothing. And you'll be worth nothing without it. You need to stop pretending everything's fine and face the reality of it."

My breath catches in my throat, a tight coil wrapping around my chest, squeezing until I can barely breathe. Her words hit me like a slap, each one sharper than the last. It's clear now – my life in the city, the name I built for myself, it all meant nothing to her. In her eyes, I'm nothing but a failure. The grief of losing my father those years ago, the cold neglect from my mother – it all crashes down on me in waves. The weight of those quiet years of regret and isolation presses into my bones, and now, with my mother's relentless push to sell what's left of them, it feels like I'm drowning in it. The heartache of losing my father and grandfather, the suffocating pressure to let go – it's all too much. The world spins faster, and I'm not sure I can catch my breath.

"I'm not giving up mom, not yet. I have to see it through. For myself." I speak with the little amount of strength I have left within me. Silence can be heard down the line. I can feel my mother's resentment through the phone, frustration and grief vibrate between us.

Until my mom finally speaks up, "I just want what's best for you." She speaks softly, yet her voice is nothing but thick with disappointment. "You are so strong, Blair, but you are alone out there. Don't you want to come back?" My heart aches with the words, but I know I can't go back yet.

"I'm not alone mom. I'm figuring things out. I need time to do that." I whisper, my eyes start to burn.

"I don't want you to regret it, Blair. Before it is too late to change your mind."

"I won't regret it. I promise."

When the call soon ends, I sit in silence, staring at my phone screen. My mom rescheduled to come to Copper Creek next week, saying she had an important business meeting. No matter how much I love my mom, her words sink deep, pulling me into a sea of sorrow. I'm lost in a whirlwind, unsure of what I'm fighting for anymore – the ranch or my own sense of self. But one truth cuts through the fog: I can't walk away from this ranch until I discover who I am without the life I left behind.

I hear soft footsteps coming up the stairs and a quiet knock on my door. Cole cracks the door open. He must have heard my conversation with my mother. I don't say a word, I don't want to explain myself. I don't want to talk about my mom guilt or my father's

death. Not here, not with him. Yet, when Cole's eyes meet mine, the noise in my brain seems to be put on mute.
"You, okay?" He asks softly, his voice is deep with concern.
"I will be, I just need some time alone." I whisper. With a nod of Cole's head, he doesn't push any further. Instead, he softly clicks my door shut and retreats back downstairs. Although Cole's presence holds the weight of my unspoken words, making me feel less alone, I can't help but break down over the overwhelming pressure my mother has placed on my shoulders.

I decide to bury myself in work to escape the suffocating weight of my mother's words. I spend the morning in the stable with Bluebell, hoping the routine will clear my mind. With Milo off today, the barn is quiet, save for the rhythmic stomps of hooves and the soft rustle of hay. As I brush Bluebell's mane, my thoughts race, a tangled mess I can't outrun. The pressure my mom has put on me to sell the ranch and "move on" clings to me, no matter how hard I try to shake it off.
I wrestle with the thought in my mind – should I just give in to my mom's wishes, sell the ranch, and return to the city? It feels like a betrayal, like I'm turning my back on my father's and grandfather's legacies, on everything I've worked so hard to build.

But at the same time, it feels like I'm failing my mom, like I'm letting her down by holding on to something she wants me to let go.

As I continue to brush Bluebells mane, a swell of emotions rushes into me. My eyes start to burn and before I know it, silent tears run down my face. I finally let my guard down since arriving here at the ranch. I cry for my father and not getting a proper chance to say goodbye. I cry at what grief does to a person – my mom. I cry for myself.

I don't know what I'm doing or where to go from here, but what I do know is that I need to find peace with it. I press my face against Bluebells mane, the familiar smell of grass and straw remind me of my grandfather. The memory of him teaching me how to ride for the first time flashes behind my closed eyes, reminding me of what this land meant to him.

After feeding all the horses, I head back towards the house. I see Cole standing on the pouch, leaning against the railing, waiting for me. He doesn't ask about my phone call this morning, instead he gives me the space I asked for.

A moment of quiet understanding settles between us. I step onto the porch and lean against the balcony beside him, our gazes drifting over the ranch. We stand so close, our shoulders grazing lightly, and I can't help but feel the weight of yesterday's kiss lingering in my mind. Something shifted then, a magnetic pull that finally drew us together, like two magnets unable to resist. The memory of his lips on mine, the rasp of his stubble against my skin, and the way his large hands fit so perfectly around my waist floods my senses.

I try not to think about all the other things he can do with his mouth, yet the apex in between my thighs start to heat and throb.

"You know what makes this place feel like home?" His voice cuts through my thoughts, and I turn my face toward him, hoping he doesn't notice the flush creeping up my cheeks. "It's nothing to do with the house or lands... it is the memories and the rooted traditions. Whether it's the gruelling work, the quiet moments, or just being surrounded by the people I care about, this ranch *stays*. It's a representation of stable and an unchanging home that I can come back to, no matter where life takes me. That is why I love this ranch so much. It kept my family going after all the hardships."

Cole's gaze catches mine, unspoken words passing between us – telling me that running isn't my only choice. I glance out over the ranch, the sun warming the earth, the grass turning a deeper green with the promise of new beginnings.

"When my father died and mom packed up our stuff and left, I felt... an intense feeling of guilt." I swallow, "Guilt for not being present when my father passed, guilt for not sticking here at the ranch. My home became... quiet. Nothing like the peaceful quiet here. It was isolating and cold. My Mom and I relationship became tarnished, as if all our happy memories died with my dad. All our dynamic now is her expectations she places on me." As a stray tear falls down my cheek, Cole embraces me in his arms.

The smell of his soap and pine engulfs me, as he presses a small kiss on the top of my head.

"Blair, you can't carry that guilt forever. I know it feels like you should've been there, but none of us can predict the future. I think your dad would want you to live without that weight, to remember the good time you had, not the ones you missed." He sighs, "I won't tell you want to do, Blair. I'll tell you this. No matter what choice you make, you don't have to face it alone. You've got people who care about you. *Hell*, even I care about you. And I just want you to find peace – whether that's here, back in the city, or somewhere you haven't even imagined yet."

I take a deep breath, letting Cole's words wash over me, grounding me in the moment. Maybe he's right. Maybe it's time to stop letting my mother dictate my choices, to stop living under the weight of her expectations. I step out of Cole's arms, feeling a shift inside me – a sense of clarity I didn't know I needed.

"Thank you, Cole."

"Anytime, sweets." He says softly, brushing a stray hair behind my ear. Making me tingle all over.

"I'm going to get some work done," I mutter more to myself than to him. Cole smirks, his gaze lingering on me, neither of us making a move to break the moment. His eyes drift to my lips, and just as I feel the tension between us build, Elijah Sullivan's truck rumbles up the driveway. He steps out, wearing that damn devilish smirk of his. "Sorry to interrupt, but Cole, could I talk to you for a sec? Or are you too busy?"

Cole grumbles beside me, his hand on my face cups my jaw. His thumb trailing over my bottom lip, not even caring his best friend is here to witness. His eyes snap up to mine and says, "We'll finish this later." Then marches off the porch and towards Eli, who has a shit eating grin plastered on his face.

I roll my eyes and step off the porch, heading toward the stables with a newfound resolve. It's time to stop letting others dictate my path – time to start making my own choices.

Chapter 12

Cole

"What the hell do you want?" I snap at Eli, glancing over my shoulder to make sure Blair isn't within earshot. The urge to kiss her again is relentless, lingering in my mind since yesterday. Her lips were sweet, and I can't help but wonder if everything else about her would be just as intoxicating.

"Helloooo? Earth to Walker?" Eli waves his hand in front of my face, trying to get my attention. "Did you hear anything about what I just said?"

I roll my eyes, "No, why are you here?"

Eli gasps dramatically, his eyes wide as saucers. He stomps his foot on the ground like a child throwing a tantrum. "Seriously, dude? You finally start talking to a girl, and now you're ignoring me? You're forgetting our friendship? What about those matching sweaters my grandma knitted for us? Did those mean *nothing* to you?"

"I'm not dating her–" I sigh, rubbing my temples as the headache from this conversation sets in. "Elijah, you're my best friend. Nothing's gonna change that."

I can't believe we're actually arguing over this.

He crosses his arms and pouts, a sting of mumbles leaving his mouth, "Maybe if I saw you wearing that sweater, I would believe you."

"Eli." I snap.

"*What?!*"

"Why are you here?" The day's barely started, and I'm already running on empty.

"Alright, alright, fine. I'll tell you but promise me you won't get mad." *Oh, great.* This can't be good.

"Just spit it out," I sigh, already regretting this conversation.

"Well..." He scratches the back of his neck, looking like he's about to confess a crime. "You know how they have the country fair every year, right? Well, this year they're doing a–" Eli pauses, clears his throat, and rushes through the next part, like he's trying to barrel through the sentence like he's bracing for impact. "They're doing bronc riding, and I might've... sorta... signed you up for it."

I blink, processing his words, before I slowly turn to face him, my jaw tightening. "*You did what?*"

Eli laughs nervously, the sound shaky, like he knows exactly how this is going to go down.

"Look, Cole, I understand that you *might* be upset but just hear me out, I–"

"Elijah! Are you fucking crazy?!" I throw my hands in the air. "I haven't done bronc riding in years!" I'm furious.

"Look, I know you're pissed, but hear me out," Eli continues, his voice strained. "The prize is forty grand, Cole. *Forty thousand dollars.* You could put that towards the ranch, maybe even buy it off Blair."

I close my eyes, letting his words settle in. The world feels like it's spinning too fast. My mind is racing, but somewhere in the blur, Eli's point lodges itself in my thoughts. I could do it. I could buy the ranch. I could make it mine again.

But then my mind drifts back to yesterday – the heat of the moment, the kiss we shared. It was everything I didn't know I wanted, everything I didn't know I needed.

But if I win this competition, if I buy the ranch from Blair, would she resent me for it? Would she feel like I betrayed her, or worse, like I used her for my own gain? The thought twists in my gut. I don't know what's more dangerous – losing the ranch or losing Blair.

I shake my head, trying to push aside the jumble of feelings swirling inside me. The idea of competing in this saddle bronc contest feels wrong, especially if it means buying the ranch from Blair. She's worked so hard to make it hers, to breathe new life into the place. I don't want to do anything that'll jeopardize that, no matter how much my bank account could use the forty grand.

"I'm not so sure about this, Eli. I'm not ready to use something like this for my own gain, especially if it means messing things up with Blair."

Eli, of course, doesn't get it. He's all wide-eyed and persistent, leaning in like he's about to close some kind of deal. "Look, Cole, I get it. You're all tangled up in your feelings for her but hear me out. This could be the solution you need. You're stuck between a rock and a hard place. If you win, you have the money to buy the ranch. It's practical. No more waiting around, no more feeling like you're walking on eggshells. You can fix things, take control."

Rodeo Hearts

I can feel my pulse picking up as the pressure mounts. "I don't know, man. The ranch... it means so much more than just a place to live. It's history, it's legacy. Blair's putting her heart into this. I'm not sure she'd understand if I went ahead with this."

Eli sighs dramatically, his hands thrown in the air like he's trying to make a point that's obvious to everyone but me. "Come on, Cole! You think Blair wants to see you struggle? If you win this thing, you're giving yourself a shot at saving what you've *both* worked so hard for. You don't have to throw the ranch away just to get the money. And if Blair's as serious as you say, she'll understand that. Hell, she might even be glad you finally made a move."

I stare at him, still unsure, but the gears in my head are starting to grind. Eli's right in some twisted way. I've been stuck in this limbo between my past and my future, and maybe this is the push I need. But is it worth it?

"Just think about it," Eli adds, his voice softening. "You have a chance to make it right. And I know you want to make things work with the ranch. But you have to take that first step."

I nod slowly, though doubt still churns in my chest. "I'll think about it," I say, but the weight of the decision presses down on me harder than ever.

"Seriously, where are you taking me?" Blair's voice cuts through the silence, her curiosity evident as she's been firing questions since I told her to get into my truck after dinner. I glance at her from the corner of my eye, watching as she squints against the dark sky outside, clearly trying to figure out where we're headed.

I pull up to the spot and cut the engine, stepping out into the crisp night air. As I round the truck, I open the door for Blair – because, of course, I'm a gentleman. She flashes me a soft smile, murmuring a quick thanks before scanning her surroundings, her eyes darting around, searching for any hint of where we are.

After a long day, I lean against my truck, my gaze fixed on Blair. There's something calming about this place I brought her to – the stillness, like the world is wrapped in a soft blanket. Her silhouette is outlined by the moonlight, her face tilted up to the sky. I've seen the stars countless times before, but as I climb into the truck bed, pulling the mattress I'd tossed in earlier, and gesture for Blair to join me, the stars feel a little brighter, a little closer, as if the night itself is holding its breath.

As Blair settles onto the mattress, her fingers lightly trace the blankets I arranged for us, almost as if she's unsure whether she should let herself get comfortable. But when I pull the blankets over us and settle in beside her, I offer her a reassuring smile. The space between us is small, but it doesn't feel cramped. If anything, it feels like we've found a quiet corner of the world that's just for us, perfectly ours.

"So, *this* is where you were taking me." She sighs up to the sky, I can't help but look at her. Her eyes are wide, reflecting the light off the stars. Her heart shaped face is soft, as if she is truly comfortable – her usual stress slips away. "It's beautiful."

I glance up at the sky with a smirk. "Yeah, thought I'd give you a better view than the one from the porch." I look down at her, teasing. "Hard to beat the view out here, though."

She turns toward me, a playful smile tugging at her lips. "I meant the stars, not you, cowboy."

I raise my eyebrow, mocking offence, "Hey! I'm a pretty good view myself."

She laughs softly, the cool night breeze carrying the sound, and for a moment, it feels like the world lightens. Her laugh has that effect – the kind that lifts the weight from your chest, even if just for a second, as if we're momentarily free from everything waiting for us back home.

"Well, I guess you *are* kinda little cute." She shrugs teasingly. I can't help but not laugh inwardly at the way she says it, that maybe, just maybe, I am more than a cowboy with a rugged smile.

"I'm *kinda* cute." I scoff and nudge her with my elbow, my voice low and teasing when I say, "And here I thought we were just getting on, Blair."

She bumps me back with her shoulder. "Are you always this big headed?"

"No bigger than the stars," I say, leaning back on my arms, a hint of anticipation in my voice. "Do you ever get the feeling that the stars are watching us?"

Blair hums beside me, shuffling a little closer to my side.

She smiles softly when she says, "I've always thought of the stars as loved ones who've passed on," she says softly, pointing up to one particularly bright star. "The ones that shine the brightest – those are the people you love most. And new stars appear every day, so yeah... I like to think they watch over us."

I pause for a moment, staring at the night sky. "What about the ones that fade?" I ask quietly.

Her expression shifts, a slight frown tugging at her lips. "Maybe they're the ones forgotten, lost in people's minds," she murmurs.

I can't help but feel the weight of it. "Sounds sad."

She shrugs; her gaze distant but firm. "That's part of why I came back. To make sure my grandfather's legacy didn't fade. To keep my father's memory rooted in the land, in the place he loved."

A heavy weight pushes down on my chest. I think back to my conversation with Eli today. The thought of buying the land off Blair doesn't seem like a promising idea anymore.

She whispers softly again, "When you live in a city for a few years, you don't see the stars. Maybe that is why I forgot to come back after a long time."

I pull my gaze back up to the sky, "I don't think you ever forgot, Blair. The stars are always there, you just need to remember."

We sit there for a beat, watching the world pass around us, letting our thoughts sink in. "This is... lovely, thank you, Cole." Blair speaks softly.

Rodeo Hearts

"You're just saying that because I'm the one who set this thing up." I reach behind her and grab her ponytail, giving it a tug. "Your welcome."
"You're too much, you know that right?"
"What can I say, I know how to treat a lady."
I glance at her, her eyes flick away. She traps her smile between her teeth. "Do you star gaze often?"
"Yeah." I sigh; I grin playfully at her. "Though I don't usually have company."
She hums, "Lucky for you, I'm the *best* company."
I chuckle, "Yeah? You don't seem like the kinda girl to blend in."
She narrows her eyes, "Nope. I like to stand out from a crowd."
"Hmm, I figured you are the kinda girl who knows what she wants. And right now... what is it that you want?" I whisper deeply.
"I don't want anything, what makes you say that?"
"Oh Blair, I know a challenge when I can see one. It's okay though, I'm good at getting what I want." I shuffle closer towards her, until out stomachs are touching.
"I told you; I don't want anything." Her breath is huskily, almost breathless.
"Come on sweet, aren't you a little curious?"
She lets out a soft laugh, "You really think you could make me want something, don't you."
I smirk playfully, our lips grazing as I say, "I don't think baby, I know."
I find myself lost in the depths of her eyes, the moonlight and stars reflecting like shimmering

whirlpools in them. My heart picks up its pace as I start to close the distance between us. But just as I'm about to get any closer, Blair shoots up, her hands flying to her mouth as she gasps, "Cole, look! The Northern lights!"
I glance upward, my breath catching at the sight. Green and purple hues swirl across the sky like liquid, moving in waves as if the heavens themselves were alive. "What the hell... Cole. This is amazing!" Blair's excitement is infectious, and I can't help but smile as I watch her face light up, eyes wide with wonder.
"Did you know about this?" she asks, her voice high-pitched with awe. Her enthusiasm is so pure it makes my chest tighten.
I shrug, feigning nonchalance, though a small grin tugs at my lips. "Don't get too excited. This happens around here on the regular."
Blair's eyes go wide, a look of disbelief spreading across her face. She stretches her arms out toward the sky, as if trying to touch the colours dancing above us. "If this is regular, I want to come here every night!" She turns to me with a bright, joyful smile, and before I know it, she wraps her arms around me in a spontaneous hug.
I still, my arms by my sides, unsure how to process the sudden closeness. "Thank you, Cole," she whispers softly in my ear before pressing a deep kiss to my lips.
I'm frozen for a moment, caught in the magic of her kiss, the lights above, and the feeling of her against me. She doesn't know that this happens only once a

year, but it doesn't matter. Right here, right now, I wouldn't want to experience it with anyone else.

Chapter 13

Blair

The last thing I expected to see this morning was five sets of eyes staring at me from the breakfast table. Actually, scratch that, the last thing I expected to see is my best friend sitting at the table with four rowdy cowboys. "*What the fuc–*"
"Surprise!" Sadie jumps up from her chair, throwing her arms around me in a tight hug. "I missed you so much."
I freeze for a second, my hands awkwardly hanging at my sides as the guys at the table smirk, clearly entertained by the look of shock plastered on my face. I pull back slightly, holding her at arm's length. "First of all, I've been gone for, like, two weeks," I say, trying to regain my composure. "And secondly – what the hell are you doing here?"
The boys chuckle sipping their morning coffee, Sadie's smiles softly, "After the phone call the other day, I thought you could do with a familiar face."
"How did you even find this place?" I ask, watching her casually settle into a chair at the breakfast table, taking a sip from her coffee mug like she owns the place.
"I have my ways," she replies, casting a playful glance at Cole, the mischievous gleam in her eyes impossible to miss. I raise an eyebrow.

I came here to escape the madness of city life – not exactly expecting surprises. But as my gaze drifts over to Cole, I catch him staring back at me, his dark eyes holding mine with a quiet intensity. I never thought I'd see him like this – sitting at the table, surrounded by family and my best friend, sharing coffee like it's the most natural thing in the world. The scene feels almost... domestic.

"Don't worry, Blair. These fine gentlemen have been keeping me company since I arrived a few hours ago." Sadie smirks into her cup.

I place my hands on my hips, "You *knew* about this?" Cole shrugs, his gaze casual but the hint of a smile tugging at the corner of his lips. "Figured it might be nice to have a little peace and quiet without you harassing me for once."

I scoff, though the memory of last night lingers – stargazing, his hand just a little too close, the way it felt right in a way I didn't want to admit. "Sure, right," I mutter, walking to the counter to grab a mug. I fill it with coffee, trying to shake the heat of our earlier moments from my skin, and walk back to the table.

The group is chatting and laughing, but Cole nudges Milo down the bench, creating a gap between them. Without saying a word, I slide into the seat, the warmth of the mug a strange contrast to the cool tension that hums between us. My thigh brushes his as I settle in, and for a split second, neither of us moves. The noise of the table fades away, and suddenly, it feels like we're the only two people in the room, wrapped up in something unsaid.

"You know..." Milo says quietly, leaning toward me as Cole talks with Eli. "Cole doesn't usually invite people he doesn't know, but he made an exception for you."

"I know," I reply, glancing back at him. "Believe me, it's just as unexpected for me as it is for you." My eyes sweep over the guys, lingering for a moment before I speak up a little louder. "So, you all just came for breakfast?"

Eli grins, looking entirely too calm for an unsuspected situation. "I'm not the one to turn down a good breakfast." He shrugs, stretching his arms high above his head, a deliberate flex of his muscles that doesn't go unnoticed. There's a casual confidence in the way he moves, like he knows exactly what he's doing. He looks down at Sadie and says, "So, what is your plan darlin'? I know you aren't just here for breakfast, anything else you are here for?"

We all groan and roll our eyes, "Yeah, just ignore Eli, he is always like this. Likes to flirt with anything with a pair of tits." Milo calls to Sadie.

"I think I'll survive," Sadie says, holding her left hand in the air. Showing off the most obnoxiously large rock on her ring finger. "You might want to dial it down a notch. I am already spoken for."

I shake my head. Although Sadie has been engaged for two years to an *cough* asshole *cough*, she claims that she is still in love. Sadie has been engaged for two years to her high school sweetheart, and while she puts on a brave face, we all know that her so-called fairytale romance has been anything but smooth. But Sadie's the queen of acting like everything's perfect, even if it's clear she's been doubting it for a while now.

"Never said I haven't hooked up with someone who is engaged." Eli pumps his eyebrows at Sadie, "Engagement rings don't frighten me."

I chuckle and glance at Cole, who sits quietly beside me. I can see a small smile hidden underneath the mug he brings to his lips. He sits oozing with calm energy, no matter how much everyone jokes around, his presence beside remains comfortably quiet beside me. His posture is relaxed as if he always knows that he is going to be a part of the chaos, still, he never becomes immersed by it.

As the chatter continues to pick up round the table, I am left to my own simmering thoughts. The boys joke around, Eli flirty remarks hang in the air like a bad perfume, and Sadie's laugh rings in my ears. The close proximity of Cole beside me, burns like the coffee in my mug. The space between us is just wide enough for comfort but close enough that I can feel the heat of his body transfer over to mine.

It's strange to think I have only been here for barely two weeks; with people I barely know. Yet, despite it all, I have never felt more like myself here... *with him.*

Sadie's voice slices through my thoughts, the playful remarks from Eli pull me back to reality.

"Seriously." Sadie scoffs, "I already just told you; my hair is auburn. *NOT RED*, Elijah."

"Darlin,' call me Eli. Elijah sounds too formal." Eli purrs.

"No." Sadie folds her arms under her chest.

"Why not?"

"Because I don't know you close enough to call you, Eli."

"Well, if you wanted to be *closer*, you could've just asked, *Red*."

We all groan. I look over towards Sadie, a small smile plays on her face, as if she is enjoying the attention she is getting from Eli. My gaze unintentionally flicks to Coles. Like an anchor in deep water, I feel as if Cole is keeping me at bay. For the fleeting moment, I wonder about the latest of my feelings. The isolation. The sudden closeness of the group of outsiders, and a man who seems to keep, me at peace without even lifting his finger.

"So, Blair," Travis smirks at me across the table, "What are your plans now that this one has found you?" He gestures towards Sadie, who is currently in a battle with a flirty Eli.

"I don't know." I mutter down into my cup; I watch as the dark liquid steams. "I never thought I would get company; I was just going to have a quiet day myself." I shift under the gaze of the group.

I catch the sympathetic look in Sadie's eyes, but there is also a glimpse of excitement too. She knows better than anyone that I crave distance, especially after my old life back home. But at the same time, I know she enjoys seeing me this way. Unbalanced, not thought out, no professionalism.

"Come on, Blair." Sadie hollers at the head of the table. "You are always so serious. Don't you want to have a little fun?"

The boys murmur in agreement. The underlying truth is, I've needed a change. Although, I never thought it would come in the version of her and four rowdy cowboys.

"Maybe a little fun wouldn't hurt me." I shrug, trying to act nonchalant despite the butterflies flying in my stomach.

"Well, if you are planning on staying around, you are going to need to get used to the chaos." Cole's voice cuts deeply within the group, his eyes meeting mine for the first time this conversation has started. "We don't really do quiet here, do we, Blair?"

His words hang heavily in the air, I feel like I'm frozen in time. The chatter from the table fades away completely as I slowly nod my head in agreement.

"No." I say, "I guess not."

Before I get the chance to expand my conversation with Cole, Eli pipes up, drawing everyone's attention when he says, "Did you guys know that Cole is entering a competition for this year's Misty Pines Festival?"

The babble from the table halt, the attention starting to shift. Cole's body tenses next to mine. His whole dementor changing as his once soft gaze snaps furiously towards Eli.

"You weren't supposed to tell anyone." He hisses lowly; it is clear that Eli has opened the door that Cole was trying desperately to keep closed.

"Opps." Eli smirks and leans back in his chair, enjoying the storm that is brewing in Cole's eyes.

I glance between the two of them. It's like watching a show unfold before me. I don't know if I should sit back and observe or lean in. The usual calmness of Cole has completely disappeared. It looks he might just loose his shit with Eli.

As if sensing a fight about to break out over the breakfast table, Travis chuckles softly. "Come on, Cole. You know Eli doesn't have a filter. He'll tell the whole town if he gets a chance."

"*Hell yeah.*" Eli smirk, "What the point of keeping a secret so juicy if it isn't going to be spilled."

"It's not the kind of thing I want people to know yet." Cole sighs, clearly trying rein in his temper.

I lean forward, the interest getting the better of me. "What is this competition for?" I feel sincerely interested now. I feel like I am learning something entirely new about Cole – something he keeps locked away.

His eyes land on mine, they soften when he says, "Misty Pines Festival happens every year locally. They hold all kinds of competition, livestock, cooking, farming, the works. This year they are doing a bronc riding competition." His eyes snap back to Eli's, "And this idiot signed me up… *without* me knowing."

"What the hell is a 'bronc riding' competition?" Sadie asks, as if he spoke a different language.

Eli springs out his seat, the excitement radiating off him. "It's a rodeo event, and basically you have to stay on a bucking horse until the time runs out."

"So, bull riding but with a horse?" Sadie asks.

Milo chuckles, "Darlin' it is much different to bull riding."

"And is this... safe." I look over to Cole, he shrugs slightly.

"I used to do it back in the day, I figured it could be fun."

"You didn't answer my questi–"

Eli scoffs, interrupting me, "Fun? Seriously dude, it is a competition. You are going to take home that first place. Mark my words."

Milo hums, "He is as competitive as they come, never backs down from a challenge. Even if it kills him."

I can't help but smile when I peek over at Cole. His posture seems taller now. It seems that the competition isn't just an event to him. It is something that matters. To prove to himself that maybe he is more than the ranch.

I see the determination bubbling within him. I see the spark in his eyes. The investment.

"I'll be rooting for you." My words slip out before I have a chance to catch them.

Looking down at me, a brief flicker of surprise plasters his face. but then he nods, a small smile playing on his lips. "Thanks."

As the conversation move on, I can't seem to shake the quiet moment between Cole and me.

I feel like I'm starting to figure out Cole in a way that goes way beyond the calm, mysterious cowboy who likes to stare at the stars with me at night.

Chapter 14

Cole

As a 'participation reward' – or so Eli and Travis called it – for my impulsive decision to compete in the Misty Pines Festival, we all ended up at The Tipsy to celebrate. The bar is buzzing with a mix of locals and tourists, but my gaze doesn't waver from her. The girl in the white sundress, her cowboy boots clicking against the worn wooden floor, and a cold beer cradled in her hands. She's the only one that matters in this crowded room.

When Blair walked out the house looking like *that,* it made me want to throw her over my shoulder and lock her away for only me to keep. The slight flush on her cheeks from the humid bar and the bright smile plastered on her face makes my pulse beat that little bit faster underneath my skin.

I bring the glass of whiskey to my lips, my eyes never leaving her as the men around her stare with hungry eyes, practically drooling as she talks to Sadie. My grip tightens around my glass, my knuckles turning white, as yet *another* guy steps up to ask her to dance.

"That caveman glare won't win her over, man," Milo chuckles beside me. I drag my gaze away from Blair, shifting my focus to our table. Travis is still, as always, lost in the TV. Eli wears that mischievous grin of his, the one that always makes me question what he's up to. And Milo? He's lounging across the bench like he's royalty, taking up more space than anyone should have the right to.

"If anything, it will scare the poor girl off."

"What the fuck is a *'caveman look'*?" I grunt, leaning over Eli's shoulder, my eyes following as she politely turns down *another* guy.

"Like this." Eli starts to morph his face into the so called *'caveman look.'* He pouts his lips, juts out his chin, narrow his eyes and pulls down his brows.

"You look like a fucking idiot than a caveman." I scoff.

"Hey!" Offended, Eli crosses his arms over his chest, I real pout now plays on his lips. "At least I can get any girl I want, and I don't need to sit from across the room waiting for her to pick me to dance, like some sixth grader."

I roll my eyes, "I'm not waiting for her to pick me to dance. I don't even want to dance with her."

Eli, Milo, and Travis laugh. As if what I just said was hilarious.

"What's so funny?"

Travis grins, "So, hypothetically if she was dance with another cowboy right now, what would you do?"

My hold on my glass becomes a death grip, the idea of another man touching her makes my skin feel like it is scorching.

"I'll tell him to take his fucking hands off what's mine." I seethe into my glass.

"I wouldn't look at the dance floor, if I were you." Milo mumbles beside me.

My gaze snaps up to the floor. The loud beat of the music and the hard footsteps hitting the wooden dance floor, sends vibration throughout the bar and deep into my bones.

I catch sight of the white dress clinging perfectly on Blair. The sight almost looks so beautiful, watching her dance, happy and carefree. However, what diminishes that beauty is a meaty palm slithered around her lower back, large shoulders and a sly grin plastered on a face.

I watch the scene playout before me. Song, after song, after song. I feel like time has slowed down, like the man above is giving me a torturing punishment for the way I first treated Blair when she arrived.

I sling back another whiskey as Sadie walks over towards our table, breathless and sweaty from the dancing.

Grabbing Eli's drink, she takes a heavy gulp and sighs wistfully. "Damn, I love cowboys."

"Cowboys like me?" Eli smirks pumping his eyebrows as Sadie pulls a chair up beside Travis.

She rolls her eyes, "Fuck no, you are where I draw the line, Elijah. I'm not into cowboys... *like you.*"

Eli groans into his hands, "Goddamn you, *Red.*"

I continue to watch Blair. Although she is dancing with a fool, it's nice to see her feel like she is finally in a place where she belongs. Despite the rustic setting of the bar, the dim lights and the smell of old beer and sweat. She looks like she is at home. The thought stirs something in my chest, a flutter I can't ignore. I've never really considered the possibility of Blair staying here for good, but now that I do, it hits me – Copper Creek wouldn't be the same without her. Maybe, just maybe, she's the missing piece I didn't even know I was looking for.

"Got any nerves yet, Cole?" Sadie leans in closer, raising her voice to cut through the thumping country music, trying to make sure I hear every word.

"This guy doesn't get nervous," Milo says, slapping a hand on my shoulder. "He used to do this for years back in the day. This'll be a walk in the park for him."

I stare down at my empty glass, Milo's words echoing in my head. He's right – I don't get nervous. But this pressure? It feels like a weight pressing down on my chest, squeezing the air out of me. The realisation hits me like a punch to the gut – soon, the spotlight will be on me. People will be watching, depending on me to win. And the thought of it makes it harder to breathe.

If I win that trophy and the cash, the plan is clear – I'll use it to buy the ranch from Blair. But every time I think about it; a sickening guilt twists in my stomach. The idea of lying to her, of betraying her trust, it all seems too much.

"You should ask her to dance." Sadie yells over the table, a knowing smirk plastered on her face. "We all know you like her."

"I—I don't!" I snap, trying to convince myself more than Sadie that there's nothing between us.

Sadie raises an eyebrow, her smirk widening. "Oh yeah? So, staring at her all-night means nothing?"

Before I can come up with a rebuttal, Isabelle Bishop appears in front of our table. She's standing too close, her eyes locked onto mine with an intensity that almost feels predatory. A look of hunger, desperate and eager, spreads across her face as she leans against the table, her posture a strange mix of desire and purpose. Her lips curve into a smile that's more possessive than welcoming. I feel the heat of her gaze burning into me, and I shift, suddenly too aware of how uncomfortable this all feels.

The last thing I need right now is Isabelle's attempt at pulling my attention away, especially when Blair is out there on the dance floor with someone else.

Isabelle leans in, practically resting on the edge of personal space. Her voice drips with an exaggerated sweetness as she says, "Hey, Cole. I saw you from across the dance floor. Want to come dance with me?"

Her words hang in the air, blending with the thumping beat of the country song that pulses through the bar. A mix of irritation and frustration bubbles inside me. Isabelle might be conventionally attractive, but it's obvious she's the type who chases after any guy with a pulse in this town.

Even if I tried to fight it, my thoughts of Blair have never seemed to stop since stepping foot in here. The idea of another women near me, especially Isabelle, just makes the knot pull tighter in my stomach.

Before I can even respond, Sadie's voice rings out over the noise, cutting through the crowd.

"Come on, Cole. She clearly doesn't have a dance partner. Don't leave her hanging!"
I glance over at Travis and Milo, both staring at the scene with wide eyes. Eli's amused smirk only adds to the pressure. I shift uncomfortably in my chair, hoping to ease the tension crawling up my spine.
"Come on, one dance, and then we can *chat*," Isabelle insists, leaning in closer. Her perfume hits me like a wave – too heavy, too much. It's nothing like the soft, fresh scent of tangerines and lavender I find myself remembering instead.
I feel a small sting in my chest. The thought of Isabelle thinking she could get me so... easily, the assumption that I would fall for her little act.
"Sorry, he already has a partner." A familiar soft voice eases the small ache in my chest. As Isabelle leans away from the table, my sight lands on an angel standing tall with confidence in a pair of cowboy boots.
Isabelle's gaze sweeps over Blair, taking her in from head to toe, sizing up the competition. Her smile widens, but it's more forced than ever as she addresses Blair. "Sorry, and you are?"
Blair smirks and stalks forward, her footsteps matching the fast pace of my heart. When she gets close enough to me and our table, she bypasses Isabelle and places herself directly onto my lap, hooking her arm around my shoulder.
Instinctively my arms warp around her waist, my skin looks dark against Blair's angel white dress.

Blair leans back into me, her voice calm as she responds, "I'm Blair Reynolds." She eyes Isabelle with the same cool appraisal, taking her in from head to toe. "And you are?"

Scoffing she folds her arms against her chest, "Isabelle Bishop." She states, as if Blair was supposed to know *exactly* who she is.

The girl in my arms chuckles, I revel in the feel of her body vibrating against mine. Her warmth transfers through me, sending my body in a relaxing state. With the feel of her back against my chest, the way her body settles comfortably into my arms. It makes the room around me completely fade away until it's only us. Her and me.

Isabelle shifts uncomfortably, her eyes flicking over Blair, still resting in my lap. They narrow as they settle on Blair's face, but Blair remains unfazed. Her chin rests effortlessly on my shoulder, an expression of calm confidence, as if she belongs exactly where she is.

"Well, I was offering Cole a dance, but I can see you're clearly... *busy.*" She forces a smile, her voice dripping in sarcasm.

"Seems like it." Blair responds casually, yet I can't help but notice the underlying challenge stitched between her words. I can't help but smile at Blair holding her ground, even in unwanted fights.

With a huff, Isabelle nods curtly before turning her attention to my brother, her entire demeanour shifting. "*Milo*, will you be my partner?" she asks, her voice dripping with sweetness.

Milo nearly chokes on his drink, eyes wide with shock, like a deer caught in headlights. "Sorry, darlin', I –"

"I think he'd *love* to!" Sadie interrupts, her voice loud and playful as she gives Milo a mischievous wink.

Milo grits his teeth, his morals clearly being tested as he reluctantly stands, shooting a glare at Sadie. Before he can protest further, Isabelle tugs him by the arm, practically dragging him toward the dance floor. Meanwhile, Sadie raises her drink in the air, grinning wickedly as she cheers him on with a teasing, rueful smile.

I feel fingers dig into my neck; I small shiver runs down the base of my spine as Blair leans closer, whispering, "That was fun," I can hear the small tease hidden in her voice, "But I think you owe me a dance now."

The suggestion makes excitement sprout within me, the gleam of playfulness in her eyes is hard to ignore. My arms wrap tighter around her waist. "Hmm, guess I do, don't I?"

My voice has more heat than I expected. The way she looks so perfect in my arms, the confidence and aura around her, it's getting harder and harder to resist.

She beams at me with a smile, "Come on, cowboy. No time to waste."

I wish I could sit in the back of the bar with Blair in my arms forever. In our own little world were everything seems to fade. However, when I stand, and place Blair gently on her feet, when she pulls me onto the dance floor, everything starts to feel right. Everything feels as if it is falling into place.

Her body sways gently against mine, her hot breath fans across my neck, and her fingertips grazes through the strands if my hair.

Her words almost get lost within the music, "You okay... with this?" I can hear the concern in her voice, something I'm not used to hearing.

I meet her gaze, brushing the pads of my fingers behind her neck, "Yeah, I'm good." But the reality is I don't know what the hell I am anymore. The tension stuck between us, the attraction that I can no longer ignore, it's so much more extreme than I anticipated. Yet, swaying here with Blair. It feels right. It feels as if I have waited for this my whole life.

Blair smiles, her fingers tangle in mine as we continue to dance. I let myself become lost in the moment. The crowd fades and it's just us – standing in a dimly lit, empty dance floor – with the soft beats of the music.

I lean in closer. My forehead rests against hers. Our hot breaths mingle together, when she smiles, our lips graze.

It's in this moment I don't care about the eyes that will be on me, I don't care who is watching. So, when I kiss Blair, I kiss her as if it is only us on the dance floor. I don't pay any attention to the gawking eyes, or my brother dancing woodenly with Isabelle Bishop in the corner.

I focus on the feel of Blair's lips against mine. I focus on her.

Chapter 15

Blair

I lose track of how many songs have played, each one flowing seamlessly into the next. Every time I start to pull away, Cole pulls me right back in. It's magnetic. It's intoxicating. Like a high I never want to come down from.

When the beats of the country song fade away – indicating another song has ended – I smile up at Cole, "Hey, do you think you could let me go for a few seconds? I need to use the bathroom."

His body vibrates against mine; a wide smile is on his face; his dark eyes look black in the dimly lit dance floor. "I finally got you were I want you, and you want to run away from me?" He smirks, giving me a playful eye roll and whispers in my ear. "Be quick, I have a feeling Isabelle is waiting for you to leave so she can pounce."

I feel my heart flutter as his playful, hot breath fans across the side of my face. Everything with Cole is intense, but nothing mattered when he was standing this close, his body brushing against mine.

"I'm not running away from you." I chuckle, "I just need a break, okay? And if Isabelle does happen to pounce on you, I will come and save you… *again.*"

His lips pull up into his signature underwear melting smirk, "Alright, hurry back sweets. I don't want to come chasing after you."

"Promise I will be quick."

I push my way through the crowd, nerves twisting in my stomach. Isabelle won't make this easy, I know that much. The thought of her eyes sweeping over Cole, of her deliberate moves, makes my head spin. Maybe they're meant for each other, both so well-liked, so at home in Misty Pines. But that thought vanishes the moment I glance back and catch Cole's gaze – his eyes steady on mine, a knowing look in his expression.

The way he looks at me, like I'm the only thing that matters in the room, lightens the weight in my chest. The idea that he'll be there when I return comforts me more than I want to admit.

As I push open the bathroom door, the noise of the bar becomes a dull thump. Walking over to the sink, I splash a handful of water on my face, the instant relief of the cool liquid settles down my racing heart rate.

I replay the events of tonight in my mind – the kiss with Cole, the way he made me feel like we were the only two people in the room. It was as if he'd awakened something inside me, brought me to life in a way I didn't expect.

I turn toward my reflection, trying to gather my scattered thoughts, but the sudden creak of the bathroom door interrupts my focus, slicing through the stillness.

"Well, look who is taking a break."

I freeze; my hands braced on the porcelain sink as Isabelle's voice slithers towards me.

"I was wondering when you would show up." My tone is flat when I smirk at her, the determination to not show any weakness rushes through me.

Her laugh is sharp and biting, a cold edge to it. "You really think you've got him fooled, don't you?" she sneers, her voice dripping with sarcasm. "You think Cole would actually be interested in someone like you?" She scoffs, the sound of her heels clicking against the floor echoing as she strides forward, each step purposeful.

I square my shoulders, and face her, "You don't know *anything* about me or Cole."

"Oh, I know more than you think." She smirks, closing the distance between us. The small bathroom seems to shrink with her presence, the air growing thick and suffocating.

"He is playing with your feelings, sweetie. Do you really think you are his type. You are just a distraction."

I feel my stomach twist. The way Isabelle thinks she has a claim on Cole, makes me feel sick with disgust.

I laugh bitterly, "I'm not playing you're game, so why don't you piss off and bother someone else."

Isabelle's expression twists into something darker, "You think you can take him away from me?" She spat, "You have no clue what you are up against."

Before I could even reply, I hear the sharp sounds of muffled footsteps, follow closely by a familiar voice. "Blair?"

The deep voice was laced with strong concern and urgency which sent a relief to wash over me. I knew who that man was.

Cole.

Not caring about entering the women's restroom, Cole pushes open the door, his eyes widen as he spots, Isabelle confronting me. The shock immediately disappears and is replaced by irritation. "Is there a problem in here?" Although his voice is calm, there is a warning hidden with his voice which doesn't go unnoticed by Isabelle.

"Nothing that concerns you, Cole." Her eyes narrow, unwilling to back down.

I catch Cole's gaze over Isabelle's shoulder, and in that brief moment, his protective energy envelops me. It's as if his presence fills the small bathroom, wrapping me in a shield of care and quiet strength.

"You need to leave." Cole's voice was firm, he steps further into the bathroom. "*Now.*"

I watch Isabelle's lips curl up in a sneer, her eyes dart between us. Before exiting the bathroom, she hisses into my ear for only me to hear. "Remember what I said. You are no match for him." Turning on her heels she storms out the bathroom, leaving nothing but her echoing sounds of her heels behind her.

"Thanks." I release a breath I didn't know I was holding, the tension in my chest melts away as I take in Cole. For the first time, in a long time, I have felt truly safe.

"I will always have your back, Blair." He steps closer, the toe of his boots brush against mine, his tall frame towers over me. His large hands cup my cheeks, and he looks deep into my eyes. "What did she say to you?"

"Nothing. It's not important." I gulp, watching his jaw clench. His fingers tighten ever so slightly on my face.

"Blair. Tell me what she said." His voice is dark, lethal. Like a dark panther stalking his prey.

I shake my head, "I told you. It was noth–"

I'm instantly cut off with his lips pressing aggressively on mine. I'm so caught off guard, that my legs almost give out beneath me. However, when strong golden arms wrap around my hips, I start to float.

Pushing me against the bathroom wall, Cole deepens the kiss. His tongue sweeps my bottom lip, a silent request for entry. As I part my lips, his soft tongue delves deeply into my mouth, licking softly against my own.

His hands travel past my waist, over my hips, and around the back of my thighs, giving them a gentle squeeze. Wrapping my arms around his neck, I pull myself up against him, linking my legs around his hips.

He moves me towards the bathroom countertop and sits me down, all while he continues to kiss me ferociously. Since I am sitting on the countertop,

Rodeo Hearts

Cole stands high over me, allowing him to delve his tongue deeper, as if he is looking for the answer I won't give him. As he starts to knead my thighs, I can't help but let the small moan slip out my lips, echoing in the empty bathroom. One hand leaves my thigh – leaving the feeling of a burning hot handprint on my skin – and grasps my jaw, pulling our mouths barely apart, his plump lips graze mine when he speaks. "You gonna tell me, Blair?" His voice oozes in desire.

As I shake my head, he makes a *tsks* sound with his tongue, displeased and pulls away, walking towards the door. "If you aren't going to tell me, Blair…" He pauses in front of the door, just when I think he is about to leave, he twists the lock. The sound echoes throughout the bathroom, goosebumps form over my flesh, and I instinctively squeeze the ache between my thighs. "I'm going to have to make you." He whispers darkly.

I gulp as he propels towards me, his dark eyes trained on me. When he is standing in front of me, I feel as if he is stripping me bare, looking deeply into my soul.

Kneeling onto the ground, he clutches my hips and pulls me to the edge. His eyes are staring deeply between my legs.

Pushing my thighs apart, he starts to pull up the white fabric of my dress, his eyes widen when he catches sight of my wet bare pussy.

"You been like this all night?" He shakes his head, his hands move up the inside of my thighs until he meets my centre, pulling my lips apart each side with his thumbs. "Have you been exposed and soaking, sweets? Hoping someone can help you fill the need?" His hot breath whispers against my thighs, waiting for my answer. One of his thumbs glide up my centre.

"Yes." I whimper, shimming my hips forward, begging for some relief.

He chuckles darkly; the sound makes my nipples tighten. "You want me to suck on your pussy, Blair? Relieve that ache?"

I squirm on the bathroom counter, "*Yes.* Please, Cole."

His voice is breathless when he says, "Be quiet for me, baby."

The fan of his hot breath is replaced by a wet mouth. As I moan loudly at the contact, my hands fly to my lips, trying to hide my pleasure to the bar.

I feel Cole's body vibrate against mine. His tongue drifts up between my slit and delves in, like a man who has been starved for days.

He laps up my wetness, his fingers press hard into my thighs, no doubt leaving bruises of his fingerprints. Then, when he inserts one finger, it starts to become so much. When I have adjusted to the size, he adds another and rises his head from between my legs.

"You like that." He looks up at me, his dark eyes look hooded in the dim lights, his cheeks are tinted a pink flush, and a dirty smirk is placed on his face.

"Yeah." I moan breathlessly. I feel the pressure beginning to build at the base of my spine, the ball of electricity becoming more powerful with each fast pump of his fingers.

However, Cole slows his pace. The buzz of power diminishing. I look down at him, finding a wicked smirk on his face.

"I'll let you come, if you agree to tell me what *she* said." His practically hisses the words.

"Cole." I whine, angling my hips closer to his face, begging for a release.

"Come on, baby." His breathing is hot on my pulsing pussy, "Tell me and I will give you what you want."

He picks up the pace again, edging me closer, then continues to slow down. It's pure agony, I feel like I am sitting of a ledge, the wind starting to sway me back and forth. Though, I am unable to fall.

"She said… all I was, was a distraction." The words tumble from my lips. The feeling of Cole's fingers stops. Looking down, I watch a dark look past over his face, he grinds his morals before he speaks.

"You are distracting." Before my thoughts take over, he places a tender kiss on my thigh. "You intoxicate me. You fascinate me." He places kisses up my thighs until he ends near the centre. "If anything, Blair, you make me feel *alive*."

He places a punishing kiss on my pussy. He kisses and sucks until I'm grinding against his face. His fingers pick up that harsh pace, hitting the soft spot inside me, like he knows I'm about to come.

He pulls away, the stars start to form in my eyes when he says, "Come for me."

Then he does something unexpected. He spits on my pussy, his saliva mixes with my juices. And it's enough to make me erupt.

Once I come down from my high, Cole stands, a proud smirk gracing his face. Grabbing some paper towels, he cleans me up gently, as if I am made of glass. Hopping off the counter, my legs feel like jelly, but once a strong arm wraps around my waist, I am pulled securely into the cowboys side.

I look down his body, unable to miss the huge bulge in his pants. Before I have the chance to speak, he interrupts me. "Don't even think about it."

"But I don't think –"

"Blair." He glances down at my face, all serious.

"Cole." I challenge.

He rolls his eyes, a small smile on his face, "Come on, let's get back to the group before they start wondering where we have disappeared to." He places a quick kiss on my lips, before opening the bathroom door.

As it creaks open, we are met with our familiar red head. Her hand raised in a fist, as if she was about to knock. "*Oh.* Hey guys!" She smiles, all cheery, but deep down I think she knows *exactly* what just happened. "I was wondering where you ran off too."

I glance at Cole. A horrible case of déjà vu hits me.

"Is that right?" Cole narrows his eyes at Sadie.

"Yup. Anyways, I'm just going to use the bathroom." She smiles and gives a non-discrete look towards me as she passes.

As we start to walk away, she calls from the bathroom one last time. "Why does it smell like sex in here?"
I hide my chuckle into Coles side. *Only Sadie.*

Chapter 16

Cole

Me: *Hey, won't be around today. Practicing for comp. If you need anything just text.*

Sweets: *Oh okay, any work for me to do around the ranch?*

Me: *No. Milo has got it covered.*

Sweets: *Okay, do you want me to come help you practice?*
Sweets: *If not, totally cool. I can hang with Sadie.*
Sweets: *Actually, scratch that, she's heading into town. I'm not going, don't feel like it.*
Sweets: *Cole, you there???*

Maybe I shouldn't have knocked back that many whiskeys last night.

My head is pounding, and I feel like I'm teetering on the edge of death. The morning sun beats down on the ranch, its heat making me sweat out the remnants of last night's drinks as I force myself through practice for the competition.

The dust from the arena sticks to my skin like glue. The sweat drips down my neck as I bind the rope around the horn of the saddle.

I've won countless of times as a teenager, spent endless hours training for this moment – on the mechanical bull my brother uses for his competitions, and perfecting my skills on the saddle. But this time, it's the real deal. The bronc is wild and unpredictable, it's power legendary. The history of leather-clad riders getting tossed faster than you can blink has scared many into never trying again.

As I swing my leg over the horse, a rush of familiarity and nostalgia hits me, like sand sticking to my skin.

"Alright, let's see what you've got." I give the horse a firm pat on its neck, guiding it into position. Shifting my weight, I slide my feet into the stirrups, adjusting my grip on the rope, every movement feeling like second nature.

I squeeze the horse, and it instantly rears up, its powerful muscles coiling beneath me. The bronc starts bucking violently, twisting left and right in a desperate attempt to throw me off. I grip the rope as best I can, but with each vicious buck, I'm tossed like a ragdoll, my body flying in every direction as the horse fights to shake me loose.

We move in sync, but with each wild jerk of the horse, I feel my control slipping. My hand tightens, cramping as I struggle to hold on. The bronc bucks, her hooves slamming into the air as she fights to throw me. I brace myself, but she's too much. With a violent twist, she spins, and I lose my grip on the saddle. The rope burns through my palm as it slips from my fingers, and I'm airborne, the world spinning as I crash to the dirt.

As my body connects to the ground, the eruption of dust bursts in the air. The bronc flies around the arena, clearly agitated and proud at the fact that it managed to get the better of me.

I release a heavy sigh, trying to focus on catching my breath. Yet when I hear the scuff of boots on gravel, my sense come on high alert.

It would be so embarrassing if my brother caught me, laying on the ground coved in muck and sweat.

But, when I look up through the dust, I catch Blair standing with her arms crossed and an unreadable expression on her face. I watch her as her eyes dart around the small expanse on the arena – me laying on the ground covered in sweat and dust and the wild horse, bucking and running around the expanse of the arena.

For the position on the ground, I take her in. Her hair in tied back in a ponytail, running down the length of her back, she is wearing her usual cowboy boots and flannel. I smile at the thought of who she is starting to become, it's as if she has stripped back into the previous version of herself, I was acquainted with a decade ago.

"Hey, sweets." I call from my position on the ground. Her eyes snap back to me, her weight of her stare lands on my shoulders. "Didn't expect to see you here."

She walks closer to the rails, "I was stopping by." She pauses for a beat, studying my form sprawled on the ground. "You, okay?"

As she approaches the gates, the sound of metal scraping fills the air as she begins to unlock them. My heart races, and I push myself off the ground, ignoring the ache in my body. I rush toward her, blocking her from opening the gates, my hand gripping the metal firmly to stop her from going any further.

"You can't come in here. It's not safe." I grip the gate locking myself back in with the wild beast. I thumb over my shoulder, "If you come in here and get hurt, I won't forgive myself."

I watch her eyes soften, she traps her plump lip in between her teeth before she says, "I thought you were hurt."

I stare deeply into Blairs eyes, the idea of her rushing to my aid even with a dangerous creature nearby brings an uncomfortable warmth across my chest.

I shake my head. "Doesn't matter. You do not come in here, if that is in here. Got it?" I angle my head towards the horse.

"Got it." She nods hesitantly, her big eyes stare up at mine, the way the sun casts across her features makes me grateful that there is a gate separating us.

Turning away, it takes a few times to get the horse under control. Leading her back towards the middle of the ring, I take a peek to see if Blair is still there.

True to form, she leans casually against the fence, arms crossed, eyes fixed on me without a word.

As I start to prep the rope, a soft voice speaks, "You didn't answer my question."

Tying the knot as tight as it can go, I then look over my shoulder to Blair. "I'm good, Blair."

She softly smiles, her gaze snaps to her hands, fidgeting. "Okay, good. So, you are good. I'm good. But... are we good?"

I turn fully, giving her all my attention. "Are we good?" I repeat her question, raising a brow.

She coughs, "Well after last night... you have kinda been avoiding me. I haven't seen you today. And I thought maybe... you didn't like it. Or me?"

The silence wraps around us, broken only by the rhythmic pounding of hooves in the dirt, the low rumble of cattle in the distance, the soft chatter of birds in the trees, and the gentle rustle of leaves in the wind. It creates a kind of white noise, drowning out the chaos of my thoughts.

As much as it irks me to admit it, I've been so consumed by this competition, by the secret plan, by the drive to win, that I haven't had a single moment to address what happened between Blair and me last night. The truth weighs on me more than I care to acknowledge. I came into this with the sole intention of winning, of securing enough to buy the ranch from her, to protect the legacy of her grandfather – but at what cost? I shouldn't have let things go as far as they did in that bathroom.

But she is like a drug I can't get enough of. She is my line.

I sigh, "Blair, I'm sorry for not seeing you today. I have been... busy. I can assure you that we are good." I smirk, rubbing my hand along my jaw, "And I *definitely* liked it."

I watch as a red tint surges to her cheeks. I chuckle as I retake my position on the horse.

"How is Sadie? She enjoying the country life? Must be a cultural shock for her." I call towards Blair, wrapping my hand around the rope securely. The muscles bunch underneath me.

"Oh yeah, she loves it here. She said she is finally living her dream, after reading all of them cowboy romance books." I hear Blair chuckle.

"Is that right?" I smirk. "What is she up to now? Don't tell me she is reading one of those books."

"Nah, she took my car, went into town. Said she has to, *'Find a better place with reception.'* So, I guess the city hasn't left her yet." She chuckles.

"Hmm, she is probably in the biggest mall she can find, looking for Wi-Fi and a latte."

She shrugs, "Can't blame her. Some habits are hard to break. But she is getting there."

I grin, but as the horse shifts beneath me, my focus shifts. Hooves dig into the ground; her head start to whip – a warning that chaos is about to unfold.

"Don't overdo it, Cole. There is only so much practice you can do before you wear yourself out." Blair calls.

I give a small nod; my grip tightens into a steel fist as I squeeze my thighs. The horse comes violently alive. Hooves fly in the air, smoky dirt consumes the space, the ringing in my ears intensives as I concentrate on staying on the saddle.

To Sadie, this life may be a shockwave for her, but for me, it is all I know.

I grind my teeth, mentally counting the everlasting seconds. My muscles ache underneath my skin as I get thrown around on a saddle. But I'm not stopping. Not until I prove to myself that maybe... just maybe I can be more than this ranch.

The wild thrashing turns into a steady trot, my body trembles with adrenaline, the aftershock of the ride vibrates inside me.

The ringing that was once in my ears is replaced by high pitch cheering. Dismounting, I look over to the loud sound of encouragement. Jumping up and down, hands clapping, Blair smiles vibrantly, "You did it! That was amazing! I'm so proud of you, Cole."

I feel my breath catch in my throat. Without even thinking, I rush directly towards Blair, although the fence is tall, my height and her standing on the bottom post, allows us to be face to face.

Grabbing her jaw, I kiss the sweet lips. I savour the way her lips mould against mine. Sweeping my tongue along her lips, she opens her mouth, allowing me to deepen the kiss.

I grip her ponytail with my other hand hard. As soft moan leaves her lips, I pull away an inch, resting my forehead against hers.

"What was that for?" She asks breathlessly, running her tongue along her pink lips.

"It wasn't for anything. I wanted too." I smile. Watching that familiar red float across her cheeks.
"Do you want to learn something new?" I smirk and raise a brow.
She pulls away – her eyes expand – clearly off guard.
"Um." She hesitates, trapping her lip between her teeth, again.
Reaching over I pull the plump pink lip out between her teeth. "Come on, sweets, promise it will be fun." I smirk, tilting my head.
"Okay." She releases within a breath.
Jumping the fence, I grab her small hand in my large one. I lead her out the stables, and across the yard, towards the fun.

Chapter 17

Blair

When Cole yanks the dusty cover off the old piece of machinery in front of me, his grin wide with pride, a wave of guilt washes over me. This was *not* what I had imagined when he promised fun.
"Well, what do you think?" He smirks, hands on his hips, his hat tipped low on his head.
I take in the worn leather, the cracks cutting through the skin of the machinery. I have seen mechanic bull machines before, but none have ever been this... rustic?
I release a small cough. "It's definitely something." I state, taking in the thin mats that are thrown haphazardly on the ground, clearly not soft enough to brace an impact of a fall.
Cole chuckles, tilting his head towards the ceiling of one of the weathered sheds near the house – thankfully, not the pink one. "Smartass." He whispers under his breath.
"So, is this how you learn?" I put my hands in my back pockets, nodding my head towards the bucking machine.
"Yeah, this isn't mine though, it's Milo's. He keeps it here cause he is always on the move. You know? With his competitions."

I nod my head. Through the grapevine apparently Milo is set to become the next world champion in bull riding. Yet with his down to earth and calm personality, you would never of think it.

"How about a ride?" He tips his head in the direction of the death trap.

"Hell no. I don't know the first thing about bull riding, let alone *fake* machinal bull riding."

He laughs again, finding my anxiety amusing. "How about this," Reaching behind him, Cole pulls out a small remote with a long cable attached to the machine. "I'll go first, and you can control the speed." He tosses the remote in my direction. "Then, once you see how unscary it is. You can have a go. Deal?"

I gulp and look down at the small remote in my hands. As scary as getting bucked off may sound, the thought of flying Cole around is all too amusing to pass up.

"Deal." I watch as he positions himself on the machine. He demonstrates as he goes, giving me instructions on where to position my thighs and legs, how to place my hands and arms.

However, as I watch, I don't listen to a word he is saying. I focus on the thick thighs bracketing the leather. The veiny hand griping the rope. The way his bicep tightens as he demonstrates how to lock into place.

"You got that, Blair?" He asks, disrupting my thoughts. Pulling my eyes away from his thighs, mouth dry, he smirks at catching me.

"Yup." I cough, clearing my throat.

"Whenever you are ready." He nods at the remote in my hands.

Pressing a button the machine comes to life. The leather groans against the weight of Cole. I press another button, the machine thrusts forward, launching Cole with it. Continuing to press the buttons, the mechanism starts to up it's speed, although Cole sit stays firmly seated, one arm raised in the air, like he is a pro.

I watch the machine drive onward, Cole's hips thrust along with it. As fun as I thought this would be, it is also extremely distracting. It's like I'm watching in slow motion, the way his hips move, the way his thighs squeeze.

I lick my lips, pressing another button, the mechanism launches forward harshly, causing Cole's grip to loosen. As a result, he ends up on the thin mats with a heavy *oofth*.

I laugh, "Maybe you are right, this is kinda fun."

He laughs breathlessly on the ground. "Come on sweets. It's your turn."

"Nah, I'm good." I place the remote on the machine, "I think that is enough riding for today."

He gets up from the ground, shaking his head. "Nope, not what we agreed upon." He picks his hat off the ground, placing it on my head. "Get on the damn thing." He whispers.

I gulp. I know exactly what wearing a cowboys hat means. What makes me more tense is the fact that it is *his* hat.

Straddling the machine, I take in a deep breath, the nerves of falling run throughout my body, making my hands tremble. I'm taken back to my first days arriving at Copper Creek. When Bluebell, spooked and threw me off the saddle. The pain shot through all parts of my body as I contacted the ground. Although the mats sit inches below my feet, the thought of falling sits makes me jitter.

However, when a warm body encases mine behind me, the nerves dissipate, leaving the feelings of excitement in its wake.

Reaching forward, Cole reaches for my hands, latching them on the rope in front of me. "We are going to do this one a little differently." He whispers lowly in my ears, causing the hairs on the back of my neck to stand up pin straight. "We are going to ride this one together. However, this time you are going to hold on whilst I control the speed and the way I finger fuck you."

I gulp, shifting against the leather. He grabs the base of my ponytail, giving it a rough tug. "Would you like that?"

I nod, unable to find the words.

"Tell me, baby. Would you like it if I finger fuck you whilst you ride this bull?"

Oh, dear lord.

"Yes." I whisper.

I feel him hum against my back as his large fingers unbutton the top of my jeans.

As his fingers brush the top of my panties, he begins to operate the machine. The feeling of his body pushing up against mine with each thrust, makes my insides melt. Pulling one arm around my waist, he presses into me further, his large fingers, dig into the front of my panties, traveling down until he finds my wet heat.

He hums against my neck, "You like this, baby?" He starts to suck on my neck as his fingers travel along my slit.

The feeling of him thrusting from behind and the feeling of his fingers slowly pushing into me, it all feels too much.

I moan as Cole sinks his fingers in deeply, the machine making it that extra deeper. I hear a groan fall from Coles lips, as he increases the speed of the machine, his fingers start to pump faster.

"Fuck, baby. You look so good taking me. You are doing so well." He whispers into my neck, licking the words into my skin.

I whimper as his thumb rotates over my clit. The bundle of nerves pulse. The wetness only intensifies the feeling.

I start to feel electricity at the base of my spine. Upping the speed one final time, Cole urges me to come on his fingers.

Stars explode in my vison, as I start erupting over Cole's fingers. It feels as if fireworks has burst within me, throwing me off balance.

As I come down from my high, Cole pulls his fingers out from my panties, and put the fingers covered in my juices in his mouth, moaning.

"Fuck," He whispers. "You taste so good baby." He gives me a deep kiss. Allowing me to taste myself mixed with him in his mouth.

Pulling away he smirks, "See, wasn't *that* scary."

I roll my eyes and lean back into Cole warmth. His arms wrap around my waist, pulling me flush against my chest. Looping the top button of my jeans, he rests his head on my shoulder.

We sit contently on top of the piece of the machinery, both basking in the feeling of our bodies flat together. It's not often we get a chance to watch the world go by – the work of the ranch keeps us both busy and occupied – yet, as I sit on the worn leather with Cole it's the first time, I can finally let my thoughts catch up with me.

As Cole's strong arms slithers around me, the world seems to pause, just for a second. My pulse races, and I feel the tenderness of his touch seep into every inch of me. It's like I'm suddenly living one of those cowboy romance novels Sadie is always reading about.

Only this isn't a book. This is real, this is occurring, and my heart is battling to keep up with the emotions swamping through me. The connection I feel in this moment is undeniable, and it feels like it's been alive inside me all along, just waiting to break free.

Chapter 18

Cole

I've been pushing myself harder each day in preparation for the Misty Pines Festival, training relentlessly for the past week. In a month, I'll be performing in front of hundreds, maybe even thousands – spectators, judges, locals – all watching my every move. The thought alone makes my stomach tighten. It's the very reason I walked away from bronc riding years ago – the crushing pressure, the weight of everyone's expectations, and the terrifying reality of things going wrong, of death lurking just a breath away.

Copper Creek was teetering on the edge, struggling to stay afloat. When I saw it was on the brink of collapse, that's when I packed away my ambitions, rolled up my sleeves and started working, doing whatever it took to keep the place from collapsing under the pressure.

Walking back into the house, the silence feels uncomfortable. Sadie left town a couple of days ago, claiming that *'her husband wants her.'* – whatever that means. So, when I don't see Blair in her usual spot, tucked up on the couch scrolling on her phone, I know something is immediately wrong.

I check the whole of the first floor, coming up empty with her presence. Taking the stairs two at a time, that's when I hear the heavy sounds of heaving from the bathroom in the hall.

I race towards the bathroom; I place my ear against the door. "Blair, you, okay?" I breathe heavily; my hand grasps the metal handle. Before thinking better of it I force myself through the door before she even has a chance to answer.

"Cole, I'm fine." A small voice calls. Peering down, Blair sits on the floor in a small ball, her hands stretched over the toilet bowl, her face ghostly white. Without even thinking, I crouch down eye level to Blair and put the back of my hand on her forehead.

"Shit, Blair. You're burning up." Before she can brush me off, she leans over the bowl. I quickly move in, gently pulling her hair back from her face, one hand cradling her head while the other rubs soothing circles on her back.

After finishing throwing her guts up, she flushes the toilet and wobbly stands. Reaching into the bathroom cabinet, she grabs her toothbrush and starts to silently brush her teeth, as if my presence isn't even there.

After beats of silence, she turns her pale face towards me, her toothbrush still in her mouth as she mumbles the words, "What?"

I raise my brow and pull my arms across my chest. "You are sick."

She shrugs, "I have been sick for a couple of days. It's not a big deal."

I stare blankly at her. "You have been sick *for days*?" I pull my thumb and forefinger towards my face, pinching the bridge of my nose. "And you didn't think to tell me!" I hiss.

Now it is her turn to stare blankly. Her pale white face is enhanced by the bright bathroom lights. "Cole, it happens every month. I told you it's no big deal."

"What do you mean *'it happens every month'*?" I gape at her. "Jesus, Blair. We need to get you to a doctor."

Without even thinking, I pull Blair up into my arms, bridal style, and rush out of the bathroom, foregoing the fact she isn't wearing any pants, and her toothbrush is still in her mouth.

Thrashing in my arms, she yells around her toothbrush. "Put me down you idiot! Do I seriously need to spell it out for you! I'm on my period, asshole!"

I pause in my tracks, Blair sits silently in my arms, her face is painted in a look that screams, *'You are such a fucking idiot.'* As I stare at her face.

"Oh." I whisper.

"Yeah, *'Oh.'* Now put me down, you picking me up like a ragdoll makes me want to throw up again." She sighs.

With a small nod, I turn. However, when I walk down the hall, I march straight past the bathroom, and I open the last door in the hall. My bedroom.

As we enter, Blair looks around wide eyed, clearly off guard. I dismiss her reaction as we enter my en-suite bathroom. Flicking on the lights I place her on the countertop and turn towards the bath that I never thought I would ever use. Until now.

Rodeo Hearts

I turn the faucet, letting the water run until it's warm. As I walk back to Blair, I crouch down and rummage through the bathroom cabinet under the sink. *I know I have it somewhere.*

"What are you doing?" Blair voice wavers, uncertainty floats within her vocal cords.

Pulling the tangerine scented bubble bath out the cabinet, I peek up at Blair. Despite the fact she is clearly sick. She looks adorably pretty, clutching her pink toothbrush in her hand.

Standing I pull it out her hands and place in the glass cup with my own, then bracket my hands either side of her bare thighs, caging her in. "Taking care of you." I rasp, tucking a stray lock of her hair behind her ear.

"But you have a competition to practice for." She whispers.

I shake my head. "You are more important, Blair. I would've taken care of you day one if you asked."

The bathroom begins to steam up as I pull away, grabbing the bottle of bubble bath. I pour the clear liquid into the rushing water, and soon, the scent of tangerines fills the air. Glancing over at Blair, I give her a soft smile, reassuring her that I'll be right back. Stepping into the hall, I pull out my phone and text the guys.

Me: *Quick question. How do you take care of a girl when she's on her period?*

Eli: Dude, how the hell are we supposed to know?! We've never been on the receiving end of that.
Eli: Also, I never dated a girl long enough to find out.

Milo: Yeah... shocking, huh?

Travis: Chocolate. They love chocolate. Trust me on that one.

Milo: Oh? Speaking from personal experience, are we, Trav?

Eli: OOOOHHH. Does Trav have a girlfriend we don't know about?!?!

Travis: I have a little sister, you jerks.

Me: You guys are no help at all.

Travis: Fine. Here's the secret: Chocolate, heating pads, ibuprofen, pads, tampons... basically, the whole drugstore. Oh, and whatever she says she actually wants. But mostly chocolate. Always chocolate.

Putting my phone in my back pocket, I grab some towels from the linen closet and make my way back to Blair.
As I open my bathroom door, I am hit with a fog of sticky scented steam. The humidity of the bathroom

covers the mirror in mist, drips of condensation fall fast down the glass. Looking over towards the bath, I almost miss the chestnut hair that is placed messily on the top of a head. The bubbles encase Blair's entire body, only her head can be seen through the glistening white foam.

As I place the towel on the side, I know I should probably leave. Let her relax. However, I impulsively walk over towards Blair and sit quietly on the floor next to the giant bath. Her eyes are closed, there is a slight flush on her face. I almost think she is asleep until she opens one eye and peeks over the bath at me.

"Hi." She hushes with a soft smile.

"Hi." I whisper. The only sounds in the bathroom that can be heard is the crinkle of bubbles and the drips of water leaking out the faucet. As she closes her eyes again, I take in her face, the paleness in her face has completely washed away, now replaced with a light dusting of pink from the heat of the bathroom. "Do you always get this sick?"

She sighs, pushing her head back and sinks further into the bubbles. "Yeah. It's okay though, it's the joys of being a woman." She smirks.

I chuckle softly beside her, but as soon as I see her eyebrows furrow, creating a deep crease on her forehead, concern begins to swell in my chest.

"Hey, are you okay?" I reach over the bubbles and brush a stray lock of chestnut behind her ear.

She shifts, her body rubbing against the white porcelain causing loud teeth grinding screeching to

fill the steaming room. "Just peachy." Pulling her hand out from the mountain of bubbles, she gives a weak thumbs up and mumbles. "If *'peachy'* means feeling like I am being stabbed by a thousand knifes." I take her small hand in mine, gently swiping the bubble residue off her knuckles with my thumb. She looks up at me with a soft smile, letting out a deep, calming exhale. "That feels a little better. Thanks."
With a small nod, I kiss the back of her knuckle – tasting the flavour of tangerines on her soft skin – and shift back on my ankles. Dropping her hand, I move behind Blair and place my large hands on her shoulders. She jumps at the contact. "What are you doing?"
I lean down; my face nuzzles her neck. "I said, taking care of you." Before she has the chance to reply, I start working on the knots in her neck. She groans, tipping her head back, her eyes closed. I smirk, watching my thumbs swirl around the back of her neck and dip lower into her shoulder. I gather the bubbles on my thumbs and fingers, whirling them over her soft skin, releasing the tension in her muscles.
I dip my callous fingers into her collar bone and run them back up along her neck, although I can feel the flutter of her pulse and the deep ragged breaths she takes, this only feels warm-hearted.
"How did you learn to do this? I didn't know a robust cowboy could also be an amazing masseuse." Blair laughs as she cups her hands, rising a clump of bubble from the bath, and blows them. The clear

foam flies across the bathroom, over the edge of the bath.
I roll my eyes and chuckle at her childishness. "When your brother is a bull rider for a living, you have to find some way to shut up his whining."
Blair, shoulders shake underneath my hands. "Is that right?" She laughs.
"Yeah. After all his competition I used to act like his own personal massage therapist. I used to travel with him to his competitions sometimes. Well, that was until..." I pause. My body completely locks up.
"Until...?" Blair's voice cuts through the silence, and I feel her shoulders tense, her expectation hanging in the air. She's waiting for me to finish the sentence, waiting for me to fill in the gap.
I hesitate, my tongue suddenly feeling heavy in my mouth. I know I should just say it, get it over with, but the words feel like they're stuck in my throat. The last thing I want is for Blair to know about my father, about how he's been slowly slipping away. It feels like a weakness I can't afford to show her. The last thing I need is for her to see me as less than what I've worked so hard to become – a man who can handle everything, no matter how much is thrown at him.
Taking a deep breath, I finally mutter, "Until my dad got sick..." My voice falters, and I hate that it does. I quickly look away, trying to regain my composure, but the weight of the secret is heavy on my chest.

It feels like the air around us is suffocating, thick with all the things I don't want to say. I can feel Blair's eyes on me, waiting for the rest of it.

I swallow hard before continuing, "And your grandfather passed. And... there was no one left to keep the place going."

I feel the words stick to my tongue, bitter in my mouth. It's not just that my father's sick; it's that I've had to carry all of it alone. The ranch, the debts, the whole damn thing. The weight of it all has been crushing. I don't want her to see how much it's been eating away at me. I can't let her see that.

But it's out now. And I can't take it back.

Blair whips toward me sharply, her face wrinkled with concern, her brows furrowed in a way that makes her look exposed in a way I'm not used to seeing. The weight of her expression pulls at my chest, and I feel her apology before the words even leave her mouth.

"Cole, I am so sorry."

Her hands clasp my own. Her eyes lock onto mine, and I see something I can't quite name – remorse, grief, and a kind of guilt that falls deeper than the surface of what's been said. It's more than just the sympathy for my father's sickness, or the sadness for the loss of her grandfather. No, the look in her eyes speaks volume – It's an apology for more than that.

The look she shows me says she is sorry for abandoning the ranch when we needed her. The look she shows me is realisation – the burden of her family legacy shouldn't solely be placed on *my* shoulders.

For a fleeting moment I want to draw this woman in my arms. Tell her that everything will be okay. But the reality is that it isn't. Not until everything need to be said.

"I didn't want to leave." She whispers, "But after the fight my mom and grandfather had... I thought I didn't have a choice. That maybe it was better to stay away from the ranch." She squeezes my hands tightly. "I thought... I thought that you would be okay without me here. That you could handle the place just fine on your own."

I shake my head, trying to get rid of the frustration bubbling in my chest. I understand what she is saying. But she should've been here. With me.

"When my dad got sick. This place was hanging by a thread, Blair. I didn't know if I could handle the job on my own. Milo is too famous, too good to give up his bull riding. Dad was too sick, too weak. I had no choice but to try." My voice comes out rougher than intended. "We needed you, Blair. I needed you."

I watch her lip tremble and tears weld in her eyes. She pulls her hands away. "I know. I know, Cole. I thought staying away would solve all the problems. But I was wrong, and I see that now."

Our thoughts float within the steam. The ranch. Her family's legacy. My father. Her grandfather. The choices that we have both made. The pain we have been carrying without acknowledgment.

I lean down closer to Blair, my forehead rests against hers. I can't pretend everything is fine. Yet, I am yearning to work through it if she is at my side.

"I can't do this alone, Blair. You can't run away and hide, expecting problems will disappear."

"I'm here now, Cole. Right here, standing with you. I'll do whatever it takes to make this right. Make it right between us… for the ranch. For your dad."

As I look into her eyes, I feel the weight of her words press forcefully on my chest. I hear a promise that everything will be fixed.

Her nose brush mine, for the first time I feel like we have finally bridged the gap of which we were too afraid. There is no more silence. No more distance.

Looking into her eyes, the regret has entirely been washed away. replaced with something completely new.

Hope.

Chapter 19

Blair

When I wake up, I find myself lying on what feels like a cloud. I know instantly something's off. The soft, warm light filtering through the curtains touches my skin like a gentle caress, and the air around me smells of fresh pine and citrus, like tangerines just picked from a tree.

I shift against the mound of pillows that cradle me, my body still heavy with sleep, reluctant to leave the warmth. But as the fog of slumber begins to lift, I blink my eyes open and take in the room around me.

And that's when I realise – I'm not in my own bed.

I'm in Cole's.

The cozy blankets wrap around my body, binding me in the scent that is exactly like his flannel shirts. As I start thrashing around on the bed, trying to unwrap myself from sheets, I pause.

Next to me on the bed, lays a small woven basket that I have never seen before. With curiosity getting the better of me, I push myself up – wincing slightly from the intense cramp – and reach towards the basket.

The pink tissue paper crinkles as I pluck apart the gift. The small basket is filled with all sorts: pads, tampons, ibuprofen, soft fluffy socks, lavender candle and most importantly *chocolate*.

Getting to the bottom of the basket, my eyes widen at the hot water bottle, the cover is a soft pink, matching the crinkle paper. Tucked underneath is a small note. Picking it up with shaking hands, the familiar messy scrawl of handwriting was instantly recognisable.

Blair,

I know it's not much, but I figured you might need some of these. Take it easy today, and don't be too proud to ask for anything else you need. You're tough, but even tough people need a little help sometimes.

P.S: I figured since you like pink SO MUCH that you decided to paint my barn, I thought I could get you something for yourself to match. (took me a while to find the correct shade of pink.)

Cole.

I read the note again with a lump lodged in the back of my throat. A simple gesture, yet it was so thoughtful that my heart was aching. Although the gifts are practical, it had a touch for care embedded in them. It made me feel seen, understood.
I glance around the bedroom, clutching the note to my chest like a teenager who's just received a note from her crush.

My fingers skim the edge of the woven basket. The thought of Cole picking out all this stuff for me, makes me feel wanted in a way I have never felt before. The basket doesn't feel like straw folded together, it feels like I'm looking at pieces of me and him intertwined together, dancing in a pattern.

I take a deep breath and carefully unwrap a piece of the gifted chocolate. As it touches my lips, the sweet, rich flavour bursts across my tastebuds. As I continue to chew on the sweetness, I feel my discomfort start to dissipate. I'm not sure if it is the chocolate or the kind gestures – but I finally allow myself to unwind. Placing the items back in the basket. I settle back against the pillows and pull the backets up to my chin. The warmth and the scent of lavender starts to pull me under.

The last thought on my mind is that maybe – just maybe – that things are starting to change for the better.

When I feel the trickle of something wet in between my thighs, my eyes instantly snap open and I shoot out of the bed like I have been electrocuted. Although the room is basked in darkness, the glow of the moonlight highlights the very, *very* dark stain on Cole's bedsheets. My hands instantly fly towards my mouth, trying to muffle my loud gasp from the cowboy downstairs.

"Shit, shit, shit." I whisper quietly as I run into Cole bathroom. Flicking on the lights, I yank open the bathroom cabinet, looking for anything to remove the crime scene I have left on Cole's bed.

Coming up empty, I grab the next best thing, a washcloth and run it under the tap. Glancing up to the mirror, I catch my refection. After my bath, I decided it would be a *great* idea to wear a grey set of pyjamas for bed. Although, that *'great'* idea resulted in a dark blood-soaked stain at my crotch.

With stinging eyes, I race across Cole's bedroom with a soaking wet washcloth. The water cascades from the flannel all over the carpets of his room. However, the last thing I am worried about is a little water on his carpet.

Getting down on my knees, I move to furiously scrubbing the giant red splodge in the middle of Cole's cloud soft bed. Yet, the more I brush the wet cloth back and forth, the stain starts to become worst and worst.

The sting in my eyes sharpens, transforming into a steady stream of tears that race down my cheeks. I move in a rhythm now – back and forth between the bathroom and the bed. The cloth in my hands, soaked and heavy, mirrors the tears that won't seem to stop falling.

My shoulders and arms start to ache, my knees burn from the friction of the bed and carpet. *"FUCK!"*

As soon as the loud word leaves my lips, the thunder of footsteps pounds up the stairs, the house groaning underneath his weight. Realising my mistake, I dash towards Cole's bathroom door before he has a chance to witness the state I am in. As the bedroom door blasts open; the bathroom door slams shut with a clink of a lock.

My breathing is ragged, as I listen to the silence on the other side of the door – my ear pressing against the wood. I hear nothing. It sounds like there is no one in the room. The thought that I have imagined the door slamming open enters my brain for a fleeting moment. Though, when a deep voice calls my name, I screw my eyes shut with dread. This is going to be *awkward*.

"Blair?"

"Yeah?" I gulp, my voice waving an octave higher.

"You, okay?"

"I'm great!" My voice cracks with emotion, trying to make my voice sound as cheery as possible.

There is no doubt that he can see the massive crime scene I felt on his bed. Embarrassment washes over me, at the image of him walking into his bedroom to find that disgusting puddle of blood on his sheets. I can imagine the look of horror and repulse etched into his face. He has probably *never* had to deal with a girl bleeding on his bed. I bet he has never been with a girl with a period as bad as mine. Nausea bathes throughout my body, before I even have time to think, I run towards the toilet and spew the embarrassment out of me.

I hear the door rattle, the knob twisting, the loud banging.

Then the sounds all cut out. Replaced with ringing.

My ears feel on fire, I feel like I am having an out of body experience.

Yet, when strong hands grab my shoulders, the ringing completely halts.

Staring into concerned mahogany brown eyes, I feel my body relax in Cole's grasp. His fingers tighten as he grips my shoulders, his furrowed brows create a deep groove on his forehead.

"I'm so sorry." I mutter, before Cole has a chance to say anything. My body starts to shake in a sob. When Cole's arms start to wrap around my waist to comfort me on his lap, I twist away. "*No!* Stop. I'm disgusting. I'm bleeding everywhere, I don't want to get blood on you!"

Cole sighs deeply, "Goddamn, Blair. I don't give a fuck. Come here." Before I can even put up a fight, Cole drags me into his lap. One of his hands drapes over my thigh, whilst the over cradles my head against his chest. "You scared the shit out of me." His breath whispers in my hair.

"I'm sorry." I whisper. "I'm... I'm *so* embarrassed." My body starts to shake again with my sobs. "I – I can pay for the –"

"Don't even think about it." Cole cuts me off harshly. "You have nothing to be embarrassed about. I should've check up on you more. You don't have to apologize for having a beautiful healthy body, sweets."

I slap away my tears. "I wouldn't class leaving a crime scene on your bed '*beautiful*.'"

Cole begins to rock me in his arms, his fingers dust the top of my thighs. "Shhh…" He hushes against my hair, "Everything about you is beautiful, Blair." He chuckles, "Blood and all."

I slap my hand against his chest. "You are so gross." When I glance at his face, a playful smirk tugs at the corner of his lips, but something behind him grabs my attention. "*What the HELL?!?!*"

"What?!" He startles in my arms, his eyes travel down my body, as if he is assessing any injures that have magically appeared since being in his arms.

"*YOU BROKE THE DOOR?!*" Hanging on by one hinge, wooden splinters sprawl across the tiles and the metal doorknob laying abandoned, I gape over Cole's shoulder towards the plank of wood which used to be the bathroom door.

"I had to get to you." He replies like it's not a big deal.

"So, you had to break the door?" I snap.

He chuckles, "How about we talk about this later." He pulls me tighter towards his chest and stands. "Let's get you cleaned up."

Placing me on the countertop like before, Cole walks over to the bath and turns the tap, letting a steady stream of hot water flow before adding the same bubble bath as earlier.

As he starts to make his way out the bathroom to get some fresh towels, I speak softly.

"Thank you. For the bath. For the basket. For all of this."

He turns in spot to face me, a lazy smile on his face, "You don't need to thank me, Blair. I would do anything for you."
And with that, he leaves me wide eyed with the sounds of rushing water and a broken door.

Chapter 20

Cole

As I walk down the sterile, fluorescent-lit hallway, a shiver of nerves crawls down my spine.

Each visit should've made me numb to the sight of the frail, wrinkled bodies in these rooms, but it never gets easier. And now, standing outside Jesse Walker's door – the man who feels like a hollow echo of my father – I freeze.

I could walk out of this care home right now, and my dad wouldn't even know. He wouldn't remember I was here, wouldn't feel the absence of me. The silence between us would stretch on, untouched.

But I can't leave. Even when the weight of it all presses too heavily on my chest, I can't walk away. Not when I catch those brief flashes of recognition behind his foggy eyes, like a spark of who I am still flickers somewhere inside him. Not when he reaches out – tentative, frail – but trusting, and places his hand in mine.

I wish I could turn off the dull pain in my chest, the frustration that swells every time I see him lost, detached from the world around him. But the reality is no matter how tough it gets; I'm still his son. And maybe, in the moments when he's not looking at me like a stranger, he still remembers that too.

So, when my hand grasps the handle of his door, I drown out the impulse of avoidance and enter the quiet room.

As my eyes scan the familiar space, I spot him in his usual spot – sitting in the worn chair, gazing out the window at a world that feels so distant from him now.

"Hey, dad." My voice is soft, careful, as I approach.

With clouded eyes, my dad slowly looks up at me. I can see the confusion flicker across his face, but beneath it, there's a trace of recognition, buried deep in the fog.

"Hello..." He hesitates, his brows furrowing as though trying to summon something lost. "C... Cole?"

I swallow, my chest tightening. "Hi, dad." I smile gently, pulling up a chair beside him, the weight of the moment settling over me.

"Cole... what are you doing here, son?" Whispering breathlessly, a bewildered look plasters onto his old looking face.

"I came to see how my old man is doing." I smile, but it feels anything but playful.

The lines on his face soften, trying hard to understand. "I'm fine... fine. You don't need to waste your time with me. You should go, son."

"I'm not wasting my time, dad." I place my firm hand into his weak one. The contrast striking. "You're my dad. I want to be here... with you."

I watch his cloudy eyes well up, tears threatening to spill like a mist creeping through a forgotten forest. The fog of his memory distorts the once bright blue,

turning it into something distant, unreachable. It's almost unbearable to see.
But then, with the tremor of a hand, he places it on mine. And for a fleeting moment, the fog seems to part, just enough for clarity to break through.
"You've always been good to me, son," he whispers, his voice fragile but full of something undeniable.
Those words land heavy, sinking deep into me, wrapping around my chest in a way I didn't expect.
I feel something warm slip down my cheek, a tear that falls and lands with a soft splatter on my jeans, leaving a dark stain on the denim. "I'm here, dad. Always here."
The soft hum of the radio in the corner fills the stillness as we both gaze out the window, watching the world drift by. My dad's voice breaks the silence, quiet but steady. "You know... you seem different."
I stiffen, unsure where this conversation could end up.
My dad never made sense these days, so it is normal for him to end up off topic. However, when his gaze lingers on my face, I feel on edge.
"Different?" I cough. "Different, how?"
I watch as his eyes study my face, trying to focus. When his lips turn into a faint smile, he says. "It's not your face... that's not what I see. It is something *deeper*... something inside of you has changed. Like you aren't... closed off."
I feel my heart skip a once steady beat. It was known that my father was the insightful one. Even with the fog of dementia that wraps around him, there is still

a small part of him hidden and locked away. I feel a spark of warmth light within my chest. My dad is right, even if I try hide it. Maybe I have changed. "I'm getting older, dad. Maybe it is an age thing." I chuckle trying to brush him off. However, I know my dad better than anyone. He couldn't be fooled that easy.

"No, it's not that. It's something inside you. It's like you have shredded something heavy, It's nothing to do with age."

I blink blankly at my father. I'm not sure to laugh or be speechless. I have been so caught up in the ranch, my competition, my friends. That I haven't stopped to think about how much I have changed because of... her. "I guess I have been figuring things out."

My dad nodded, a knowing glint in his eyes, "I can see it. You're not carrying it all by yourself... are you?"

I could deny it all I wanted; I could keep this between me and my dad observations. But the tightness in my chest tells me the truth is hanging in the air, thick and undeniable. "I guess not."

The radio whispers softly in the background, but the silence in the room hangs heavy, almost suffocating. My father speak with a depth I haven't seen before. "Whatever it is, keep it close, son." He whispers softly, "It's been a long time since I have seen this in you. You've got more of *her* in you than you realise."

I knew exactly who my dad meant.

Blair.

Maybe she has been a steady force that I never knew deep down that I needed.

"I'll try, dad. I'll try, I promise." My voice feels thick with emotion. I watch my dad's eyes soften even further, catching a flicker of my old man I used to remember.

"You don't have to do it all alone, son. Not anymore. And it's okay to let someone else share the load. You've been carrying it on your own for too long."

I pause, letting the words sink deep into my bones. "I'm trying." I finally speak, exhaling a heavy sigh, letting the frustration slip from my chest. "But it's so *damn* hard."

He chuckles with a soft understanding. "It is hard for all of us to let go of something that we are so accustomed to. But the hardest part is to let someone help you carry it."

He offered me a small smile, the corners of his mouth crinkling softly, a quiet, tender expression that only a father could give his son. "I'm proud of you, remember that."

"Thanks, dad." I nodded slowly, feeling the emotions swell up in my throat.

It's here, as I sit next to my father, I finally start to truly realise that *this* was what it felt like to be on the right path. And it wasn't just the ranch, the land or the legacy Blair's grandfather and my father left behind.

It was because I had Blair by my side, helping me rebuild Copper Creek, piece by piece.

And maybe, just maybe, that is what I need to keep moving forward.

Chapter 21

Blair

I stand in the doorway, my fingers gripping the frame so tightly that my nails dig into the wood, leaving shallow indents. My gaze follows my mother as she paces the length of the living room, her steps slow and purposeful, each one filled with quiet tension.

I knew this visit was inevitable, but watching her pace the small stretch of the living room – so composed, so deliberate – stirs a tight, uneasy knot in my stomach.

The ranch felt foreign with my mom here, like it was being scrutinized, measured for its worth. It wasn't the familiar, cozy space I knew so well – it was a showpiece, a thing to be examined, not lived in. The warmth had been replaced by a cold, clinical air, and I couldn't shake the feeling that everything was being weighed.

The sound of the sharp clicks of my mother's heels echo against the wooden floorboards. With each step she took, I feel the knot tighten in my churring stomach. The designer pantsuit customed tailored to her frame, the polished black heels, the perfectly styled hair and make-up. The existence of her presses onto my chest.

This isn't a conversation I have been hoping to have today. Not after the years it ultimately took to come back here, to prove that Copper Creek was the right decision.

"I don't understand why you insist on holding onto this place, Blair." Her icy gaze shifts from the room to lock onto me, her hands settling firmly on her hips. The mother I once knew is gone, replaced by someone all business, all control. "It's falling at the seams, and it's not like you have a future here. This place is stuck in the past."

My heart sinks, a weight pressing down on my chest. My fingers dig into the doorframe, knuckles whitening as I try to steady myself. I've heard this before – the cold dismissal in her voice, the belief that I could just walk away from this place, this legacy. But each time, it lands harder, like an old wound that never fully heals.

"I can't just *sell* it mom." I speak firmly. The ranch is my home. It's not just a piece of land or property; it's everything. Every memory, every piece of work my grandfather and my dad put into this place, every oath I have made.

My mom's gaze was sharp, cold, and calculated as she eyed me. "You can't keep running this place forever. This place needs a lot of money to survive, money you don't have, Blair. This place is starting to sink, and you are drowning with it. It's true."

My breath gets lodged in my throat, the truth of it weighs heavily on my chest. I have worked myself to the bone on this ranch, yet I can't help but become swayed by my mother opinions. Maybe she is right, I don't have the money. The ranch is struggling and

it's not getting easier. The legacy my grandfather has passed on might not be as salvageable as I thought. The thought of letting go felt physically painful. Yet, I can't keep pretending that the ranch will magically fix itself.
"I don't want to let go of it, mom." My voice feels thick with emotion, wavering as I continue. "I can't let go, it's the last I have of dad."
Her eyes soften ever so slightly on her hard face. "I understand, Blair. But you have to let go of the past. You had such a bright future ahead of you. You are not wasting your life on a dusty ranch. Holding onto a place because you feel obligated to isn't a life I want for you. The ranch is not your future anymore."
I knew my mom spoke from a place of practicality – years of success, stability, and wealth shaping her every word. But no matter how much sense she made, the guilt still clung to me like a heavy cloak. The family legacy, lingering over my shoulders like a ghost, was impossible to shake. Out here, though, on this ranch, it was different. All the numbers and investments faded away. What mattered here was the memories – the love, the family.
I shake my head, removing the hypnotising, motherly trance fogging my brain. "This is *my* home. This is my father's home. This is my grandfather's home. I can't throw it away, even if it is falling apart."
Her sigh is sharp. "You don't have the resources or funds to fix this place up. Just let me help you, Blair. We can sell; you can move onto something better. This place has had its time. It's time for something new."

The words that leave her lips feels like she has physically slapped me. I have spent weeks fixing up this place. And now my mother is asking me to let go of something that is truly mine. The decision hangs heavy on my shoulders.

"I... I don't know what to do." My voice is barely above a whisper.

The sound of gravel crunching under tires reaches my ears just before the front door bursts open. Cole strides in, his brows furrowed with concern, his gaze sweeping the room – and then landing on the stranger. The tension in his posture is clear as he takes in the unfamiliar presence.

His gaze shifts between me and my mother, his expression unreadable, but there's something beneath it – something unspoken – that makes me feel less alone in this moment. He doesn't say a word, but his presence is steady, anchoring me in the silence.

My mother spared a quick glance at him. Her eyes narrowed as she says, "So, is this the solution, Blair? This... *cowboy?* Is that seriously want you want for your life?" Her voice is filled with venom, sour and lance with judgement.

It was all familiar.

"You don't know anything about him or me." I snap, my tone of my voice shaper than I intended. "You've never cared to know."

My mom looked at me across the room, her gaze cutting through the space between us, cold and condescending. The silence stretched, thick and suffocating, wrapping around my chest and making each breath feel heavier, like I couldn't pull enough air into my lungs.

"This ranch clearly means a lot to your daughter, ma'am. It is more than a business arrangement or a piece of land." Cole's deep voice breaks the silence filtering in the room.

His words felt like an anchor in the eye of the storm my mother has tried to create. His understanding, his support, as grateful as I am it startles me how much is words etch deep into my heart.

My mother's perfectly manicured brow arches, her mind racing to process this unexpected defiance. But when the words don't come, I catch a glimpse of a crack in her usual composure. I don't want to disappoint her, but I'm not ready to let go of this place – not now, not yet.

"Maybe I don't have the answer yet, mom." I stand tall, squaring my shoulders. "I don't know what the future holds, but I know that I'm not ready to let of Copper Creek just yet."

I watch as she exhales a heavy sigh. "I don't want you to make a mistake, Blair. You deserve more than this."

The lump in my throat feels heavy, but I swallow it down. "I'll think about it. I promise. I'll figure it out."

"I know you will," she says, her voice tinged with something softer, but still distant. "Don't take too long."

A resigned expression settles over her features as she gives a sharp nod and turns toward the door.

Without so much as a glance at the tall cowboy in the doorway, she strides past him and out the front door, her steps cold and decisive, before disappearing into her car.

The sound of her wheels crunching over the gravel fades into the distance, and I let out a shaky breath, releasing the tension in my chest. When I turn toward Cole, he's still there, moving closer, his presence steady.

He stops just in front of me, his hands reaching up, warm and sure, to gently cup my face. His rough fingers brush over my skin, grounding me.

"You, okay?" he asks, his voice low, as if testing the weight of my emotions.

I hesitate, unsure of how to answer, how to feel. But when I meet his gaze, I find something that steadies the storm inside me – something that reminds me I'm not alone in all of this.

"I don't know," I whisper, the words thick with uncertainty. "But... I can figure it out. I have to."

He nods, his dark eyes unwavering, filled with something that feels like unspoken strength. "Whatever you decide, we're in this together."

The words settle into my chest, a promise, a lifeline.

I managed a small, grateful smile, feeling the weight on my shoulders lighten just a little. Maybe it wasn't all about letting go. Maybe it was about learning to fight for what mattered most.

Chapter 22

Cole

The faint glow of the morning sun struggles to break through the foggy windows of The Tipsy. The smell of greasy breakfast food lingers in the air, weaving between the mismatched tables of the usual crowd: a few bleary-eyed regulars, a group of construction workers nursing their brutal hangovers, and then there's Milo, Eli, Travis, and Blair.

Sitting on a worn barstool, a stack of the white fluffy pancakes stands in front of me. My hand hovers over the dark syrup bottle hesitantly. I can't seem to shift my focus away from the pretty brunette on the other side of the bar – happily sipping her coffee.

The unexpected arrival of Blair's mother sent me back into reality. The woman arrived like a storm – forceful, demanding, and relentless, as if she hadn't disappeared from the ranch for years. As hard as Blair tried to hide the tension in the air, it was clear when she stepped back onto Copper Creek, it was never meant to be a simple and friendly visit.

It didn't take a genius to see the shift between Blair and her mother. The women pushed and prodded, each word like a calculated move in a game neither of them seemed willing to lose. Her mother didn't waste any time trying to persuade Blair to sell the ranch, to unload the land that had been in Blair's family for generations. The land that had, in many ways, defined the Reynolds legacy. Yet, despite the pressure of her mother's words, Blair didn't buckle. She stood her ground, her spine stiff with resolve. I could see the determination in her eyes as she refused to let her mother dictate her future, even if it meant standing alone.

But what really struck me was how Blair handled the situation. She wasn't the lost city girl anymore. She wasn't the same woman who'd walked into this place thinking she could just walk away from it all. The woman standing before her mother now had the grit and strength of someone who knew what she wanted – and wasn't going to let anyone, even her mother, stand in the way.

I could feel the shift too. My mind started to drift back to the plan Eli, and I had set in motion – how we'd intended to buy the ranch from Blair, to finally take it off her hands. The idea had made sense at the time. A piece of land like Copper Creek didn't deserve to be left to rot. We'd use it, build it back up, and make it profitable again. But now, after watching Blair in action, something was nagging at me.

Maybe it was the look in her eyes, or the fire she had in her that I hadn't noticed before. She wasn't the pushover I had expected. She was tough, determined, and unwilling to let anyone push her into a corner, not even her own mother. It made me doubt everything I'd told myself about the deal.

Was this really what Blair needed? Or was I just part of the problem – another person trying to get their hands on Copper Creek for their own benefit? Eli had been so certain about the sale, but now... now I wasn't so sure. I didn't want to be the one to break her spirit. I didn't want to be the one who took something from her just because it was easier than fighting for it.

I watched Blair and her mother, the tension thick between them. It was clear the battle wasn't just about the ranch – it was about control, legacy, and what each of them believed they were entitled to. And suddenly, I found myself wondering whether I was just another player in a game I didn't even fully understand.

The small slashes of sunshine cut across her features harshly. It's almost alarming how gorgeous she looks. The way her hair falls loosely down her back, the brightness of her eyes, and the plush pink tinting her lips.

I feel the pulse in my neck quicken, a light flutter turning into a steady beat.

I feel the room starting to fade. The gruff conversations, the clinks of dishes, even the laughter for Travis and Eli – it's all drowned out at the sight of *her*.

Blair. Sitting there, her face submerged in those stray sunbeams, looking like something straight out of a daydream. I could probably sit here for hours and just examine her, trace the lines of her face, the way her smile lifts one side of her lips ever so slightly like she's in on some private joke. It's maddening how every little thing about her seems to draw me in deeper.

"I know you think you are being subtle, but you are giving Blair more eyes than a bull staring down a red flag." Milo disrupts my thoughts, shoving my shoulder with his own. However, it doesn't take my eyes off the girl at the bar top as I mumble. "I'm not even doing anything."
"Think he is going to ask her out today, or have another pancake-induced existential crisis?" Eli 'whispers' to Travis. Loud enough for the whole bar – *including Blair* – to hear.
Travis smiles down into his plate, cutting into his greasy bacon causing it to crunch under the pressure of his knife. "Giving the state of his hair, I reckon this is crisis number three."
I drag a palm over my face, the sticky residue of syrup smears across my nose. The last thing I need is for these idiots to embarrass me in front of the regulars and my so called '*crush*.' "Can you guys just let me eat in peace, please?"
Milo chuckles at my side, his shoulders shake heavily. Picking up a piece of toast he shoves it into his mouth with a big bite, and winks over towards Blair.
It takes me everything to not pounce at him and throw him across the bar. So, with a small twitch of my eye, I start to slowly cut into my breakfast.
"Peace is overrated, brother. But I guess I can let you have your *moment* with the pancakes." He smirks, as he watches Blair give us a small wave from across the room.

Blair raises an eyebrow, her lips curling into a teasing smirk as she stirs her coffee. "You know, Cole, if I didn't know any better, I'd say your breakfast is about to turn into a science experiment. How much syrup can one man ingest before his blood type changes?" She laughs lightly, watching me squirm as I nearly choke on my pancake.

"Yeah... well it's the only thing helping me keep awake at this point." I cough.

"You are a walking disaster, Cole. A real *true romantic* you are." Travis sighs heavily.

Eli snorts, "Romantic? Sure. But not in the 'bring her flowers' kind of way. More like 'stand on the edge of a cliff and contemplate life's deep mysteries' kind of way."

Milo laughs as I groan into my sugary breakfast. "Like this? *'Do I, Cole, have what it takes to finally ask Blair out? Or will I drown in my stack of pancakes?'"*

I roll my eyes, pulling my hands down my faces, trying to add some distant from the idiot cowboys. "You guys are the worst."

Travis observes me with half-lidded eyes and adds, "Honestly, Cole. If you don't ask her out, I'm pretty sure you are going to end up looking like one of those sad, syrup drenched pancakes."

Glancing down at my plate, I dig into the 'sad' looking soaked stack. Part of me wonders if I should just drown in the sugary liquid and call it a day. However, Milo doesn't give up as he leans in and says, "What is the worst that could happen? She could say no?

You can just get back to eating your pancakes like nothing happened."

"Thank you for the confident boost, brother." I mutter, gazing over towards an amused Blair, clearly entertained by our antics across the bar.

Without missing a moment to add some spice, she leans in slightly, her voice just loud enough to hear over the quiet murmurs of the bar. With a grin that is a little too mischievous for comfort she chuckles, "You know you could just skip the pancakes and ask me out instead."

For a brief moment it feels as if time has stopped. My breath gets clinched in my throat, and every muscle become tighter, my whole body becoming locked. The entire bar becomes silent, as if it were empty. The casual conversation of the regulars pauses in the face of Blair's challenge.

Without missing a moment to embarrass a friend, Eli slaps a callous hand on my shoulder, causing an echo throughout the bar. "See? Wasn't so hard, was it?"

"Yeah, now you can go back to your breakfast without spilling syrup on your pants." Travis snickers into his breakfast.

As I stand too quickly, my attempt at looking cool falters, my legs unsteady beneath me. I nearly knock over my plate of pancakes and stumble over my chair, but somehow, I regain my balance, forcing myself to walk across the bar toward Blair. With each step, a mix of determination and panic pulses through me, leaving my nerves jittering uncontrollably.

Reaching her table, I let out an unstable breath and rub the clammy inside of my palms down the length of my thighs. Clearing my throat, I try and throw out the words. However, as if the air is conspiring against me, the words become lodged in my throat. "Blair – I – um – I was wondering if you… I mean, if you are free sometime, would you…"

Blair raises her brow, pulling her cup of coffee up to her plump lips, trying to hide her amused smirk. As she takes a tactical sip of her drink, she gives me a look that makes me understand that she isn't going to make it easy for me. "Let me guess, you are asking me out? Or is this another one of your *'I need some more syrup crisis'*?"

I groan and slouch forward on the bar top next to Blair, feeling the heat rising in my cheeks. "Okay, yes! I am asking you out. Are you free tonight?"

I watch Blair's eyes gloss over as she thinks carefully about my question. Letting the silence hang longer than necessary, her lips curl into a playful smile. "Well, I suppose I could squeeze you into my tight routine of fixing the farm. But I'll need to check."

I feel my heart sink deep within my chest. Yet, before I have the chance to spiral down a deep wormhole, Blair bursts into a bubble of laughter, the sound is light and full of warmth, just like the morning sun shining over Misty Pines. Reaching out, her small delicate hand clasps my shoulder. Giving a reassuring squeeze, she smiles, "Of course I will go out with you, Cole. God, you *really* got to work on your dramatic pauses."

She rolls her eyes playfully as the bar erupts in laughter and cheers – as if they were in with the joke the entire time.

From across the bar, I look towards my group of friends. Eli raises his mug of coffee into the air as if it was a pint of beer. "Finally, only took you, what? A month of living together?" A large grin spreads rapidly across his face.

Travis squints his eyes as if he is deeply moved. "A love story meant for the ages. Someone cue the soundtrack."

Trying to get my bearings I walk back towards my empty chair and sink down. My breakfast has been long forgotten now, yet the feeling of relief was undeniable. As I catch Blair's eyes from my seat, there is no doubt I look like an idiot with a constant smile stuck permanently on my face.

As the laughter continues to carry throughout the bar, I finally allow myself to relax, my stare never strays Blair's. Today felt like the beginning of something new. For once, I am not going to let this slip though my fingers.

Chapter 23

Blair

Sadie: Okay, you have to give me the details about tonight. I need a full play-by-play.

Sadie: Is Cole picking you up in a horse-drawn carriage, or is he rolling up in that truck of his with some 'I'm-a-cowboy-but-make-it-casual' vibe?

Sadie: What's the plan, Blair? Are you gonna make him look cool with that rugged cowboy thing, or are you just going to show up and blow his mind with your way better style?

Sadie: Also, please tell me you're wearing something you can eat candy floss in. I need to know this date is sweet on all levels.

Sadie: Oh, and if you can manage to sneak in a quicky on the Ferris wheel that would really make my night. 😉

Sadie: Now go, make your cowgirl dreams come true, and report back with full debrief tomorrow!

The bright neon lights of the Misty Pines Festival casts over and into the dark sky with an array of greens, reds, blues, and yellows. The air was thick with the smell of sweet candy floss, earthy smells of salty popcorn, and sizzling with atmosphere with the fried greasy food.

The place was packed with local and vacationers all dressed clad in denim. The thumping of music and laughter was thrust into the atmosphere as people milled around, enjoyed the games, rides and enjoyed the lively environment.

When I walked into the festival with Cole an hour ago, it was safe to say that we were both a bundle of nerves. I was trying to play it cool, but my stomach kept doing backflips at the sight of all the glinting lights, the glamour of carnival games, and the exotic yet satisfying buzz of excitement in the air.

Cole, on the other hand, was trying – key word *trying* – to hide how out of his element he was. He had his usual cowboy swagger, but there was a slight tension to his jaw, as if he weren't quite sure if he should be back steering cattle or throwing darts at a balloon.

Wandering aimlessly pass crowded booths, I felt Cole's hand brush against my own every now and then, making me feel as if we are grounded and floating all at once. Although we weren't holding hands – not just yet – it is clear that it felt as if we were one tiny breath away from the moment. As childish as it seems, that thought made me feel giddy.

Out of the corner of my eye, I could see Cole sizing up the rides, his mind clearly working overtime. He was probably trying to figure out how to avoid getting me on the Ferris wheel – or maybe he was just deciding how badly he'd embarrass himself by clutching the metal bars like it was the rope in a rodeo.

But what made him really tense, was the festival barker calling out prizes for a simple ring toss game.
"Alright, darlin,' ready for a big challenge?" I drawl in my most southern accent, nudging the nerves out of Cole's body with my elbow.
He rolls his eyes and gives me a cheeky smile – a smile that makes my heart do a little happy dance. "I guess we can see if I am as good at tossing rings as I am at herding our cattle." He chuckles, gazing across the small booth with obnoxiously large stuffed animals hung over the backwall behind the flying rings. Although his voice sounded confident, I could see a gleam of worries in his dark eyes.
"Yeah, right. You are a *cowboy*, not a ring master." I laugh softly as we step up towards the booth preparing for the mayhem to follow.
It was clear it wasn't just a carnival date; it felt like the start of something I can't define yet. Maybe it was Cole trying to play it cool whilst I could feel his heart beating in sync with mine. Or maybe it was first date jitters I felt – trying not to let on that I was just unsure what would happen next after this night.

As the plastic ring cut through the air, it completely misses the bottle necks and clatters onto the floor.
"*YES!*" I throw my hands in the sweet, scented air as the lights inside the booth bursts into colour, signalling my win.

Cole lets out a low whistle, hands on his hips as he tries to hide his impressed grin. "Alright, alright, you won. But it's not over."

I smirk over towards the cowboy and smugly hand over my ticket, basking in my victorious win. "I'll take... *him*." Pointing towards the wall of stuffed animals, I pick out the largest teddy bear. Clutching the teddy in between my arms, my new fluffy friend's feet drags across the ground as we walk away from the booth.

I feel Cole's body brush against my back as we make our way through the throngs of people, towards the outer most part of the festival. The loud chatter and screams starts to become muted.

"And I thought you couldn't get any softer." Cole chuckles, as he pulls his phone out to take a photo of me and my winnings.

I laugh, hoisting the teddy higher in between my arms, "Don't get used to it, cowboy. Now that I won, I think you owe me a ride."

I watch his eyebrows raise, a small crease forming on his forehead. "A ride? You mean the Ferris Wheel?" He looks over towards the tall structure standing proudly in the centre on the festival, lights glittering brightly. "You sure about that?"

I grin, amused to see a new side of the fearless cowboy I first met when arriving in Misty Pines. "Not afraid, are you?"

"Afraid? Never" He shrugs, a hint of a challenge filters within his voice as he says, "But are you sure you want to sit in a little seat with me for the whole ride? I'm a big guy."

"I think I can handle it." I feel my smile widen with playfulness.

Every step we take towards the wheel, I try not to laugh at Cole's frazzled dementor. When we climb into the creaky booth, we ascend slowly into the dark sky. Reaching the top, I feel the cool breeze of the festival whip into my face as I look down below at the busy crowd, the lit-up rides, and the packed stalls. "You know, this is actually kind of perfect." I sigh, leaning farther over the edge to look over the land.

Cole glances over towards me, his chocolate eyes soften as he stares at my features. "Perfect? You aren't freaked out or anything?"

I shake my head, my own eyes bore into his, "I'm not really scared of heights, Cole. And I'm not scared of you, either."

The words stir within the wind around us, the quiet admission hanging between us, both teasing and genuine. Cole shifts within his seat, his thigh brushing against mine, warming me against the gusts of chilly air. He grins boyishly, breaking the small moment. "Well, glad you're not scared of me. Although let's keep that a secret, I want to keep my reputation as *'tough cowboy'*." He winks.

I laugh as we start to descend from the sky, "Oh, don't worry. Your reputation is safe with me."

As we hop of the ride, Cole never mention anything about the lingering tension between us, choosing to

leave it in the dark sky instead. With an outstretched arm, he smiles "You ready for the next one?"
Linking my arm through his, I smile up at him. "Lead the way, cowboy."

The festival lights continued to cast neon hues into the night sky across the dusty fairgrounds. The energy of the crowd continued to grow with each passing hour into the night sky, yet as I head towards the long queue of the portapotties it was getting harder to overlook my developing discomfort.
Enjoying the night with Cole – snorting at his jokes and challenging him at stalls – it all felt amazing to have this night with him. However, I have been holding in for *too long*, and the need to go was getting urgent.
As soon as the plastic door opened, I rushed past the line of elderly women – calling a dismissive *"Sorry!"* over my shoulder – and thrown myself into the portapotty.
As I finish up relieving myself, I give my hands a quick sanitise and rush out the door. The smell of the grimy toilet is replaced with the sweet aroma of candy floss and the saltiness of the pretzel stand nearby – with a recognisable cowboy waiting in line.
With a small smile, I readjust my jacket, yet when I glance up, I freeze when I spot a man leaning against the row of toilets, with predatory looking eyes.

Glancing around, I scan the throngs of people, hoping he is just waiting for someone, but there was no one there in sight. Pushing off the stall, he starts to swagger over with a bit of unease. With his boots dragging across the earth and the slight hues of red across his cheeks, it's more than obvious that this man has had a little *too* much to drink. His grin grows on his face has he edges nearer, which does nothing but grow the sense of unease across my skin.

"Well, well." His voice was oily and low, slow as he moved closer. "A pretty thing like you alone at a festival? Ain't that dangerous?"

I feel my stomach drop as I take an instinctive step back, trying to make as much distance as possible. "I'm not alone." My eyes screw shut at my shaky voice. "Go away."

Not listening, the man moves a few inches closer, eating up the distance. Grinning wider, his breath reeks of alcohol as he slurs, pulling a sweaty arm around my shoulders pushing me tight against his body, "I'm not going to bite, sweetheart."

I have delt with men in the city, with strange behaviours. Following home, catcalling, unwanted flirting. However, in my years of living in a city, a hand has never been laid on me.

I recoil in his tight grip, trying to wrench out of his grasp. "Let go of me!" I snap firmly, yet my protests to leave his arms only intensifies his clamp around my body. Just as I try to twist out the steel arm branding my shoulders, a voice deep and authoritative cuts clearly throughout the oblivious loud laughing crowd. "*Hey! Get your hands off her.*"

The familiar voice makes the small pulse in my neck spike, although I didn't have the time to react before the man was jerked roughly away from me.

As the heavy weight lifts from my body, the pressure fades, leaving a wave of relief in its place. I inhale deeply, the sweet scent of the air filling my lungs as I try to calm the jittering nerves that still hum beneath my skin.

My heart pounds in my chest, but it's not from fear anymore. I turn towards the familiar voice, my emotions shifting, replaced by something else – something that makes my stomach flip with anticipation.

Standing all rugged – broad frame and eyes as hard as stone – Cole stood there, towering over the man that had put his hands on me. His jaw was clenched, his arms were crossed over his chest, stance wide and protective, like a lion ready to pounce.

The air around us crackled like sparklers with tension. Cole's eyes never left the man's face – which has completely drained of colour – his voice is low but fortified with barely restrained fury.

"She told you let go." Cole said, ice-cold, almost dangerous.

The cocky grin on the creep's face faltered, only for a second. Recovering, he puffs his chest out, "What's it to you, Walker? You think you can intimidate me?"

I stand there with my feet frozen from the intensity of Cole's ice-cold voice. I never even considered the fact that Cole could know this guy.

My pulse is still racing – though it's not from the deep fear. It was the intensity between the stranger and Cole. Every muscle in his body was tense and locked, fists clenched tight at his sides, ready to strike if necessary.
I knew he could handle this situation. He had the strength and power – yet it was his presence that seemed to fill the air that both unsettled and impressed me at the same time. He was dangerous. But there was something oddly… protective about it.
I watch as the man hesitates again. His red eyed gaze travels towards me and back to Cole, as if he is weighing his options. Though the cowboy who makes my heartbeat faster stands there firm and tall, his steady stare never leaving the creeps face.
"Whatever." The man takes a stumbling step backwards after what felt like an eternity. "She's not even worth it anyways." He sneer, before stalking off behind a few stalls.
Exhaling sharply, I bring a hand towards my chest trying to calm down the fast beat. The thought of saying thank you hangs on the tip on my tongue, but I just find myself staring at Cole instead.
Turning his still stone-cold eyes towards me, his voice is still uncharacteristically low and clipped. "Are you okay?"
I feel my throat clog with a whirlwind of emotions, unable to know how to respond. "I – I'm fine." My voice comes out barely a whisper. "He just… I didn't expect that." My next words tumble out my mouth before I have a chance to catch them. "I didn't need help."

I watch the cowboy's eyes flicker with confusion, something flashes over his harsh features of his face. "You think I am going to let some guy touch you?" His voice comes out sharp, as if he has been just as effected by the situation as me. "You don't get to decide that. That isn't your call, Blair."
I blink against the heat of his words. "I can handle myself, Cole," My voice now colder, a new sharpness creeping in as I brush pass him. "I didn't ask you to be my knight in shining armour."
He doesn't move, he watches me with an unreadable expression, though I can see his muscle in his jaw tick, as if he were holding back. "Well, sometimes it's not about what you want."
I stop in my tacks with my back towards him. My chest becomes tighter as I manage to speak the words, "I didn't ask you to do it. I don't need you." The words come out sharper than intended, but the fight for control, for independence, had finally boiled over. I was too used to not needing anyone, I was used to standing alone. I don't need anyone to stick by me, certainly not a cowboy I may or may not have feelings for.
But when he stepped closer, his presence looms behind me heavily. I could feel the heat radiating off him. "You're wrong about that." His voice was steady. "You think you don't need me. But I am not going anywhere, *sweets*."
His hot breath travels the expanse of my neck, as his large hands grip my hips tightly and spins me towards him. Swallowing I stare into his warm chocolate eyes. I was angry – angry at the creep for

putting his hand on me, angry at myself for needing someone in that moment, and angry towards Cole for making the situation feel as if I didn't know how to handle it.

Although, when I continue look into his eyes – eyes that never seem to damn waver – I realise that maybe, just maybe, he was just protecting me. He was trying to make me see something, something about us, about what we are becoming.

"I don't need you, Cole." My breath catches in my throat. My voice is quiet, yet the words hang loud in the air.

He didn't reply, instead he just stare intently at my face, watching with a blank expression. There was tension that no one could understand, bursting between us like fireworks.

Yet, when the cowboy took a step back, his gaze was softer than I have ever seen it before. The fleeting thought that maybe, just maybe, that I'm not as indifferent as I wanted to be.

"Maybe not." Cole speaks gently, heat erupting in his dark eyes. "But I'm not going anywhere."

Chapter 24

Cole

The drive back to Copper Creek was a quiet one, broken only by the hum of the engine and the crunch of gravel under the tires. Blair sat in the passenger seat, her arms resting loosely across her chest, her gaze distant as it drifted out the window into the vast, dark expanse of the fields.

Outside, the world had drifted into sleep, save for the occasional flicker of farm lights and the distant, soft glow of towns far off in the distance.

It was well past midnight now, and the moon hung high, casting a pale, otherworldly light over the land. The fields seemed to glow, bathed in that ethereal illumination, as if touched by something beyond this world's reach.

As my truck rumbles down the dirt road, the silver light bathes Blair in an almost surreal brightened glow, her brown hair almost looks black in the light, flowing gently in the wind from the rolled down windows. The shiny strands that get caught in the moonlight almost looks like silk, reflecting the striking features of her face and the soft curve of her pale neck.

For a moment, I pull my eyes off the road a stare at her profile. My grip on the steering wheel tightens ever so slightly as I study her. It's almost alarming how *gorgeous* she looks in this light – how the simple quiet moment seems to make everything about her stand out.

I can't remember the last time I have been so struck by a person – by the way she carried herself, the way her presence seemed to fill the truck without her even saying a word, simply breathing blew me away.

I fight to keep my attention on the dirt road, but there was something in this moment that felt like there was a storm building on the horizon I wasn't prepared for. Blair isn't the type to make small talk, fill the space with useless words. Except, I could feel the tension growing between us, it was simmering underneath the surface. Ready to bubble over.

Shifting in her seat, she pulls her knees up to her chest, her arms overlapping her legs as she pulls them tight. For a moment, I swear she closes her eyes, the road acts like a lullaby throughout the truck. Yet, I can tell her mind is far from quiet.

The thoughts of the Misty Pines Festival swirl through the vehicle, replaying moments that we *both* weren't expecting.

"She's not even worth it anyways."

My knuckles turn white as I grip the steering wheel tightly. I grind my teeth at the thought of the prick – how he had the nerve to lay a hand on Blair. I have never had the urge to rearrange a guy's in the face like I did tonight.

My eyes flicker back towards Blair. She was glancing out the window, again. She could think that my behaviour was irrational, but I couldn't stand by and let a woman – especially Blair – be harassed by a man.

"Blair?" My voice is barely a whisper, swallowed by the sound of the gravel crunching beneath the tires.

She turns her head just enough to meet my gaze, her light eyes locking with mine for a fleeting moment. In that brief second, the unspoken tension between us feels heavier than ever. She doesn't say anything, and neither do I. Instead, I find myself staring at the winding dirt road ahead, the way it stretches out toward Copper Creek, trying to drown out the weight of everything hanging in the silence.

And just like that, the stillness thickened once more, tighter than before. The air between us felt thick with unspoken things, charged and raw, making it impossible to find the right words.

Leaning her head back with furrowed brows, she stares at the horizon, like she is unable to get her thoughts together.

I follow, trying to gather thoughts of my own. No matter how hard she can deny, it is obvious that there is storm inside of her that is growing stronger by the day.

I couldn't sleep. As soon as I pulled up to the house, Blair hopped out of my truck and ran inside the front door before I could even cut the engine. The house was deathly quiet when I entered after Blair, the only sound the soft click of the door behind me.

I glance around, the silence settling in like a thick fog, heavy and suffocating. Blair's already gone, slipping into the shadows of the hallway, and I don't know what she's running from – or if I even want to know.

But that doesn't explain why I'm lying in bed now, in the dead of night, straining to hear if the girl who might be slipping through my fingers is still awake.

The room is pitch black, but my mind is louder than the dark, the thoughts echoing in the silence. I can't shake the image of Blair fading into the house, her back to me, shoulders rigid as if she's trying to outrun something – or someone.

I groan and throw my pillow over my head, trying to block the noise of my racing thoughts surrounding my head, but it only seems to make it worse. Every creak of the loose floorboards. Every whisper of the cool wind against my window. It sends the pulse in my neck into overdrive.

I roll over and check the time on my phone.

3:37AM

I know she's awake. I can feel it in the air. She's probably lying there, wide-eyed, like me – how could she sleep after everything? But I can't make myself go to her. Not yet. She hasn't said a word about what happened, about whatever it is that's haunting her.

Part of me wants to march down the hall, pound on her door, shatter the silence that's settled between us. But the smarter part – though it feels like a weak excuse – tells me to stay put. Let her come to me if she wants to. Let her make the first move, if she's ready.

Still, I lie there, waiting. Listening for something to change.

That's when I hear it, a dull thud coming in the direction of Blair bedroom.

I quickly throw the covers aside and rush to the door, expecting to see Blair halfway down the hall on her way to my room. But when I open it, there's no sign of her. I pause, shaking my head in confusion.

Fucking idiot.

Of course she isn't coming to your room.

Why would she?

That when I hear it again, a little louder this time – a dull thud. Creeping down the hall, I land myself in front of her door. My fingers curl around the cool doorknob, the door rattling under the pressure of my knuckles pressing into the wood. A knock echoes through the silence. I clear my throat, the sound too loud in the quiet. "Blair? You, okay?" I press my ear to the door, straining to hear if she is awake.

Thud.

Thud.

Thud.

"Cole." She says breathlessly.

She must've been asleep after all. She must be shocked that I'm knocking on her door at this time in the morning.

However, when I push the door open a crack, I almost pass away at what I am seeing.

Blair sits in the middle of her bed, covers thrown on the floor. Wearing nothing but an oversized tee, she straddles a pillow between her golden thighs. Her hands are holding the front of the pillow with a tight grip – to the point her knuckles turn white. Her brown hair hangs messily down her back, and over her shoulders, framing her apple red face and shocked lust filled eyes.

My eyes *must* be deceiving me. I *must* be dreaming. I bring my knuckles to my eyes and rub them hard. *Nope definitely not dreaming.* "What the fu-"

"*GET OUT!*" She screams, throwing herself off the bed, trying to push me out into the dark hall. Yet, I stand unmoveable like a brick wall as I gawk at her. She continues to push her small hands into my chest. "Please, get out! Oh, this is so *embarrassing.*"

"Were you…"

"*NO!* Nope, no." She continues to flail her arms, her face turning even redder.

"Moaning my name?" I ask.

She stop her attempts to push me into the dark hallway. Her eyes cast down towards her toes as she shuffles on her feet. "I- um." She coughs.

I smirk, amused about finding something Blair Reynolds is shy about. "You were, *weren't you?*" I stalk further into her room and towards her. Every step I take, she mirrors backwards until her back is pressed between the wall and myself. I take her heart-shaped face between my hands; I smirk at the heat frying her face.

She has nowhere to go. Nowhere to hide. Nowhere to run.

She swallows, "Yes."

"*Fuck.*"

She tries to wiggle her way out between my body and the wall as she says, "I'm so sorry. God this is so embarrassing. I must be making you feel so uncomfortable right now. After our date tonight, it's clear I'm not worth it and I'm going to be too much work. So maybe we should just cut whatever this is early and-"

"I'm going to stop you right there."

She freezes on the spot; an audible gulp works in her throat. Her lips part as if she is about to rush into another sorry, though, I don't give her the chance to say any more. My hand wraps lightly around her neck before she can pull away completely. "You don't get to decide that for me."

I watch her eyes dart around the room as if she is looking for an escape route, but her body remains glued between me and the wall, caught between tension and surrender. I can feel the heat of her skin radiating though the thin cotton of her T-shirt. I can feel her pulse thrash against my fingers on her neck. "Blair, listen to me." I whisper softly, my mouth touches feather light kisses against her lips as I hush, "You don't have to apologize about whatever you are thinking about, just… don't push me away."

She shakes her head, her hot breath fans across my face as she sighs, "But I just – I'm a mess. I don't know what I am doing half the time in this place. I have no friends here. No family. *I'm not worth it.* Can't you see? I'm trying to save you from the pain."

As I watch her eyes become misty with tears, I draw her in that extra bit closer, melting her body between mine. "You don't have to be perfect, Blair. I just want you to be real with me, that is all I am asking for."

For a long moment, she doesn't say anything. Her body stiffens slightly, as though she's still debating whether she should let me in. But when she looks up, her eyes meet mine with a vulnerability so raw, I can't help but feel the weight of it.

"I don't know if I can do this." She admits, her voice cracking. "I'm scared."

I let out a slow breath, my thumb brushes against her plush lips, "I know, me too. But I'm here. And I am not going anywhere."

I watch her face transform from rain to sunshine in a matter of seconds. I quickly chase a kiss on her lips before I pull back and walk towards the door. "Now that we have got that all cleared, I'll leave you to your… *activities*." I smirk, looking back towards Blair who is still glued to the wall, like a fly in a trap. "Sorry for interrupting."

As tempting as it might be for me to rip her shirt off and find out what is underneath, tonight I am being a gentleman – not the reckless cowboy.

And besides, everyone knows that the unwritten rule of a first date is to not have sex.

Right? *Right.*

As my hand wraps around the cool knob of the door to leave, Blair stops me in my tracks with her small hand grabbing my wrist. "Where are you going?" She licks her lips, my eyes tracking the movement of her tongue.

"To bed." My voice can be barely heard over the sound of my racing heart. Blair's touch on my skin burns despite her hand being wrapped loosely around me, I'm sure if she'd let go, I could see the traces of her hand on my skin.
"Oh." She hums, shuffling nervously on her feet.
"Do you want to-"
"Yes."
I smirk, "I didn't even finish what I was going to say."
"I'm sorry… continue." Her face flushes a bright pink, as if she is embarrassed.
"I was going to say." I lean close to Blair's face till we are only millimetres apart. "Do you want to fuck me."
She takes in a loud breath, sucking all the tension filled air into her lungs. The house is deathly quiet, as if it is waiting for the answer that I desperately want.
"*Yes.*"
Grabbing her face, I pull her into mine. Only one thought crosses my mind.
Fuck the first date rule.

Chapter 25

Blair

When I hushed that three-letter word, I knew it was going to leave me in a whole lot of trouble in the future. That said, lying on Cole's bed – which is a *cloud* – with his hands running up my legs and his hungry mouth on mine, I don't seem to care about the responsibilities that we would both to face in the morning.

His fingertips dig into the soft skin of my thighs, no doubt leaving marks in their wake. Yet, I simply need more. I need *more* of him. I need all the contact from this cowboy who is devouring my face.

A small whimper leaves my lips as he nips on my bottom lip – hard enough to draw blood – and sucks and smooths away the pain he just caused by his teeth.

"What do you want, baby?" His whispers tickle against my lips, sending my senses into overdrive.

"You." My hands rake up his back and over his messy waves on his scalp. "Only you."

He smiles as he pushes my oversized tee high up my body and over my head, leaving me completely bare for him. "You already have me, baby."

I suck in a deep breath, sucking in tension into my lungs. He always had a way of words, yet these feel raw and real.

I watch as his dark eyes travel down my heaving chest, he licks his lips as his eyes trace the soft curve of my breasts and the hardness of my nipples. Then his eyes travel lower, and lower, until he reaches the soft folds of my wetness.

For a beat we sit in silence, our deep breaths can only be heard in the nevertheless silent house. I watch as Cole shakes his head and bites his lips.

On instinct I close my legs together, rationally thinking he is disappointed. However, when he roughly grabs both of my knees with his callous hands and pulls me apart, my insecurity dissolves into dust as he says deeply, "Don't move gorgeous, I am trying to take in my view."

I feel the heat creep up my face at his words. I shift slightly on the bed, trying to soothe the ache in between my thighs. His piercing eyes snap up towards my face with a smirk. "You, okay?"

"Yeah." I croak, pushing my head further into the pillow, trying to hide my flush of shyness.

His smirk turns into a full megawatt smile, his pearly white teeth act like a beacon in the darkness. "Don't get shy on me sweets. Tell me what you want."

His hands drag up my thighs and down behind my calves. "Do want me to touch you?" He hushes.

I shake my head. "Yes."

"Do you want me to touch you here?" His fingers edge closer towards my centre, but not close enough. I shake my head, my hand gripping the sheets at the pure torture.

"No? How about here?" His fingers brush up my slick folds, dragging the wetness across my centre. Yet, he completely ignores the tight bundle of nerves, he simply drags through my folds.

"Cole." I whimper, my hips thrust in the air, trying to fight for the pressure that I so desperately need.

"Hmm?" He hums with a chuckle, clearly enjoying my suffering.

"Please, I *need* you." I rush out the words and screw my eyes shut. Yet, when his movement of his fingers stop, I slowly open my eyes and lock onto him. He sits on his knee, boxers still on but it's not hard to notice the significantly large bulge. The moonlight slips between the curtains into the dark room, cutting Cole in half with a silver light. His dilatated eyes look like black ink filled with lust, tension, and something else that I can't place. His eyebrows are furrowed, as if he is in deep thought about what I just said.

"Cole?" My voice cuts in between whatever he is thinking, pulling him back into the moment with me.

"*Fuck.*" He whispers, his gaze snaps back to my centre along with his fingers. He slowly start to rub the small bundle of nerves in a circle, causing my back to shoot off the bed. With one hand on my hip, he runs his thumb along my hipbone, tenderly trying to soothe the intense, overwhelming sensations.

When I am completely soaked, he slowly inserts a finger into my heat, and that is all it takes for me to breakdown and come over his fingers. My vision erupts in white flashes of pleasure, stars lighting up my vision like the sky.

Coming down from my high, my hazy vison disappears, leaving a beautiful cowboy in its wake. "God, Blair. You are breathtaking when you are like this." He pulls his finger out my heat and bring it towards his mouth, sucking it clean. *Shit, that's hot.* Sinking down further onto his knees, Cole leans closer towards my centre. But before he makes contact, his lust filled eyes snap towards mine. "Can I?"

One nod of my head is all it takes for him to trap his lips around my sensitive nerves. His tongue laps up my wetness, causing a whimper to leave my lips. As his lips work on my clit, he reinserts his finger back into my pussy, pumping slowly edging me closer towards my climax.

Grabbing his hair, I pull at the stands, grinding myself into his face. It's only then he slowly adds another finger, I start to lose myself. When his teeth scrape along the nerves that's when I erupt.

Pulling my arm over my head, I close my eyes and slowly come. That when I hear a rustle from the end of the bed, and a crinkle of a wrapper. Pulling the arm off my eyes, Cole sits on his knee in front of me, boxer now gone, leaving his hard cock standing tall in his hands.

"Can you handle one more, sweets?" He asks whilst rubbing his hand loosely over his shaft.

"Yes." I shake my head eagerly like a bobbly head. He chuckles, moving closer up the bed until his knees brush the back of my thighs. He slowly brushes his shaft between my wet folds, coating his cock in my last orgasm.

I whimper softly when the tip of his shaft slowly fills me up. He thrust in a couple of inches then retreat, then add another couple. With each thrust, he fills me with more and more, until he is flush against me.

Leaning down towards my face, he brushes a thumb over my cheek, and give a quick kiss before saying, "Let me show you that you *are* worth it."

I don't say anything, I can't. I feel so emotionally full. Something I can't quite understand buries itself deep between my chest. Before I get a chance to really think of it, Cole start to slowly thrust in and out of me.

I watch has his eyes roll to the back of his head at the sensation of being inside of me. With each thrust Cole gives me, it gets harder to contain my moans. As soon as he picks up the pace, my fingers fly towards his shoulders, my fingernails digging deep crevasses into his skin.

"You are taking it to well, baby." He whispers into my neck, then seals it with a kiss. "Fuck, Blair you are so tight, come for me. Come with me." He breathes in my ear.

I break around him.

As pussy clenches around him when I come, his thrust become frantic, I can feel his cock pulse inside me. He groans and stops his thrusts. His cock continues pulse, softening inside me.

Our heavy breathes are the only things that are left after the euphoric moment. Pulling himself off me, Cole walks into the bathroom without a word.

However, the anxiety driven thoughts that plagued my mine disappears as he re-enters with a warm washcloth.

He places the cloth on my centre, cleaning my body with such gentleness. The moment feels more intimate than the sex we just had. The way he takes care of me, the way he touches me like a delicate flower, it all feels too much. Before the feelings overwhelm me, Cole slides into the bed, and pulls me close to him. His large arm wraps around me like vines, binding me to him. His leg slips in between mine, wrapping me warmth.

We sit there in silence, processing what just happened. The eventful day, the date, the creep, and the intense orgasms. When I think he has fallen asleep he breaks the deathly silence with a hushed whisper.

"Your worth doesn't decrease just because someone else fails to see it, Blair. You are worth it. Always was and always will be."

I don't say anything, I keep my eyes closed, letting his words sink into my skin. As the repetitive deep breaths fill the room indicating Cole has fallen asleep, that's when I dig into that unknown feeling that has inserted itself into my chest.

No. Not my chest. My heart.

My skin prickles at the realisation. The unknown feeling has been love.

I love Cole Walker.

Chapter 26

Cole

Waking up from a deep sleep, in a cold empty bed is the last thing I wanted.

When I open my eyes and adjust to my dim surroundings, I don't see any signs that indicate Blair had been in my bedroom all night.

Her side of the bed is made up perfectly compared to the crumpled sheets on my side. The covers are tucked underneath the mattress, pillows fluffed up into clouds, and a small blanket – which I gave her when she said she was cold in the middle of the night – lays folded tightly on the end of the bed.

It is as if I dreamt the night we spent together. As if everything we shared was just a figment of my imagination.

I sit up slowly, my mind grappling with the strange weight of an illusion. The room is unnervingly still – too still. The scent of her perfume still clings to the air, sweet and citrusy, but there's something haunting about it, like a ghost that refuses to fade. But then I look around, and the room tells me a different story. The crispness of the sheets. The hollow emptiness surrounding me. Everything is telling me she's not here.

I run my hand through my hair, trying to rein in the frustration pulling tightly in my chest.

Did she leave in the middle of the night? Or did I imagine the warmth of her body intertwined in mine, the softness of her breath kissing my skin?
I glance at my alarm clock displaying the time. ***8:27AM.***
Where the hell is she?
I toss the covers aside and push myself out of bed, my feet meeting the cold floor with a sharp cringe. But the discomfort is nothing compared to the surge of unease and determination crashing through me, propelling me toward the door with a force I can't ignore.

My fingers wrap around the cold metal of the doorknob, pulling it open, bracing for the usual silence that fills the house. But instead, a soft hum floats through the air, a melody that bounces off the walls like a quiet greeting. Along with it, the rich, salty scent of bacon drifts in, mingling with the rhythm of the hums in a way that almost feels like an invitation.

For a moment, I stand there frozen, feet stuck on the cold floor like icicles, unsure whether or not I should approach or turn away. The humming is soft – comfortable, even – making me ache from the inside.

I move slowly down the hall and make my way down the stairs, drawn by the sounds that fill otherwise silent house.

I reach the bottom of the stairs and freeze, unable to move. Blair stands in front of the stove, lost in her own world, her back to me. The morning light spills across her, soft and golden, a stark contrast to the way I saw her in my truck last night. The sunlight catches in her hair, turning it into liquid gold, while the steady rhythm of her stirring the pan feels almost otherworldly, like something out of a dream.

She's here. She's real. And yet, there's something about this moment – this calm, this quiet – that feels like we're living in two worlds, blending effortlessly into one.

I take a careful step forward, but the floorboards betray me, their creak snapping Blair out of her trance. She turns, eyes wide with surprise, before quickly smoothing it over with a practiced smile.

"Morning," she says, her voice bright but tinged with something I can't quite place. "Sleep, okay?"

I don't answer for a beat, I watch her scurry around our small kitchen, placing dirty dishes into the sink.

Just as she glances over her shoulder, I give her a small nod, though it is far from the truth. "I did. Until I woke up to an empty bed." I try keep my tone light, but it comes out sharper than I intended.

Blair smile faulters for just a second, before she turns back to the sink and scrubs a pan harsher than needed. "I didn't mean to wake you." She mutters, drying her hands on a hand towel and returning towards the salty simmering bacon, hands moving in a practiced rhythm.

I take a step closer towards her, the scent of breakfast food and coffee mixing in with the tension filled air. "You didn't wake me up. I just… woke up, and you weren't there."

She doesn't look at me as she plates the food, the clink of the utensils is the only sounds that can be heard between us. I watch her closely, noting the tenseness of her shoulders, her movements rushed. Like she is trying to avoid something. *Or maybe me.*

Propping my hip on the countertop next to her, I tuck a strand of her hair behind her ear. Before I have the chance to swallow the words, they fall out of my lips. "Where did you go?"

Her stressed shoulders hike up towards her ears at my question. Instead of turning her face towards me, she whispers down at the plated food. "I – I needed some space. I thought that you'd still be sleeping."

A knot forms tight in my stomach. There is something else in her voice, hidden underneath vocal cords, gnawing at me. "Blair…" I whisper.

She finally turns; her eyes filled with unspoken emotions. "I didn't want to make things weird." She quietly says, the words breaking as she says them. "But I don't know what to do with all of *this*. I can't do *this* is we aren't together. I'm – *I'm sorry.*"

Her fragile words hangs between the air for beat before I place my hands gently on her heart shaped face and pull her closer. The unreadable emotions in her eyes disappear as I give her a small smile.

"If you wanted me to be your boyfriend, *sweets*, all you needed to do was ask. I would say yes."

"What?" I watch as her eyes widen in shock at my admission.

I chuckle. "Do you really think you could get rid of me that easily, Blair? What kinda guy do you take me for?"

"Wait, hold on. You want to be together... like a couple. Together, *together.*"
I give my head a nod, my gaze steady on hers, feeling a mix of amusement and something deeper. "Yes, together, *together.*"
She stare at me for a long moment, her gaze slipping between uncertainty and something soft. Then, the corner of her lips turn up into the faintest smile, I can almost see the weightlifting off her delicate shoulders.
"Why didn't you say that earlier?" she asks, her voice filled with playfulness.
I let a quiet laugh slip out with a shrug. "You didn't give me a chance. Besides, you seem to be doing *a lot* of thinking."
Placing her hands on my bare chest, Blair looks up with a bright smile. The gesture is simple, but it feels like everything. "Well, I do tend to overthink things."
"We both do." I lower my hands down to her waist, pulling her that little bit closer. "But I am not going anywhere."
She smiles as if it can't get bigger. "Good." She hums before closing the small gap between us, her lips meet mine in a kiss that feels like the answer to every question that's been left hanging in the air between us.
"Finally." A voice slashes through the air, breaking our moment. "Can I finally get my breakfast now, Blair?"
I blink at the sudden interruption. Whipping my head over my shoulder I spot none other than my good

friend Elijah, sitting with a smug grin at *my* breakfast table.

"What. Are. You. Doing. *Here.*" I growl, frustration clawing at my throat at the sight of my best friend sitting arrogantly in my home, demanding breakfast from *my* girlfriend.

Girlfriend, that has a nice ring to it.

Blair brings his filled plate over to the table, placing it in front of him. "Elijah was sitting out on the porch this morning when I woke up. I figured it would be rude to let him sit outside all morning on an empty stomach. Hope you don't mind."

Blair places her hand on Eli's shoulder, giving him a reassuring squeeze. The sight should make me feel proud – my friends getting along with my new girlfriend – however, the stupid smug smirk on Elijah's face makes me want to throw myself over the table, grab his breakfast, and smother it all over his arrogant face.

"Hey, Cole, could you put some clothes on? The sight of you in your underwear is *really* putting me off my delicious breakfast." Eli smirks, mouth full.

My fists ball up tight at my sides. Before I *actually* launch myself at Eli, Blair walks past with two heavy plates. The aroma of the breakfast foods wafts through the air, causing my stomach to grumble in protest.

Blair takes a seat, glancing at me with amusement in her eyes. "Ignore him." She picks up her cutlery and digs in. "Eli is just annoyed I didn't make him breakfast in bed."

"Oh, I'm not mad, just disappointed. But a guy can dream, right?" He says around the food in his mouth. I shoot him a glare, but it's hard to stay mad when the smell of salty bacon, eggs and toast fill the room. My stomach growls again, this time loud enough for Blair to hear, she raises a brow. "I think your stomach agrees with me?"

"Yeah, yeah, alright." I mutter, stalking over towards the table. I run my hand through my hair as I take a seat next to Blair. The tension from earlier has faded a bit, but the teasing from Eli still lingers.

I glance at her in my seat, grateful for the small moment of calm. As much as Eli's antics always seem to throw me off, it's easy to forget everything here when I'm next to Blair.

"Thank you, for the breakfast." I say softly, watching her expression melt.

She shrugs, a hint of a smile tugs at the corner of her lips. "Anything for my favourite cowboy."

I reach for my fork, taking a bite of the eggs, the flavours burst in my mouth as I savour the taste. It's only when I take another bite, I realise Elijah is staring at us, eyes narrowed as if he is waiting for something.

"What?" I raise a brow.

He grins, wiping his mouth with a napkin. "Nothing, just waiting for the lovebirds to make googly eyes at each other again."

Blair chuckles at my side, shaking her head as she says, "You're such a pain."

I look between my best friend and girlfriend, the corners of my mouth rise in amusement, "You are one to talk, Eli." I take I bite of my breakfast, "You're the one who seems so intent in watching our every move."

Eli raises his hands in the air, a feign surrender. "Hey, I'm just trying to enjoy my breakfast. No need to get all defensive." He takes another bite of his toast, clearly content in his role as the instigator.

Before I can reply, my phone cuts through the breakfast scented air, interrupting the warm moment. Eli and Blair continue to talk, muttering about today's plans in the background as I answer the call without bothering to check the caller ID.

"Is this Cole Walker?" A women voice calls down the line a little breathlessly. My stomach dips. My senses work in overdrive.

"Yes." Picking up on my shift of mood, Eli and Blair observe me from across the room, worried expressions filtering their faces.

"This is Misty Valley Care Centre. It's about your father."

Chapter 27

Blair

Stepping through the doors of the care facility, a quiet but persistent knot of anxiety starts to form in my stomach. The smell of the sterile disinfectant mixed with the aged wood, and the soft whispers of voices from rooms echoed down the corridor.
There was an undercurrent of sadness and uncertainty submerged in these walls. The smell of bleach in the atmosphere makes me feel detached from humanity as I walk down the hall with Cole.
A lump forms in my throat, not fully understanding on how to behave in this environment, what to say or in this case, how to face a person who has forgotten themselves.
I watch as Cole's expression tightens with every step we take further down the hall. I can feel the emotions stirring beneath the surface – grief, worry, maybe even fear. His hand feels cool in mine, and a subtle tremor runs through his fingers, quietly unravelling the calm façade he's holding onto.
"You didn't have to come, you know?" He mumbles; voice thick with emotion. "He doesn't take kindly to newcomers."
I shake my head, the image of Cole answering the phone call flashing in my mind. His brows furrowed, eyes brimming with tears, his face crumbling under the weight of it all. The thought of him facing this

alone leaves a bitter taste in my mouth. "We do this together," I murmur, the words soft, just for him. "We're a team now."

He gives a small nod of his head and murmurs, "This way."

His steps are slow, almost mechanical, as we move deeper into the care home. With every step he takes, I match it with my own, my heart racing in my chest. I know how much this visit means to him, and though I don't fully grasp the storm of emotions that seem to possess him, I can feel the heaviness of it all pressing down on us both.

As we reach his father's room, the door hangs slightly ajar. The harsh glow of the hallway lights spills into the darkness, casting long, unsettling shadows across the floor. Cole pauses, a flicker of hesitation crossing his eyes before he steps forward. I give his hand a gentle squeeze, and he glances down at me, a soft smile tugging at his lips – as if, in this moment, he realises he's not alone. That there's someone, someone beyond his family, standing by his side.

He gently pushes the door open. The room was small yet tidy, the kind of space that belonged to someone who had once lived independently but was now confined to the limitations provided by age and illness. The curtains were drawn, blocking out the morning sunshine.

My gaze immediately falls upon Cole's father. The sight stops me in my tracks. The memories of the man I knew from my childhood has been completely stripped away. The man who was strong and sturdy, a figure of quiet authority, was now crumpled up on his bed, his body jerking from erratic jitters. His hands were grasped in the air, the tremor of his limbs were violet and uncontrollable. His eyes were wide and frantic, darting around the room, looking for something that isn't there.

"Dad – dad, it's okay." Cole's voice was tight as he took a step towards his father, his face was now a picture of restraint, though it was clear that it took an overwhelming amount of effort to maintain his composer.

Kneeling beside his bed, Cole's fingers brushed gently against his father's withered shivering hand. The man's clouded eyes snapped towards Cole's; his expression etched with confusion. "No... *no*," he stuttered, voice trembling. "I – I'm not... I..."

A tightness grips my chest as I take in the sight of Cole's father. I've seen him before, but never like this. It's clear the dementia has slowly consumed him, like a dark shadow creeping deeper into his mind. The man I once knew from my childhood feels so far away now – a mere shell of the person he used to be.

I watch the helplessness in Cole's eyes as he stares steadily at his dad. His hand grasps gently onto his fathers, trying to soothe the discomfort. "Dad...It's me, Cole." His voice was low, trying to provide comfort but it was lanced with something else... like pain. "You are safe, dad."

The words didn't seem to have an influence at first. The man continued to struggle, his body rigid and

trembling, his breathing coming out in brisk bursts. "I can't... no – *no.*"
I watch as Cole's face falters, his father's suffering eating away at him with every tremor that shakes his body. Helplessness grows in his eyes, the weight of it pressing heavier with each passing second. For a moment, his gaze breaks from his father and locks onto mine. I see the struggle warring inside him – one part clinging to the man he once knew, desperate to pull him out of this fog, and another bracing for the inevitable loss that's already sinking in.
I take a careful step toward them, my hand resting gently on Cole's shoulder, a small anchor in the storm. I feel the tension in his muscles ease under my touch, the weight of it loosening just a little.
"You're not alone," I murmur, my voice a quiet promise. "We're in this together."
My words make Cole's jaw tighten, but he nods, his chocolate eyes never leaving his father. He keeps holding his dad's hand, murmuring words that seem to barely cut through the storm of confusion swirling in the old man's mind. Over and over, he repeats the same words, as if hoping they'll reach him, even just for a moment. "It's me, dad... It's okay... *You are safe.*"
The fit seemed to subside, the storm has past its highest peak, yet remnants still remain floating inside. The jerking has stopped, heavy shallow breaths filled the room, this time they were less frantic. His eyes were glossed over with turmoil and despair, still swimming in a sea filled with confusion.

Cole didn't move. He stayed kneeled by the bed, hands clutching onto his father's for dear life. Relief and sorrow was carved deep into his face, the lines drawn tighter than I have ever seen them before.
I take a few steps back and lean against the door frame. A wave of inability washed over my body as I take in the sight of my boyfriend and his dad. I couldn't fix this. I can't undo the cruel illness that has taken over Cole's father, stealing him away day by day, piece by piece. But what I could do is be there. For Cole. For his father. For *both* of them.
The room was still, safe from the laboured breathing and the soft whispers of Cole's deep voice. My hand shoots to my chest, heart aching at the sight of a man trying to hold it all together, a young man taking on two roles – son and caretaker.
After a long stretch of silence, the old man finally seemed to settle, his body now slackened, his breathing slowing. He wasn't entirely at piece – the dementia has taken too much of that – but for a moment, the storm has passed.
I take a deep breath, filling my lungs with the sterile air as Cole turns away from the bed. His eyes were wet with tears, though he held a blank expression as if he is trying to block out the hurt, trying to make sense of the rough piece of his life.
Reaching out I cup his cheek, his stubble bites into my tender touch, though I offer him some discreet strength that he desperately needs.
"How are you holding up?" My voice is soft but firm with concern.

He blinks and gives me a tight smile that doesn't reach the eyes. "I don't know anymore." He admits quietly. "Some days feels like... I am losing him all over again."
There wasn't an easy fix with this pain. No easy answers. All I could do was stand by his side, share the burden, and help though a moment were it feels as if everything is slipping away.
I wrap my arms around his neck, drawing him in close, letting him feel the steady rhythm of my heart beating in my chest.
For just a moment, there was no talk of dementia, no talk of overwhelming responsibilities. It was just us, holding onto each other, two people trying to make sense of a world where it felt as if everything was slipping in between our fingers.

The sun has now dipped down to the horizon, the cool crisp air gusts into my face as I sit on the porch with a mug of tea. I watch the golden light spill across the land of Copper Creek, casting long dark shadows over the wide-open plains.
After the morning event, Cole has disappeared somewhere on the ranch.
"I need to practice." Was the first thing he said after a short silent drive home – he hasn't been back since. When he disappeared down to the stables, a queasy feeling erupted in my stomach. The distant look in his eyes, the flash of tied down emotions, and

the stress carved into his face, was all it took for me to call Eli.

As much as I long to be by his side, I knew Cole needed someone who wasn't me. It wasn't that I didn't want to be with him – it was just that sometimes, having his best friend around might be what he truly needed. Someone who could look out for him in ways I couldn't, someone who knew him the way I didn't yet.

As I stare blankly at Eli's truck, mind racing with thoughts of Cole. My phone vibrates in my pocket. Pulling out the slick black screen, I look at the flashing familiar name.

Mom: Incoming call.

My stomach twists. My thumb hovers over the big red *decline* button – already knowing what this call is going to be about. Yet, my thumb slides hesitantly across the screen, answering the call. "Hey, mom." My voice comes out quieter than I intended, the lack of confidence in my speech evident.

"Blair." My mom's voice rung out sharply down the speaker, disrupting the quiet tranquillity around me. "I have been thinking about the ranch. We need to talk."

Of course, it's about the ranch. It's *always* about this ranch.

A wave of dread tightens my chest, but I push it down, straightening my shoulders and forcing a façade of confidence, as if somehow, she could sense me – feel the strength I'm desperately trying to project.

"Alright, what's going on? I'm listening."

There was a pause, the air suddenly felt too thick to breathe. "I've made my mind up." My mom's voice continued down the line, her voice ice cold. "*I'm* selling the ranch."
"Selling the ranch?" My breath clogged in my throat as I repeated her ice-cold words. "You've got to be kidding me. We have talked about this before. You can't just –"
"I *can*, and I *will*." Her words cut me off sharper than the knife she has just lodged into my heart. "You've been gone months, Blair. What is left for you there? The ranch is a burden. I'm not letting you waste any more money on something that is falling apart. It's time to sell."
My mind races with a thousand thoughts. I've grown up on this ranch; it's a part of my family's legacy. For the first time, I finally have a place I can truly call home.
I grip my phone tighter, fighting to keep my voice steady. "Mom, you don't understand. This ranch has been in our family for generations. You can't just sell it –"
"There is nothing to understand." She snaps down the line, the frustration radiating through the phone. "I have had enough of the upkeep and the repairs – it's all too much. You don't live here anymore, Blair. You have got your own life, and frankly, I don't see you rushing back here anytime soon."
"I have *always planned* to come back." I feel my pulse in my neck quicken as I try to rein in my growing anger. "Look, things has just been *complicated*, you know that."

"You have been saying that for months, Blair. I am tired of waiting on you to decide. It's time to move forward."
I stay silent on the line, letting her words sink into my skin. Every step forward she expects me to take, feels like two steps back. A storm of frustration and guilt churns inside me. I haven't been home in months, but I've never had the chance to visit the ranch as much as I wanted – until now. Life with Cole swept me up in a way I never expected, and now the life I've finally begun to feel is truly mine is slowly slipping through my fingers.
"You don't even care, do you?" Although I am firm, hurt intertwines with my voice. "You don't care about what this means to me. About what it means to *us*."
A sharp dismissive sigh can be heard over the faint howls of the wind. "Don't even dare to try and guilt me, Blair. I'm doing what is best for us. You have to be realistic. We need to sell the ranch before it costs us more than it's worth. You are going to thank me later."
My hand grips the wooden railing in front of me, steadying myself from the ground that seems to start shifting underneath me. "I don't want to sell it, mom. *I don't want to lose this place.*"
She sighs again, "If this is about the cowboy, I –"
"This has *nothing* to do with him. This is about *me*, mom. *Please.*" My voice cracks as I beg.
"Too bad." She shot back, "This is happening, I already have an agent lined up. I have made the decision."

I close my eyes, trying to keep myself from spiralling into a dark panic. My mom's control over the situation feels like a vice wrapped around my chest. The ranch, the memories, everything that I have been trying to hold onto – it's all slipping between my fingers. "Mom, please... can't you wait a little longer? I'm sure if I –"
"No. No more waiting. No more indecision. I have made the choice, it's done."
I wanted to yell, to scream, demand my mom to stop trying to take the memories away from me – make her understand. But the words get trapped in my throat. I know there was nothing I could do that could change her mind.
I try blink back the tears welling up in my eyes. "I'll think about it, okay? Just – just give me some time."
"It's a done deal. You have had the time. Don't even try to talk me out of this, Blair."
My chest tightens at the finality in my mom's voice. The sharpness of her words rang in my ear. "I'll talk to you later." My voice is numb, my heart heavy in my chest.
As I stand on the porch, I look out towards that land that I have failed to take care of, the land that I thought of as home. The thought of losing the ranch was unbearable but now it seems inevitable, out of my control.
My mom's cold, unrelenting push to sell makes me feel like I'm caught between two worlds – one slipping away, the other just beginning to feel like home.

Chapter 28

Cole

The wind in the grass brushes the scents of hay and earth into my face. I was dripping in sweat, dirt clung to my skin, a reminder of the intense practice I'd thrown myself into since returning from the care home.

My grip on the rope tightened at the thought of my father. His manic episodes happened rarely, but when they did strike, it hit harder each time – serving as a harsh reminder that I was losing him, little by little, faster than I realised.

The horse shifts on its feet, hooves digging in the ground impatiently, eager for a ride.

I glanced over at Eli. He was watching me thoroughly, arms calmly crossed over his chest. I knew Blair had something to do with him showing up, but he hadn't said a word during my practice – just stood there, silently observing.

I urge the bronc forward, the horse kicks up a cloud of dirt as it took off, bucking furiously in unpredictable bursts. I grip the rope tightly, using every ounce of my strength to hold on, twisting and turning as the animal beneath me fights for control.

However, when the rope slips out of my sweaty grasp, the horse kicks powerfully sending me flying off it's back and face first into the dirt. The deafening thud of hooves echoes through the ground, matching the frantic rhythm of my racing heart.

Groaning I push myself to stand. Brushing off the dust on my shirt, I peer over towards Elijah who is now leaned up against the fence, his eyes narrowed. There was no point in hiding, he knew me long enough to acknowledge that I was running from something.

I nod my head and hesitantly make my way over towards him, shaking out the stiffness in my arms. As I come up to the fence, Eli's eyes narrows as he says, "You're balance was all off. You are riding like a damn manic." His voice was laced with concern, "What are you running from."

I wipe my brow with the outside of my hand, trying to calm my ragged breathing. I don't meet my best friend eyes when I say, "Just getting ready for the competition next week." Though, it was all a lie. "I need to be sharp."

Eli shook his head, a small smirk tugging at the corner of his lips. "Bullshit, you're always sharp. You're avoiding something. Talk to me, brother."

"There is nothing to talk about."

He didn't buy it. Eli catches the flash of frustration in my eyes, "Come on, You've have been acting off ever since that phone call this morning. You are distracted, and I know why. It's your dad, isn't it?"

I went still, keeping my back to Eli as I made my way toward the stables, avoiding his question – training forgotten in that moment. I knew he wasn't the type to give up easily.

So, when he caught up and stood in front of me, his words echo in the barn as he pressed, "You are carrying all the weight, aren't you? Do you think fixing things with Blair, fixing this ranch, is going to fix everything else? You think that buying the ranch is going to make you feel better about your dad?"
Anger and guilt mix inside me. "It's not just about the ranch, Eli." My voice is quiet but filled with rough emotion. "It's about proving I can do it. Proving that I... I'm not like *him*."
Eli stare softens, yet his words are firm, "You're not like him. You *aren't* him. He chose to focus more on the ranch that his sons. That is on him, not you."
My lips press into a thin line as I feel the muscles in my neck flex as I look over the barn. "You don't get it. Milo doesn't even care. He is gone all the time. And now... now it's all up to me to fix everything. The ranch. The money. My dad... I have to do it."
He steps an inch closer, arms crossed as he meets my eyes. "Fix what, exactly? Do you think that winning this and the money is going to make everything better? You know that plan was stupid when I first said it. What happened? What is going to happen when Blair finds out? She isn't a damsel in distress. You can't take something that is a part of her family just because you feel the need to fix yours."
My fists ball at the side of my thighs. "She doesn't get any of this, Eli." I snap. "She has stated many times that this ranch is a burden for her if anything I am doing her a favour. If I buy it, I can fix her

problems. Make things right. Maybe – maybe I can make it right with my dad."

Eli's brows furrow. "By buying the ranch off her? By fixing *her* problems without giving her a say?"

"I have been watching this place fall apart for *years*. My dad is a mess. Milo… Milo is busy building a name for himself. I'm the one who has to step up. I'm the one who needs to fix it all."

The rawness can be heard as I spill my thoughts to my best friend. It felt like everything was eating me alive. My shoulders were heavy from the weight I have been carrying – I couldn't hold it in anymore.

Eli sighs. "Look, I know everything is messed up at the moment. But you can't bury it by buying Blair out without her understanding why. This isn't just your decision."

There was silence. My gaze fell to the ground for a brief moment, letting Eli's words hang in the air like a thick fog that I couldn't escape. But before I had the chance to respond, I couldn't keep the question in any longer.

"What changed, Eli?" My voice was low but edged with frustration. "What changed your mind about the plan?"

Eli hesitated, his eyes avoiding mine as if the answer was hard to find. He shifted uneasily, glancing around like the room had suddenly grown too small. A part of me was already regretting bringing it up, but it had to be said.

"I – I don't know, man," he finally muttered, rubbing the back of his neck like he had just woken from a dream. "I'm just... not so sure anymore."

Not sure? That wasn't what I wanted to hear. My heart sank, my jaw tightening as the doubt crept in. This wasn't the conversation I'd been expecting. We had a plan. We were supposed to follow it through. But now, it was starting to feel like we were on the edge of something that could fall apart at any moment.

"You're not sure?" I repeated, my voice low and strained. "This is a done deal, Eli. What's there to be unsure about?"

Eli sighed deeply, rubbing his face before meeting my eyes. "It's just... Cole, I've been thinking about it, and I don't know if we should be going after this land anymore." His voice was quieter now, the weight of his words settling in the air between us. "Blair's been through enough. Selling this ranch – her family's legacy – just feels... wrong, you know? And I have noticed a difference between you two..."

I stared at him, stunned by the shift. The Eli I knew was all about business, about getting things done, no matter the cost. But now, his usual confidence was gone. This wasn't the Eli I was used to.

"Eli, we've already made the offer. She's gonna sell it," I pressed, my voice tightening. "This is our chance. We need to close this deal and move forward."

He shook his head, looking away, clearly struggling with something deeper. "I know, but... it feels like we're taking advantage of her. She doesn't know what she's doing with this ranch. But I'm starting to feel like we'd be pushing her into a corner just for our own gain. I can't help but think we're wrong."

I ran a hand through my hair, frustration bubbling inside me. I had expected hesitation, maybe some second-guessing, but this... this felt like more than just doubts about the plan. This was a shift in his entire perspective. And it was throwing me off.

Before I could respond, the sound of footsteps outside the door broke the quiet.

Turning around, my stomach drops at the sight of Blair stood in the doorway, her arms crossed, her expression unreadable. The tension that was already in the air become sharper and heavier.

Eli's eyes widen, and my body stiffens, heart sinking in my chest. Blair's voice was quiet, though there was a clear fury laced between her words making me freeze as she talks.

"So, has *this* been the plan all along?" Her words are ice cold, filled with disbelief. "Behind *my* back?"

Chapter 29

Blair

"So, has *this* been the plan all along?" I can hardly hear my voice over the thumping beat in my chest. "Behind *my* back?"

My eyes are locked on his, watching every small shift in his body, every subtle move that betrays him. His gaze flicks away, anxiety pulling at his shoulders, beads of sweat clinging to his brow like he's fighting a storm inside.

He doesn't look like the cowboy I know, the man I've loved. Instead, he looks like a stranger – someone who's been hiding pieces of himself from me, piece by painful piece.

Eli steps closer, his eyes pleading, but I can't bring myself to meet his gaze. "Blair, please, just let me explain –" he starts, his voice thick with frustration and regret. "I didn't mean for it to happen this way. I just—" But I don't want to hear it. Not now. Not after everything. I cut him off, my voice sharp and raw.

"No, Eli. Just stop." I take a step back, the weight of his presence suffocating me. "I don't want to hear your explanations. You've already made your choices, and I'm done trying to make sense of them. So just go." The words taste bitter, but they're the only truth I can offer him.

Eli turns away, his shoulders heavy with hurt, his footsteps echoing as he disappears down the barn, leaving Cole and me in the silence that follows.

"Cole." I snap, my voice drips in irritation and pain. "Can you *look* at me?"

His dark eyes finally lock onto mine, guarded – filled with something I could only describe as regret. My heart continues to palpitate in my chest, hot burning rage rises within me. "I asked you a question."

He shifts his weight, the scuff of his boots against the floor only adding to the irritation gnawing at me. I wait. I keep waiting for him to say anything. His lips part as if he is trying to find the words, but nothing sounds right.

Nothing sounds *honest*.

"You were going to buy it… the ranch?" I say slowly – trying to make the word sound right in my head. Everything tastes bitter on my tongue as I continue, "Behind my back. You were planning to take it? Planning to take my home? *Everything?* Why didn't you tell me?"

His jaw tightens, his fists clenching at his sides, yet he stays silent. The raggedness of his breathing speaks louder than anything he could say.

"I thought we were past this, Cole?" I whisper, hurt embedding in my every syllable. "I thought we trusted each other? But you have been lying to me this whole time."

Shame hangs heavy on his posture, eyes now flickered to ground. I almost wish he would be angry

– fight, shout at me, at least I would know that he would care.

But this?

The quiet guilt eats away at the pieces that are left between us.

"Blair," he finally says, his voice barely a whisper, like my name is a weight too heavy for him to carry. "I never wanted to hurt you, but I... I thought I could fix this. I thought if I just took the ranch, everything would be okay. For both of us. Especially for you."

His words hit me like a punch to the gut. For a moment, I'm too stunned to respond. "Fix it?" I echo, the words tasting bitter in my mouth. "Fix *me*? Do you really think I need fixing? Do you think I need you making decisions for me... behind my back?" Heat floods my cheeks, my pulse quickening. "What makes you think I can't handle this? What makes you think I can't handle *us*?"

"My intension was to never control you, Blair." He tries to explain. Although his pleads only go through one ear and out the other. "I thought that... maybe if I took away the burden this ranch placed upon you, everything would become easier. I thought I was doing the right thing."

"*No, stop.*" My words come out darkly as I take a step away from the man, I thought I knew. "You have no right to make the choices for me, what I can and can't handle. That isn't something I deserve."

He takes a step towards me, shaking hands reaching out. Though, when I take another step back, the small distance between us suddenly feels like miles.

I watch his face fall, crumbling with guilt and anguish. I can't tell if he is just sorry or regretting his actions. Either way, the damage has been done.
"Cole, I – *I love you*. I fucking love you more than this god damn ranch. Couldn't you see it?" My voice cracks but I continue, "You were right, this ranch was a burden. When I first arrived here, I wanted nothing to do with this place – it was falling to pieces, nothing but dust and grime. But it was you. You showed me how to love this place, love this land. *Love you.* Yes, my grandfather's legacy is important to me, he is seeded within this land. But you, Cole, were the one that taught me everything, you were the one who helped me fix the pieces. *You.*" I shake my head, trying to shake away the feelings of regret and betrayal. "I can't do this anymore. I can't keep pretending."
"Blair, please." His voice cracks, but I can't bear to listen to a word.
I take another step back, my heartbreaking into a thousand tiny pieces. "Goodbye Cole. I need to figure this all out. Without you."
The silence that follows me out the barn feels heavier than I have ever felt. I turn, not even daring to look back as I walk towards the barn door. I can hear him calling my name, but it is all too late. It's too late for apologies, too late for excuses. I can't keep letting him think he can make outcomes for me. Not like this.
As I step out the barn, I look over the land for the last time, the memories and love that we shared – none of it feels the same anymore. For the first time, the

vibrant pink barn feels muted, exposed of its warmth, it's colour fading into something cold and lifeless. And I don't know how to get any of it back.

It's been a week since I last saw Cole. In the space of that time, I have met up with my mom and the agent to finalize plans to sell the ranch, settled overdue bills, and consumed enough ice cream that could rival the amount of my own body weight.
With said ice cream in hand, I glance around my bland apartment. I never noticed how bare the walls were, how ordinary the furniture looked, how sterile the room felt. I peek out my window and look down at the bustling city below. People swarm the streets, headlights are queued up miles down the road, the loud sounds of car horns — it all feels intense.
For the first time living in the city, I feel out of place. New York could never compare to Misty Pines. This fast-paced city seems to swallow time whole; it's constant motion leaves little room to breathe or appreciate the moments that pass.
Don't get me wrong, I love the city. Though, when I think back to my time in Misty Pines over the summer, this place feels smaller now, reduced to the way I remember it. It lacks the spark, the history that lived in every corner there. This apartment has none of that warmth. It simply *isn't* Copper Creek.
The image of Cole standing with a guilt-ridden expression has been playing on a constant loop in

my mind. I couldn't believe what I heard coming out of his mouth, the shock of hearing that his plan was to take away my home that has been in my family for generations.

I feel slashes of betrayal in the little piece of my heart that I still have felt for him. How could he make that decision for me, for us? To take away something personal and turn it into a transaction.

How did someone I love and trusted, believe that it was okay to strip away everything that was special without even caring? And worse – how didn't I see it coming? How did I never see the signs? Were they there the whole time or was I too busy wearing my rose-coloured glasses to notice?

I keep trying to move forward, shake him off my mind but thoughts of him haunt me like a ghost. His apology and regret, they all felt hallow, how do we come back from this? How do we rebuild something when the trust has been shredded into a thousand tiny pieces.

My thoughts are interrupted by a series of loud banging on my front door. I glance down at my half-melted ice cream sitting on the coffee table – my last shred of comfort – before I drag myself across the room. I unlock my door, expecting a delivery, but instead a storm of red hair burst through my doorway and into my apartment.

Clad in business attire, her heels click against the floor as she marches inside without an invitation. "Why does it smell like a cat died in here?"

I slam my door shut with much more force than necessary. "Hello, to you too."

Sadie rolls her eyes, taking a seat at the couch. She peers into the half-melted, half-empty ice cream laying abandoned on the small table and raises a brow. "How many did you have of those?"
I sigh, "Only two." She gives me a pointed stare, already knowing I'm bullshitting. After a beat of silence I give in, "Okay, fine! Maybe six or seven, I have lost count at this point."
I flop down on the couch beside her and grab my ice cream. The half-melted substance doesn't seem all that appealing now that I am looking at it. Though, I decide to busy myself by digging my spoon in the box, trying to avoid the sight of my best friend's intense eyes and worried facial expression.
"You, okay?" Sadie's voice is soft, but the intensity in her eyes cuts through the silence, making the hairs on the back of my neck stand up. It's a question laced with concern, but the weight of her gaze feels like it's drilling into me, burning into the side of my cheek as I try to hold it together.
"Why wouldn't I be?" I scoff, my eyes blinking rapidly, trying to get rid of the severe sting behind my eyes.
"I don't know," Sadie sighs, slouching down on the couch – in her fancy business attire and all – matching my lethargic posture. "I haven't heard much from you since you came back. Do I get to know what happened?" She raises a brow.
I feel my chest clench and my heart sink. The sting behind my eyes become horribly worst by every pasting second. I try and collect myself; I try to calm myself by counting to ten. That said, when I reach number three, gushes of wet, fat, salty tears travel

down my face. "It *all* went wrong." I manage to say though the sobs shuddering through my body. I try to explain the whole situation to Sadie – the conversation with my mother, the day we became official, Cole's father, his plan to buy the ranch off me – my shuddering sobs gradually fade into nothing more than a faint tremor in my voice as I finish the sentences.

I peer over towards Sadie, she never said a word since my breakdown, the occasional squeeze of her hand in mine was the only telltale sign that she was still listening.

The silence between us is thick, heavy with unspoken thoughts and raw emotion. Maybe I've said too much, maybe I've opened a door that should've stayed closed. But when a warm arm wraps around my shoulders and pulls me in tight, thoughts of those feelings completely disappear into the unknown.

"Oh, Blair." Sadie's voice cracks with emotion. "God, I am *so sorry*."

"It's fine." I breathe in her pear scent, the smell instantly calming me down from the erratic turmoil inside me. "You have nothing to be sorry for."

"No. No, I should've called you more to make sure you were okay. I'm not making excuses, but you know how things are with –"

"I know." I cut her off, not wanting to bring *him* up. "Look it's done now. I'm never going to see Cole or Copper Creek again. There isn't any point of making this a bigger deal than it needs to be. I'll get over it."

Sadie pulls back, her eyes locking onto mine, searching for any trace of what I've left unsaid, any truth hiding beneath my words.

She shakes her head hard, sending waves of red hair over her face. "This isn't happening." She states and untangles her limb from me as she stands. "You love him, right?"

I nod my head, swallowing the lump in my throat.

"Blair," Sadie says, her voice softer now but laced with urgency, "Can't you see the possibility that Cole might love you too. I know it might not seem like it right now, especially with everything that's happened, but I've seen the way he looks at you, the way he talks about you when you're not around. It's clear he doesn't want to hurt you, not really. He's just... he's confused. And scared. You're not the only one with something to lose here. He's been carrying the weight of his family, of the ranch, for so long. And it's eating him alive, Blair. But underneath all of that – underneath all the pressure and the mistakes and the distance – he loves you. He's just too afraid to admit it, to be vulnerable, to let you see how much he needs you. He loves you, and I think deep down, you know it too."

"I don't think that is –" I croak but then get immediately cut off.

"He let you paint the barn pink! He showed you his private stargazing spot. He rode the Ferris wheel even though he was scared of heights. Come on, Blair. Can't you see it?"

"But he lied to me," I say, my gaze fixed on the ground as the words spill out. "He lied about everything, behind my back. That's not love."

Sadie sighs, her voice softening. "Look, take some time to clear your head, and then we'll talk more tomorrow, okay?"

I nod, barely above a whisper. "Okay." Her arms wrap around me, a comforting warmth that momentarily eases the ache inside.

"You aren't alone, Blair. How long is it going to take for you to realise that you have an army of supporters behind you."

I don't answer. Instead, I let her words settle into the silence, sinking beneath my skin and down into my bones. Maybe, just maybe, I do have supporters. Maybe, deep down Cole does love me. But right now, none of that feels like enough. All I know is that I need to figure out a way to take back the life I had – before it slips through my fingers completely.

Chapter 30

Cole

The rain falls in heavy sheets, fat droplets stumbling from the sky, perfectly reflecting the weight of my mood in this moment. Each drop hits the glass window with a quiet rhythmic thud, a sound that mirrors the beating organ in my chest. I watch as the world outside blur into a relentless, grey, downpour – just like storm inside me, unclear and muddled.

I never thought the first place I understood, would become a place which I dreaded the most. What once felt like a refuge, a place where I could breathe and make sense of the chaos, has now turned into a reminder of everything I wish I could escape.

The familiarity has now slowly mutated into something suffocating, an echo of all the things that I have lost and failed to face. It's strange how a place that held so much clarity has changed into nothing but shadows, each corner reflecting what I've become.

I know I messed up. I can't deny it, no matter how much I want to. Blair never deserved any of this – never deserved to have something so important, so cherished, ripped away underneath her. She *trusted* me. That plan with Eli? It was reckless, stupid. I thought I had everything under my control, everything planned out, but I was blinded by my own arrogance to acknowledge how wrong it was. I wish I could undo everything I done to hurt her, but I can't. All I have now is the consequences of my own actions – and the regret. My phone sits silently in my hand, my thumb hovering over the contact name of the one person I want to explain myself to. I feel like I'm frozen in the moment, torn between the engulfing urge to reach out, and the terror of what my words might break further.

I know there isn't an easy fix, no perfect way I could make up for what I have done, but I can't help to hope, that if I say the right thing – maybe it will make a difference. Still, my thumb hovers over the screen with a tremor, as if the weight of the situation presses down on me.

What do you say when you know that you've already destroyed everything?

It's not just Blair I think about, I think about Eli. The one person who should've known better, the person that should have stop me before I lost all of my control. He was my friend, my partner in crime, but somewhere along the way, he got caught in the web of this reckless plan. I should have known better than to trust him entirely, still in my haze of desperation, I let him lead me down a path that I wouldn't be able to come back from.

Although we have been through everything together – late nights, futile decisions, even worse

Rodeo Hearts

consequences – but this? This is solely different. This isn't a mistake that we can laugh off later, not a mess that can be swept underneath a rug. This is a thing that has broken and shattered all of us – Me, Blair, even Eli.

I can't even bring myself to see him after last week. The phone call I know I have to make, the one that I have been avoiding, isn't just for Blair. It is also for Elijah too.

He is the one who got me into this mess from the start, but he is also the one who has been radio silent as I have. It's as if we are both hoping the weight of the situation will die down if we completely ignore it for long enough.

My thumb slides across the screen, opening up Elijah's contact. An assortment of fury and melancholy build up in my stomach. I don't even know how to even begin *that* conversation. What do I say to him? How do I apologize for something that I barely comprehend myself? All I know is that we've been hiding excuses for far too long.

I know I need to face this, but I can't stop thinking about how I'm making everything worse. How much pain I have caused by not owning up sooner.

The rain outside pours ruthlessly, smashing onto the windows like it is never going to end, just like this mess I have created. I can't hide in this place forever, not with this guilt, not with these thoughts.

I know I need to call Blair. It's the only way out of this storm. If it doesn't fix everything, at least it would be a step in the right direction – a direction which is

taking responsibility for the destruction I have caused.
Still, I can feel the anger boil within me, melting away the guilt. Elijah isn't just a part of this mess. He is the goddamn catalyst. I trusted him. I let him convince me that this would be a promising idea, everything would work out, we would be happy if everything were kept under control. But look where we are now. Look at what has been left in these ruins. Blair's hurt. Shattered trust. Normality unrecognisable.

The frustration surges through me, coiling tight before snapping into my fist. I slam it into the wall, the impact barely dulling the rage that courses through my veins. My phone still stays clutched in my hands, though I don't want to make the call right now. I don't want to fix this with *him* – not yet.

Not when I'm so pissed off, I can barely breathe.

I shove my phone on the table and stand, restlessness gnawing at my insides. I glance outside, the storm utterly illustrating the wild rage swirling within me.

Needing to feel something other than rage, I grab my jacket off the hook and slip on my boots. The heavy weight of the fabric sliding over my shoulders add a little comfort to the cyclone inside myself.

The rain is coming down in hard, heavy pelts, though I don't care.

Yanking the door open, a gust of cool air greets my features. I step out into the rain, letting the droplets soak my skin. It's like the storm outside is daring me to face it, to get lost in it, and I'm too angry to resist.

Rodeo Hearts

My fists are clenched tight, my breathing becomes more ragged with each step I take. I don't care where I am going, I just need to move.

The sounds of my squelchy footsteps rival the faint booms of the thunder hidden in the dark clouds. The sunny pink barn comes into view – another reminder that Blair is no longer here.

I need to practice for my competition. May as well make it count.

Even as I unlock the stable door, step inside, and prepare my horse, it's Elijah who lingers in my mind. My so-called friend, the one who let me down. And Blair – someone I can't undo the damage to, no matter how desperately I wish I could. For now, though, all I can focus on is the sound of hooves clattering against the earth and the sting of rain against my skin, hoping it will wash away some of the rage that's slowly eating me alive. I don't know if it will help. But I have to try.

Chapter 31

Blair

Me: *Meet me at my apartment when you have time.*
Me: *It's time to plan.*

Sadie: *Yes ma'am.*

As I stand in my tiny, bare box apartment I stare out the window and peer down at the busy street underneath me – the hum of the city outside does little to drown out the silence in my head.

The sharp pain of Cole's betrayal is still wedged in my heart like a knife, though after a day of sleeping on it, I have decided to brush it aside and focus on the one thing that I can still control – the ranch.

My mother has had the ranch for long enough, and I'm not letting it slip out between my fingers that easily. Though, it's not just the ranch she is selling. It's everything we've shared, everything I have fought for in silence. I knew that this day would come, in some form or another, but now that it is here, it feels like the ground is starting to crumble under my feet.

My mom has always been stubborn but this – this is *more* betrayal. I fought to keep that inheritance alive, to keep our family history alive. But now, mom is deciding to let it all go. She's handing over the keys of treasure, as if they're nothing more than worthless scraps.

I start to pace the small amount of space in my apartment. The ranch wasn't just land – it was my inheritance, my future, my history. Every grain of dirt on that property felt like my father's hand on my shoulder, guiding me. Selling it wasn't just a transaction; it was like erasing everything that made me who I am.

The more I think about my mother, the more my blood starts to simmer. She never gave me a chance. She never asked me about my opinions. Never considered my feelings, as if her own daughters voice never mattered.

I am not letting her throw away my future without a fight.

The tap of knuckles vibrate off my door halting my thoughts. As I let the redhead into my apartment, I start to continue my pacing, my frustration sprouting into the air.

My mind still races as I try to come to grips with my mom's plan to sell the ranch without any warning. The thought gnaws at me, a constant weight pressing down on my chest. Each time I let it linger, it feels like I'm losing part of myself, piece by piece.

"Okay," Sadie clear her throat, "What are we working with?"

I stop in my tracks and stare at her for a beat. "She has already signed the papers." I fidget with the sleeve of my hoodie trying to steady my growing anxiety. "The sale is in motion; I tried to talk to her, but she is done. She doesn't think I can handle the ranch anymore – like I am some outsider from New York who doesn't seem to care."

Sadie crosses her arms, leaning back on the couch, watching me with a penetrating focus. "So, we have to stop it. We can't let her walk away with something like that." She snaps her fingers, the loud nip bouncing off the walls. "Though, it's not going to be easy."

My jaw tightens, "It's not just that. I won't let her sell it to just anyone. I am not letting her hand over the keys to some stranger. It's mine, and she *knows* it."

Sadie nods her head, chewing the inside of her cheek as she thinks. "Okay. So, we need to find a way to make her think that this sale is a bad idea. Something big enough to make her second guess herself."

As I stand with narrowed eyes at my best friend, an idea flickers in my head. "She doesn't see it, but the ranch is falling apart. It's not just sentimental value. It's practically getting swallowed up by the ground it sits on. It's clear she is ignoring the mess that needs to be fixed. The broken fences, scruffy cattle, issue with some land rights..."

Sadie raises a brow, "So, if we make her think it's worse than it actually is... we could make her panic."

I feel the corners of my mouth twist into a determined smile. "Exactly. She thinks that she's all done, but she doesn't realise what she is letting go of. If I show her how much trouble the ranch is really in – how much danger it will cause, she might reconsider selling it."

Sadie pulls a notepad from her bag, her eyes narrowing in thought as she begins scribbling. I can't help but admire how effortlessly she switches into problem-solving mode. "What kinda danger are we talking? Financial problems? Legal issues? Or are we going full on disaster movie and bring in a tsunami or what?"

I lean back on the arm of the sofa, my arms folded as I listen to Sadie scrawl together our plan. "I've been looking back on some water rights issues on the property. If we could make it look like the land has been vulnerable – like the water is about to be cut off – it could be the ideal justification. I'm positive mom hasn't even touched the paperwork of the property; she won't realise how bad it's gotten. And when we show her the cost to fix everything, she will have no chance in selling it."

I watch Sadie's green eyes, glow as the plan comes together. "Oh, I like this. A little *'We've got a legal issue, and by issue we mean the ranch in going to collapse in on itself.'* I can already see her getting panicked."

I take a deep inhale through my nose, trying to calm my growing nerves. "It'll work. Once she sees that she can't handle it, I'll be the only one to help. I'll be the only option – then I can take control."

Sadie grins, she pauses and looks up from her notes, "All we need to do is make sure she doesn't get to attached to the idea of selling. What's next?"

I start to pace my small confines of my apartment, again. "Well, whatever documents we are going to show her needs to look legitimate – like we have unearthed something huge. I will start looking at some papers, see if I can dig anything up which will cost her more than what she thinks it is worth. Then we will be golden."

Sadie brushes a wild red curl out of her face, tapping her pen on her notepad. "We should also look into making the sale process trickier. Show her it isn't a quick fix. The more we slow her down, the better."

The plan was starting to take shape, "Right. We need to have everything in place before she pulls that trigger. I can't let her back out before she is too far gone."

Sadie stand and joins my pacing. "Okay, we are talking legal documents, water rights, repairs… but what if there is a chance that someone is eyeing up the ranch? What do we do then?"

I pause my pacing, "If there is someone else lined up, we're going to need to play that angle too. We could make her think that someone is trying to take it from her, that she will regret selling it to them. Though, we need to do this without tipping her off. If she gets any amount of scepticism, then it's over."

Sadie tilts her head, her eyebrows furrowed in thought. "Have you ever considered how the locals might feel if she sold it off to some city wannabe cowboys?"

"That might work. When she realises that locals might come knocking on her door with complaints, that could make a huge mess in her decisions."

Sadie grabs her jacket which she discarded on the couch when she entered. "I'm in. We'll dig up the right paperwork, find a way to make her believe she's making a mistake. If we can make her think she's losing the ranch to something – or someone – else, we'll have her right where we want her."

A storm of fear and anxiety whirls inside my stomach. However, when I take a deep breath, I brush aside the growing panic.

I'm doing the right thing. I am taking back what is rightfully mine. "Let's get to work."

Sadie give me a mischievous smile, rubbing her hands together like an evil villain. "Ready to play dirty?"

My lips curl into a smile, "Oh, I don't care if it is dirty. I just want this ranch back, and I'll do whatever it takes to do it."

We exchange a look – there was no going back now. We had a plan. And I will fight until the end to keep my mother from selling something that is rightfully mine.

Chapter 32

Cole

His frail body lays in bed, his laboured breaths fill the quiet room. I hoped coming to see my dad would distract my mind from chaos, but, unsurprisingly, it only seemed to make it worse.

His face is withered and getting paler by the day. He is sleeping more, mumbling nonsense more, *forgetting* more. The small hum of the clock in the corner ticks away, as if it is counting down on how much time I have left with my dad.

Tick.
Tick.
Tick.

The room feels suffocating, the quiet pressure of grief grows louder with each passing second. I watch the slow rise and fall of my dad chest, the effort it takes for him to breathe is too much for him. My chest feels hallow being here with him like this – present in the body but absent in every other way.

"You were always the one who kept everything together, dad." My voice pops the bubble of silence. "You always knew… what to say. Now I can barely get a single sentence out of you."

I lean back on my chair at his bedside, staring at the ceiling. It's too quiet, it's too still. I can hear my own

heartbeat race with everything that I have tried to keep bottled up – resentment, exhaustion, guilt.
I wish Blair were here, I wish I could explain myself. I wish I could tell her how much I've been holding everything in, how heavy everything feels. Though, the words never seem to come when I need them the most. The silence that follows me only makes everything harder. It feels like I am suffocating underneath the weight of everything unsaid – and Blair, she could always make me feel better.
But now it is just me, my dad, and the clock ticking away, as if time itself is slipping through my fingers.
There is a soft knock on the door, the sound of it creaking open, revealing Milo. I straighten in my chair, caught off guard by his surprise arrival. I feel the weight of the room shifts as he quietly enters. The tension thickening with every soft step her takes. Glancing at dad, a hesitant expression flashes across his face, as though he is unsure whether or not he belongs. "How is he?"
I glare at his face for a beat, the tension palpable. "He's here." I jolt my chin to the old worn man curled up on the bed. "Still here, barely. You've been *gone*, Milo. But sure, see him whilst you still can." I snap; my words loaded.
I watch him look down at his scuffed boots, guilt evident on his face. He knows that this conversation is overdue, though is unsure to handle it. He takes another cautious step towards the bed and peers down at our father, who seems completely unaware that his two sons are present in the room with him.

Milo looks anywhere but my eyes when he mumbles quietly, "I have been... busy. You know how my coach gets; I need to work my ass off to make championships... It's been a lot."
I scoff, my voice rising an octave. "A lot? Is that what you tell yourself? I've been here, Milo – I've been here *almost every day*, waiting, watching until he slips away, and you couldn't even be available to make a fucking phone call!" I shake my head, trying to rein in my temper. "We, need you, Milo, he needs you. But you... you have been too busy for any of it."
I watch my brother physically flinch, as if my words have slapped him in the face. He looks at our old man. He looks at the frailty *his* father is in, a stark reminder of everything he has been avoiding.
"I didn't want to see him like this." His tone is defensive, "I thought... I thought if I stayed away, maybe it wouldn't feel real."
A bitter laugh escapes my mouth. "Yeah, right. You thought if you stayed away long enough you wouldn't have needed to deal with it. Wouldn't have to deal with us. Do you really think you can walk in and expect us to be okay with that?"
"I'm – I'm sorry, Cole. I don't know how to make up for it. I just – I just thought I was doing the right thing, you know? By not being here, by not making things worse."
I shake my head; *does he really think that?* A lump forms in my throat, increasing in size by the growing tension and emotion in the room. "By you not being here, has made it worse." My voice cracks with sentiment. "Every day, I've had to watch dad forget

who I am, forget who he is, and you weren't even there to see it. You were never there when he shouted mom's name because he doesn't even know who is around him anymore." My vision becomes foggy with wet tears. "He doesn't *know* he is dying."
Cole looks down at the thin, frail outline on the small bed, a painful reminder of all the time that has been lost. He take a deep breath, trying to steady himself. He speaks softly, "Look, I don't know how to fix this. I can't fix it. But... I am here now." His eyes snap to mine, remorse washing over his features. "I'll be there, Cole. I'll help. Whatever you need."
Silence eats up the room. The words hanging heavily between us, like a bridge trying to form with missing pieces. I rip my gaze towards my dad, his awkward breathing pattern makes his chest rise in an uneven rhythm. My frustration melts away, replaced with something subdued – exhaustion.
"It's not about fixing it, Milo." I sigh, "It's just about... *being there*. Before it is too late."
I watch Milo, swallow hard. Looking down at his hands with guilt and grief. He doesn't know how to repair the past, but he can be present for the future.
I stand from my chair, pulling my brother into a hug. "Don't beat yourself up about it, Milo. All I am asking you to do is be there. For us. *For him.*"
He hesitates at first, his body stiff in between my arms, but then he slowly relaxes, his shoulders slumping under the weight of it all. His breathing comes out shaky, like he is trying to hold it all together, still the cracks are showing. I can feel the

guilt radiating off him, and that alone makes me ache for the both of us.

His voice is barely above a whisper, "I don't know if I can do it, Cole. I don't know how I can be here, not like this. I've been running from it... from all of this, for far too long. Now it feels too late."

I pull back slightly, looking him in the eyes, "It's never too late, Milo." I clutch his shoulders to steady the slight tremble racking through his body. "It doesn't matter how far or how long you have stayed away. What matters is what you do *now*. You don't have to fix anything... you just need to be there."

I watch his eyes gloss over, his fists clench by his side, like he is trying to keep it together long enough for this conversation to end. Nevertheless, I can see it in his eyes – the shame, the weight of all the things he should've said, should've done. It floats between us, cutting out the air until it is suffocating.

His voice cracks, "I don't know what to say to him anymore. What if he doesn't know me? What if he can't even remember I'm his son?"

The question hangs in the air unanswered. I peer over to my dad, laying ever so still in his bed, his frail body barely breathing with each sallow breath. The silence is thick between my brother and I, but I don't answer. I don't know what to say to make it easier.

"It doesn't matter if he doesn't remember you, Milo. He'll know you by your presence. That is all what we have left. Just be here. Do that for him. For me." I sigh.

I watch his eyes flicker to dad, then back to me. After a moment, it looks like he wants to say something, though, it's like the words got trapped in his throat. He nods his head, a slow, shaky motion, as if he is accepting the heaviness of the moment. "I'm sorry, Cole. For everything. I'm sorry I wasn't here before."

I softly sigh, and pull him back into a hug, slapping him on the back a few times. "It's okay, Milo. It's all we can do now – be there. Together."

For a long moment, we stand there in stillness, the ticking of the clock in the corner growing more forceful, filling the room with its relentless reminder of time slipping away. But for the first time in a long while, I don't feel as alone.

Chapter 33

Blair

I gaze up at the towering glass façade of my office building, watching as the swarm of New Yorkers rushes past, heads down, eyes locked on their phones – barely aware of my presence. For the first time, the sight of the sleek, pristine structure fills me with a sense of intimidation I've never felt before.

The folder with the carefully planted documents is tucked underneath my arm, it's weight pressing down on me, as if the entire plan is bearing down on my shoulders.

My hands tremble at the thought of knowing that I could either lose everything or save it – the ranch that has been in my family for generations.

I swallow past the lump in my throat as I walk up the steps and into the lobby. The bright white lights spring off the polished floors, and the crystal chandelier above the reception desk seems to hang like a significant reminder of this world I've stepped back into. My former colleagues are dressed to the nines, all sharp suits, and polished shoes. The contrast hits me like a wave – a jarring reminder of Misty Pines, where the furniture is worn and rustic, the pace slower, and everything feels simpler. The discomfort prickles at my skull, like the first sting of a headache.

I hurry toward the elevators, hoping to slip by before anyone notices me. As soon as the metal doors open, I step inside and quickly press the button for the top floor – my mother's office.

As the metal box continues to ascend so does my nerves. It was only months ago when I first got that letter from Cole, stating that I should either sell or fix Copper Creek. At first, my initial intension was to sell off the land – get rid of the 'burden' that my grandfather placed upon me. But somewhere along the way, my intension switched; I fell in love with the ranch. I fell in love with the land that stretched endlessly around it. I fell in love with the quiet beauty of stary nights. And somewhere between the dusk and sunsets, *I fell in love with him.*

I close my eyes as the memories flood my mind. Cole's laugh, the way he used to look at me with so much hope, the feeling of unspoken love, like we could face anything as long as we were together. I loved him, truly. Maybe that was the problem.

I tried to move on, convince myself that leaving was the best option, that it was the only way to protect myself from someone who wasn't truly by my side. Though, as much as I tell myself I made the right choice, the truth was harder to swallow. I miss him. I missed us. I missed the way he made me feel like I could take on the world. But the trust is now shattered, I couldn't undo what has been done.

The heavy doors of the elevator slide open with a soft ping, revealing the extensive hallway that leads to the large door of my mom's office. I step out of the lift hesitantly, my gaze drifting to the assistant's desk where my best friend sits, her fingers flying over the keyboard in a blur of motion. At the sound of my heel clicking against the glossy marble floor, she looks up, and without missing a beat, abandons her work. She stands and pulls me into a comforting hug. For just a moment, the knot of nerves in my stomach slackens just a little, the familiar scent of her perfume – fruity and floral – grounds me as I take in a deep, steadying breath.

"You ready to do this?" she asks, pulling away slightly to study my face.

I let out a sigh, trying to shake off the nerves crawling up inside me. "Yeah," I mutter, though it doesn't feel as convincing as I'd like.

Sadie takes my trembling hands in hers, her gaze soft but steady as she looks into my anxious eyes. "You've got this, Blair. You're not alone. I'm right here with you." She says, her voice firm, as if she's trying to banish any doubt that might linger in my mind.

I don't say anything. I simply nod my head and creep down the hall towards the office I dread. Sadie stays right on my heals, keeping to her word – *quite literally* – as I knock on the door, sending a vibration of sound into the atmosphere.

The muffle sound of footsteps can be heard on the other side, each step mimicking the brisk beat of my heart in my chest. As the door peels open, I am met with a worn looking figure with determination in her eyes – my mother. She has been intolerable for the past few months; I know this isn't going to be an easy fight. My mom decision to sell didn't come lightly and convincing her to let go of it might take more than a couple of documents.

"Blair." She sighs; exhaustion threaded in her voice. She glances over to her assistant. "Sadie. What's this about?"

I step inside her untouched office, trying to push away the knot in my stomach. Taking a seat at her desk, my mom looks nothing but like a queen on a throne. Yet, it is hard to not notice the dark circles that lie hidden underneath her eyes.

Sadie takes a seat in front of my mom, taking out her phone to reply to an email with an easy casualness that doesn't match my growing nerves.

I take a seat on the other chair opposite my mom, I pull out the methodically planned out documents from my arms and place it on the desk in front of me. The sound of paper hitting the desk echoes throughout the large space as I clear my throat and swallow down the bile. "Mom, we need to talk. It's about the ranch."

Raising a perfectly manicured brow, my mother leans back in her chair, clearly weary about having this conversation again.

She crosses her arms and lets out a resigned sigh. "We have talked about this enough, Blair. The decision has been made. I'm done dragging this out." She shakes her head, "I am done fighting with you about something that is slipping away. It's time"

Sadie casts me a look of concern in my peripheral, but I nod my head, refusing to back down. This

conversation has been trapped in my head for weeks, and I'm ready.
I lean in closer and lock eyes with my mom. "It's not too late, Mom. You don't have to sell it. I've been looking into the numbers, and I have found a lot of things – about water rights, the bills, condition of the land... this isn't the right decision to make."
My mom cautiously peels open the documents, flipping through the paper with a critical eye, not looking up. I watch her with my heart in my throat, as she reads the legal language on the documents. The silence is extensive, filling every corner of the room. I can feel the tension burning, but my mom doesn't break.
"Blair, I have told you, I have made my mind up. I am tired of watching this ranch slip in between fingers. I am not letting that place swallow me, or you, whole. Selling it is the only way forward."
My stomach twists at the sound of exhaustion in my mom's voice. Her voice cracks slightly with every word she speaks, I know this decision isn't easy for her. The weight of it all dragging her down. I can feel the sting of her words in my soul, but I am not going to back down. Not now.
"Mom, you're not alone in this. You've taught me to fight for what matters, and the ranch matters. I know it has been hard, but I *want it*. You have taught me so much, but I can't stand by and let you throw it away."
As if sensing the moment is crucial, Sadie speaks up, her tone softer, almost coaxing. "Mrs Reynolds, I know it has been hard. But think about how much

this ranch means to your family. It's not about the land. It's about the legacy, the history. It was your fathers dream, your husbands dream. If it's gone, it will be gone for good. You won't get another shot at keeping it in the family."

I watch my mother's gaze soften at her assistant words for a fraction. She looks down at the small photo frame that sits on her desk – the only object which is non-work related in her office. Her eyes linger on the photo of my dad and herself. Young with the ranch thriving in the background. Although the memories are dense, my mom doesn't show them, not yet.

Her voice is barely above a whisper as she almost speaks to herself, "I have tried. I've tried too hard, Blair. I just didn't want to watch it fall apart."

My hands grip the handles of the chair, turning my knuckles white. I take in a long breath, before I speak again. This time with more of an edge, though my voice still cracks just a little. "You're not protecting me by selling it. You're protecting yourself. You are choosing to let go of something that belongs to me, *us*. If you sell it, you're giving up on all of this – the history, the legacy, the *family*. I'm not ready to let it go. And I don't think you are either. You think that this is your burden to carry on your own. But let me help you, mom. Let me take over. I want to keep the ranch alive. I want to keep *our future alive*."

I watch my mom hand tremble as she grips the documents again, her tried eyes dart around on the paper. The silence stretches, and for a moment it seems like my mom is lost in deep thought, torn between struggle and love she still has for the ranch buried deep inside.

When she finally speaks, her voice is quiet, though filled with settle. "Maybe, you are right. I've been trying to protect you from all of this. When you first left to tend to the ranch, I realised that I didn't want you to carry that weight that I felt, them many years ago. But I can see that you aren't some little girl anymore. You're strong, Blair. You've always been strong. And maybe I have been too stubborn to admit that."

"You don't need to carry it all alone. We can fix it... *together*." I speak with all the sincerity I can muster.

She looks down at the documents that was are supposed to show the ranch decline. But when the realisation starts to sink in – it doesn't need to be this way. Not yet. Not if I can help it.

She releases a quiet breath. "Okay. You take it, and you make it work. But you have to promise me – never let it go. You will fight for it, like we both have."

My heart swell with relief, though I don't show it. I just nod, my voice full of appreciation and determination when I speak. "I will. I promise."

I peek over towards Sadie, who gives me a quick, proud nod. I feel a wave of energy – like I have just won the first round of a fight that will last a lifetime. The ranch is no longer just a dream. It is real again. And it's mine to protect.

My mom stands, rounds her desk, and places a hand on my shoulder – giving a reassuring squeeze. The weight of the years still hang between us, but for the first time in a long time, it feels like we are moving forward.

"It's yours now. Don't let me down." She smiles softly. I meet my mom eyes, the responsibility settling on my shoulders. It's not a burden – it's a second chance. A chance to fight for what is ours, to save what is left of our past, and build a future.

When I step out the office in a fit of daze, Sadie engulfs me in a warm hug, her laughter and cheers bouncing off the walls. "We did it! You did it, Blair! We saved the ranch; it is finally yours!"

I stand there for a moment, barely able to process the words. "It is," I whisper, still in disbelief that I actually won the ranch back.

As we continue down the hall in a stunned victory, Sadie grins at me. "So, ranch is saved, relationship with your mom is amended, what is the plan now?"

I let out a soft chuckle, a glint of mischief in my eyes. "I think maybe it's time to pay an old cowboy a visit."

Chapter 34

Cole

The air was thick with dust, carrying the scent of sweat and grime, and the roar of the crowd blended with the crackling voice of the announcer. But I couldn't focus on any of it – my mind was consumed by the decision that had already been made for me. Elijah stood beside me, fingers fiddling with the strap of my gear like any other day, like everything wasn't going to detonate in front of us. The bronc in the chute was twitchy, pawing at the dirt, bucking it's legs back with eagerness.

Still, it felt like everything outside this moment was slowly creeping away.

The sound of the horses, the rumble of the crowd, even Elijah's presence – it all felt so distant. The only thing that was clear was the tight knot in my stomach that has been growing for the past months. The plan that my best friend set in motion – the plan to buy the ranch off Blair.

I heard it over and over again in Elijah's voice. The enthusiasm, the certainty, as if it were the *only* way to go forward. But it never felt like *my* choice. I was backed into a corner, expected to step in and take away Blair's land, take over the place that meant everything to her. Not because I wanted it, not because I was ready, but because my best friend thought it was the right move – thought it would give me some redemption, some way to reclaim my life after everything that has gone wrong before.

Eli pulls away from my gear and straightens up. Out of the corner of my eye, I feel him studying the side of my face while I mess with my gloves. When he speaks, his voice is too calm – like it doesn't match the storm raging in my chest. "Cole, you good?" Although the question is innocent, I couldn't stop the corners of my mouth downcast in a sour grimace, I didn't know how to answer. "Yeah." The words tasted bitter on my tongue, all foreign in my mouth. "I'm fine."

I knew Elijah could see the shift in me. Glancing over to where he stood, I could see a flicker of hesitancy in his eyes that deceived his common confidence. It was as if for the first time Elijah realised that the plan wasn't as solid as he thought it would be.

When I watch his expression waver, I can't help but feel a sour satisfaction in seeing my friend question everything that he pushed for.

Maybe just maybe, Elijah was starting to understand that the weight of his choice he made without considering the consequences.

Clearing his throat, he leans in slightly. "Look, I know you are pissed about how things went down with Blair. I get it, man. But we talked about this – this is the way to move forward. You can buy the ranch, turn it around, get a fresh start. You and me both know she was planning on selling it anyway. You'll be helping her in the long run."

My jaw tightens, though I don't look away. A wave of frustration washes over me like a tsunami. I heard that line from Eli so many times, it started to sound hallow.

I ball my hands tight, trying to rein in my resentment. "She might have been ready to sell. But not to *me*, Elijah." My voice was low and sharp, barely audible over the deafening audience in the stands. "If she was ready to walk away, I wasn't even in the equation. This whole thing – you planning for me to buy the ranch like it was already a done deal – it feels like you made the decision for me, without ever asking what I wanted."

Eli staggers backwards, his face scrunching in a mixture of frustration and regret. "I thought you would see it the way I do, man. The land is worth something, isn't it? It's an opportunity."

A dark chuckle slips out between my lips. "This has nothing to do with the land, Elijah. It never was." My chest squeezes at the thought of our crumbling friendship. "It *was* about her. It will *always* be about her." My voice cracks as I continue. "Did you seriously think she wouldn't see right through me, see how I am supposed to take over, like I'm some… some replacement? A business move to fill the void she'd leave behind? You were asking me to buy her out like some *stranger*. I'm not a stranger to Blair, Elijah. I'm not a business deal. I never was."

My best friend was silent for a moment. His eyes avoid my own as he weights the words that finally hit home. "I didn't mean it like that," he whispers, though there is no conviction in his words, no apology that will undo what has already been done. The crowd blossoms to life at the next rider entering the rink. Still, I don't tear my gaze away from Eli. The bond that we once shared seems to get thinner, and thinner with every second that passes. I take a deep exhale, my voice quiet but harder than ever. "You pushed me into this. I never wanted to buy that ranch off her. I never asked for this. And the last thing I want to do is take away something that her family has worked for, for decades, and pretend it's all mine."

My own words stung as they cling in the air between us, but I didn't care anymore. The truth had to be said. Yet, something inside me throbbed. I'm not angry at Eli. I'm angry at the situation, at everything that led to this moment, at the feeling of powerlessness that has slung itself around me without even knowing.

Eli opened his mouth as if to say something, but I didn't give him the chance. I didn't want to hear his excuses. I didn't want to hear *'it's for the best.'* I just want to get on the bronc and prove something – anything – to myself.

"I need to focus." I mutter, without looking at Eli. The tension in my chest is now unbearable, leaving no space left for more words. Only the ride.

Without another glance, I make my way over to the chute. The bronc, restless and violent, kicked at the air, it's muscles rippling beneath the skin as it thrashed in the small confines of the gate.

Rodeo Hearts

Pulling myself over the chute, my heart pounds in my chest as I begin to mount the saddle. I lock my boots into the stirrups and pull the rope taut. Despite the tension between us, Elijah climbs up beside the chute and gives me a quick check. "You got this, Cole," he shouts over the roar of the crowd and the heavy, restless breaths of the animal beneath me. With a small nod, I tighten my hand. Although I was sat on top of a ferocious animal, my mind was elsewhere – fighting with the anger towards my best friend, the helpfulness of my future, and the complicated whirl of emotions with Blair.

However, my thoughts are shattered as soon as the loud buzzer rang out throughout the arena, and the gates slamming open, releasing me and the bronc with explosive power.

My body jerked with each forceful buck the animal gave me, but I held on, using every ounce of strength and muscle memory to stay mounted. My memory was sharp now. Everything – Eli, the ranch, even the crowd – faded into the background as I gripped the rope tighter with white knuckles, bracing myself from the twists and turns.

The animal was unpredictable, but I was used to that. It was the unpredictability of life, of my choice, that made me hesitate.

Then when the bronc twisted aggressively, sending me to one side, something caught my eye. *Someone* caught my eye.

In the crowd. There she was. My Blair.

Rodeo Hearts

For a split second, it felt as if time had completely froze. Though, the animal kicked brutally, forcing me back into the rhythm, yet my eyes never left Blair. Standing near the front, her posture was rigid, her ocean eyes locked on mine. *She hasn't moved on.* For a moment, she was the only person in the world, the only thing that mattered. Even if her expression was unreadable – serene yet withdrawn – there was something about the way she was watching me that hit me like a wave. She wasn't just in the crowd. She was *looking* at me.

The heat of the competition, the thudding of hooves, the sounds of the crowd – it all melted away as my chest tensed, the storm inside stilled, long enough to realise something. No matter what my best friend planned, no matter the land, no matter the ranch – we were connected by something deeper.

She had always been there for me. She wasn't just part of this situation – she was my anchor. The thought send a jolt of transparency through my body. For the first time in what felt like forever, I felt something soft. Something real. *Love.*

I held on tight to the bronc, but my mind was no longer focused on anything – not even the animal. The ride didn't matter to me anymore. It wasn't about the competition; it was about what came next. About what I could still build with Blair, the choices that still lied ahead.

As the buzzer rang out throughout the arena, signalling the ride has ended, I was heaving with exhaustion, but my mind hadn't been this clear in months. As the pickup riders dismount and herd the horse out of the arena, my legs shake as I begin to move across the dirt. But I don't head for the exit. Instead, I scan the crowd again, my gaze finally locking on Blair.

She was still there, watching me. And for the first time, I wasn't thinking about what Eli wanted, or what had been taken away from me. I was thinking about what I wanted. And maybe, just maybe, I could figure it out – if I could make thing right with her.

For the first time, in a long time, it felt like I had a chance.

Chapter 35

Blair

At the edge of the crowd, my eyes locked onto the arena. The sun hung low in the sky, stretching long, harsh shadows across the dirt and sand of the rodeo grounds. But no shadow could rival the storm raging inside me.

My heart was fluttering in my chest, and my palms were clammy as I waited for Cole to make his move. I watched him practice many of time over the past months, back when things between us were easier, back when I would believe we had all the time in the world to figure things out. But today, it felt different.

I felt like a stranger here, like so much has changed between us – like we have both drifted apart, caught in our own current of their own choices and fears.

Still, I'm here. Watching him. I couldn't look away, even though I didn't have a clue where we stood anymore. There was so much history between us – too much pain, too many unspoken words – and yet, despite everything, Cole was still Cole. The same man I loved, the same man who had always found a way to fight for what mattered.

My eyes follow every step he took towards the chute, the muscles in his back rippling underneath his shirt as he adjusted his gear. His eyes were set with determination, though when I look closer, I can see there is something else. Something delicate, a rawness that made me ache in a way I wasn't prepared for.

I could see it now – the weight of everything he was carrying. The regret. The duty. I finally understood now, more than ever, how hard it had been for him. And, despite all the anger that had been burning between us, my heart softened at the presence of it.

When the gates slammed open, the bronc shot out like a live wire. Cole's body jerked with the force, yet his grip on the rope remained steady. I could hear the rush of his breath, the quick rhythm of his chest as he fought to remain control.

The crowd emitted into a roar, but it felt muffled in my ears. All I could hear was the beat of his heart, as if I were right there, beside him, feeling everything, he felt.

Every twist the animal made felt like a reflection of our own chaotic journey – the wild and unpredictable ride that we both seemed to never get quite right.

The bronc bucked forcefully beneath him, but Cole didn't let go. His body moved with it in a perfect dance, filled with strength and control, as though he is trying to prove something – both to the crowd and himself.

My chest constricts as I watch him, my heart trapped between pride and something else.

Regret.

Because I knew deep down that he didn't want this. He didn't want to buy the ranch off me, take away something that I grow to love. He done it because he thought it was right. Because he thought it was the only way to fix things.

But the truth was, the only thing that was stolen was trust.

As the buzzer rang out, Cole launches himself off the bronc with shaky legs. The crowd erupted in applause, though I barely heard it. I was too busy looking at Cole. I couldn't tear my eyes away from him, his heaving chest, his rugged face set in a quiet triumph, yet there was no hiding the exhaustion that raked through his posture.

For a moment, I thought he might stumble, but instead, he steadied himself, his gaze sweeping over the crowd, searching for something – or someone. My heart skipped a beat. I didn't have to guess. I knew he was looking for me.

And for the first time in months, I didn't turn away.

I stayed where I was, my feet planted firmly on the ground as I watch him moving through the busy crowd. Each step Cole took felt like a statement, a silent promise that he was coming to find me after everything that had torn us apart.

The tension drained the air of every breath, leaving nothing but heaviness. But with each step he took toward me, it was as if the weight lifted, even if just for an instant.

As he pushed through the throngs of people, the world faded away into nothing but muted silence. He had finally reached me, we were only mere inches apart, and yet the space between us felt like an endless abyss.

Cole's dark eyes were soft, filled with something that I hadn't seen in a long time – vulnerability. I could see the load of everything that he had been holding back, the anxiety, the guilt.

It was a look I knew all too well – one I'd seen in the quiet moments we used to share, when he tried to hide his deepest feelings beneath layers of stubborn pride.

But now, there was nothing to hide. And it left me breathless.

His tanned hand reached out with a hesitant shake, his warmth and adrenaline transfers into my bones as his callous fingers hold gently onto my arm. The simple gesture held so much more than physical contact. It felt like he was reaching out for our broken pieces, desperate to glue them back together.

"Blair." He started; his voice breathless, thick with emotion. "I'm sorry. I am so sorry. For everything. For the way that I handled it, for not talking to you about it sooner. I should have never –"

He stopped short, his voice breaking as his gaze drops to the dirt underneath us. It was as if the words has been caught in his throat, too heavy to finish. Though, I didn't need him to say it all. I understood.

"I know, Cole." I whisper, my voice was barely audible as it trembled with the weight of everything that we have been through. "I know. I was so angry. So, hurt. I thought you were doing this to take something from me. I thought you were trying to push me aside." I look into his gloomy eyes as I continue, "But I see now… it was never about that. It was about you trying to fix something. I know that now. But you never should've had to. I never wanted to make it feel like you had to do that for me. I just wanted you to choose *us*."

When his dark eyes met mine then, it felt like for the first time in forever, I saw tenderness. It was the kind of softness I had once known in his every touch, every look – the quiet, unspoken love that had always been there, bubbling beneath the surface. Beneath the anger, beneath the hurt, beneath all the words left unspoken and the faults that had stacked up between us, it had always lingered, just out of reach. But now, in this moment, it was no longer hidden. It was raw, undeniable. His gaze held all the things he hadn't said, all the emotions he had kept buried for so long. It was a tenderness that spoke of remorse, of wanting to make things right, and of a love that had never truly gone away.

And as I looked into his eyes, I knew that this was the moment we both needed – the moment were we could finally stop pretending. No more walls. No more silence. No more space between us. Everything that had kept us apart, all the misunderstandings and the hurt, dissolved away with that one look. And for the first time in what felt like forever, I felt seen. Truly seen. Not just for the woman I was, but for everything we had been through together. And for everything we could still be.

"I *did* choose us." His voice was quiet and steady now, though, it was still filtered with an influence of disappointment. "I just... I didn't know how to. I thought buying the ranch was the only thing to do, the only way to make things right. But I see now that it wasn't about the land. It was about *you*. I've been so stupid to think that I could fix everything with a business deal."

My heart tightens in my chest. Hearing him say that was like the final piece falling into place. It felt like he finally *understood* it now.

"I'm not selling it, Cole," I say, my voice firm, even as tears swelled in my eyes, threatening to leak over. The stress of my decision pushed heavy on my chest, but I stood my ground. "I can't. I can't let go of it. Not like that." I paused, swallowing hard, trying to steady the slight shake in my voice. "It's not just land to me. It's... everything." The words seemed get caught in my throat as I searched for the right way to say it. "It's my history. My family. It's the echoes of every person who's walked the fields before me, the sweat and love they poured into that place. Everything that made me who I am, it's all here. Every recollection, every piece of myself is entwined to that land."

My eyes drop for a moment, my hands clutch the metal fence in front of me, the cold biting into my flesh as I try to hold onto something solid, something real. "I thought of selling it at first." I continue, my voice breaking ever so slightly. "I thought that would take the pain away, that I could move on and forget it all. But I was wrong. I can't, not anymore." I look up at him then, my gaze unwavering from his face. "I've tried to run away from this place. To make it easier for myself. But in the end, it's not the land that

I am trying to hold onto – it's everything that still matters between us."

A heavy silence filled the air between us, both suffocating but unusually comforting. It was like we were breathing the same air after years of being underwater.

Cole took a step forward, his face softening. His hand brushed against mine, tentative at first, but then steady as he sought the connection. "I'm sorry." He whispers again, his voice thick. "I never should've let Elijah talk me into it. I thought I was doing the right thing. I thought I was doing what would be best for us, but I was wrong. I should've listened to you. You should've been the one to make the choice, not me. I never want to take that away from you. Never."

My breath catches in my throat as I shake my head, my tears spill down my face as I utter, "I was scared, Cole. I was scared that we couldn't fix it. That it was too far gone, too broken to bring back to life. But I was wrong. I should've listened to you. I shouldn't of ran away."

His hands gently cup my face, his thumb brushing away the salty tear that had escaped down my cheek. The tenderness of his touch made my heart swell. The last tension between us seemed to melt from that simple gesture.

"You never have to run again, sweets." He murmured softly, "Not from me. Not from *us*."

For a long, quiet moment, neither of us spoke. The crowd, the noise, the world outside our bubble felt distant, muffled as we stood there, completely lost in each other. When Cole's hand slid down to my own, it felt like the weight of everything we had endured and survived slowly lift. It was as if the past months had been long, drawn-out, but now, in his hands, I felt the calm after the rain.

"I love you, Blair," He whispers, his voice breaking due to the power of the words. "I always have and always will."

A knot that I never knew I had started to unravelled around my heart with the simple, undeniable words. A smile, fragile but real, curved my lips through tears.

"I love you too, Cole." I utter back, "I have never stopped."

He then kissed me. It was soft, slow, and tender, filled with everything that we had left unsaid for far too long. His lips against mine spoke more than any word could – a silent promise, an acknowledgement of the pain, and the chance to rebuild. To try again.

When we finally pull away, he rests his forehead on mine, his breath shaky as he sighs "So... we rebuild this. Together?"

I smile through my tears, yet this time they were filled with relief. Peace. "Together."

Just like that, the storm that seemed to rage between us became quiet. There was still uncertainty ahead, still things to figure out. Still, for a first time in a long time, I knew we were in this together. That certainty, that shared commitment, was enough to make everything feel right again.

The road ahead was unknown, but at least we were walking it together. Side by side.

Chapter 36

Cole

The noise of the crowd fades into a distant roar as I stand in the middle of the arena. The seconds turn into hours. My legs are stiff from the ride, the lingering rush of adrenaline making it hard to stay still.
The anticipation is a living thing, pulsing inside me, spreading from my chest down to my fingertips. Every muscle inside me is screaming, but the storm of frustration, confusion, and regret that had thundered through me earlier is now gone. Now there is only a quiet, stable pull towards Blair, who is standing in the sea of people, just a few feet away.
The announcer's voice booms through the speakers, but I don't hear the words. Not really. The crowds energy rises and falls like waves, yet I all I can hear is the rapid rate of my heart in my ears.
The cheers are just a background noise. It's the waiting – the agonising quiet before the storm of the announcement – that is what has me on edge. Each passing second feels like a countdown, and I don't know if I am ready for what is about to come next.
I can feel Blair's gaze on me, steady and unwavering. I know she's watching, even though I haven't had the courage to glance her way.
I'm still too caught up on the load of what we've just shared, what we have confessed. The words

exchanged – the apology, the declarations – still linger in the air between us, a warmth that I can't quiet describe. They aren't just words. They're promises. They're everything I'd been holding back on for so long.
The announcers voice cuts through my thoughts, and the ovation of the crowd become deafening as the results come closer. All I can do is stand there, listening to the rumble of people, waiting, but not really caring about the competition anymore.
I have won something much bigger than any fancy ribbon or shiny trophy could ever give me.
I glance over towards Blair then. She is still standing there, her gorgeous eyes locked on mine, that quiet, knowing smile on her lips, like she is just as lost in the moment as I am. There is something in her gaze – something soft, yet steady. Something that tells me that, no matter what happens next, we have already found our way back to each other.
This time the announcers voice rings out clearer, more authoritative, as the sounds of the crowd gradually fades into a singular hum. I can barely register the words at first, still caught in the daze of everything that has happened.
But then it hits me. The world sharpen, everything snapping into focus.
"And the winner is... *Cole Walker!*"
The crowd erupts in a deafening roar, but everything around me fades into a blur. The cheers, the applause – none of it reaches me. My heart pounds in my chest, and for a second, I wonder if I'm even breathing. Victory should feel like a rush, but instead,

it feels hollow, distant. My mind is elsewhere, on one person. Her.
I step up to the podium, the microphone cold in my hand, but I don't raise it to speak just yet. The audience waits, the air thick with anticipation. I take a deep breath and, without hesitation, lean into the microphone.
"Hold up," I say, my voice steady but laced with something else – something raw. "This win isn't just mine. There's someone I need to share it with."
A few confused murmurs ripple through the crowd, but I don't care. I scan the faces in the stands, my eyes searching until they land on her – Blair. Her gaze locks with mine, and I can see the surprise and warmth in her expression.
I point the microphone toward her, my voice breaking the silence. "Blair, get up here. You're the reason I'm standing here today."
The crowd goes quiet, and then, all at once, they begin to cheer her name. Blair doesn't hesitate. She stands, her eyes never leaving mine as she makes her way toward the podium.
When she reaches me, I hand her the mic, and for the first time, I let the weight of the victory, the weight of everything, sink in. She takes the mic from me, her fingers brushing mine, sending a shock of warmth through me.
"Together," she says simply, and the world feels right again.
I smile; my heart finally able to breathe. "Together."

And then, as the cheers swell around us, we stand there, side by side, sharing the moment we've both been waiting for.

The last thing I expected was the night to end with Blair in my arms and her pillow soft lips against mine, but here we are.
As soon as I pulled up to the ranch, she was on me in a heartbeat. Her nails digging into my shoulders, her body pressed up tight against mine, as we boomerang in the hall towards my bedroom. Before we entre, she pushes me with force against the wall, trapping me in. "I missed you." She whispers against my lips, her hot breath fanning on my face.
"Oh, yeah?" I grip her hips and spin us, colliding her with the wall with a dull thud. I give her lip a playful bite, "You going to show me how much?"
She moans when my lips brush her collarbone. I smirk as I lazily drag my lips down, then up the length of her neck, finding the flutter of her pulse underneath the sensitive skin. "I asked you a question, baby." I whisper as I nip her ear, "You going to show me?"
She whimpers, filling the silent hall with her sensual sounds. "Yes."
"Good girl." I grip the back of her thighs and pull her up against me. Kicking the door open, I march over towards my bed and set her down, the moonlight spills into the room from my window, painting Blair in silver.

As we remove our clothes, we don't look away from each other's eyes. The tension in the room is thick with anticipation. As soon as the last piece of clothing hits the floor with a soft thud, I finally tear my eyes away from hers and take in the view before me.
Blair sits on my bed; her skin looks milky white compared to her dark hair in the dusk. The shining strands falls effortlessly down her back and shoulders, framing the swell of her breast and the hard points of her nipples.
"On your knees, baby. Show me how much you missed me." My voice comes out deeper and more commanding than I intend, but when Blair kneels down, that thought flies completely out the window.
Fisting my cock, I give it a few tugs, relishing in the feeling. As I move closer to Blair, I grip her hair, pulling her back to look at me. "If it gets too much, tap my thigh." My voice is softer this time, the last thing I want to do is hurt her or make her uncomfortable.
When she nods her head, she opens her mouth and places her tongue on the tip, sucking gently at first. My eyes roll to the back of my head at the contact, we've barely started, and I am already about to come.
Blair starts working on my cock, taking an inch with each passing stoke of her hands. "Fuck, Blair. You are doing so good baby, keep going." I pant.
Her moans sends a vibration around my cock. Fisting the back of her head, I gently pull her away and thrust her back in. I watch her eyes roll, I watch

as my cock moves in and out her mouth, glistening with her saliva.
Pulling out of her completely, I move her onto the bed and spread her legs. "God, Blair. You are dripping. Do you need me, baby?"
I look up from her soaked pussy, I can see a dark shade of blush painted on her cheeks at the words that leave my mouth.
Staring down at me, her chest rises and falls rapidly. "Yes, please Cole. I want you. I *need* you." She rasps.
My nostrils flare as I pull her down the bed towards me. I line up my tip to her entrance. I enjoy the feeling of her bare warmth on me for a beat before I reach over to my nightstand for a condom. But I stop when a soft hand clasps around my wrist.
Looking down at Blair, she smiles and shakes her head. "I'm clean."
I stare at her, unable to comprehend the words that left her mouth. "Sorry?"
A small chuckle leaves her lips. "I'm clean and on the pill if you wanted to try without. But if you aren't comfortable…"
"No." I shake my head. "I am completely comfortable and clean." I let my gaze travel down her body for a second, before I say, "You sure?"
She smiles delicately. "I'm sure."
I release a breath I never knew I was holding, then move back down Blair's body. Linning myself up, I lock eyes with Blair as I start to sink in.
With no barrier, the feeling feels indescribable. Blair's moans fill the room as I start to move in and

out gently. Her wetness coating over my dick almost makes me blow.

"Harder, Cole." Blair moans loudly, as I start to up the pace.

The sounds of skin slapping and panting breaths fill the dark room. Sweat clings to my brow as I try to hold back on coming. Yet, when Blair clenches around me and her back blows off the bed as she reaches her high. I let go.

I thrust harshly into her as I start to come. My hand clasps her breast, tweaking her nipple as she withers underneath me.

When our moans return to laboured pants, I collapse on top of Blair, encasing her in my warmth. Reaching my fingers to her face, I brush away the strands of hair stuck on her face. She smiles softly as she hushes, "I love you, Cole."

I smile as my lips graze hers, leaving a soft, feather-light kiss, gently hushing the words on the tip of my tongue. "I love you too, Blair. I'll always will. Thank you"

She frowns, "Thank you, for what?"

"For giving me a second chance. I would be lost if I didn't have you. So, thank you."

She smiles tenderly, "You're welcome."

That night, I stay wrapped up in Blair's warmth, content and happy. I may have won a trophy, but I won something worth much more.

Her.

Chapter 37

Blair

As I step out of the barn, the soft morning glow casts over the ranch, the sounds of the land settling into the quiet rhythm of another day. I have been focusing on the work – on the life that I can finally call my own. But there is something in the air today, a shift, like the calm before the storm.

I don't know what is coming, but I can feel it for definite.

It's when I hear a rumble of an engine, that I realise what it is.

I look toward the road, where Eli's truck is rolling up toward the ranch, slow and cautious, like he knows exactly what he's walking into. The tires crunch against the gravel, a sound that seems to stretch out longer than it should, as it comes to a stop in front of the barn. I can't say I'm surprised – this is what I've been anticipating. But even knowing it's coming, I'm not sure I'm ready for it.

Eli steps out of the truck, his posture rigid, shoulders stiff as if he's bracing for something. I watch as he walks toward me, each step measured and wary, like he's unsure of how to bridge the distance between us. For a moment, I wonder if he's even going to be able to look me in the eye. But when our gazes finally meet, there's no avoidance. No deflection. Just guilt.

It hangs heavy between us, making the air feel thicker, harder to breathe.

"Blair..." He starts; his voice softer than I remember. "I... I know I have a lot to make up for."

I want to say something – anything – but the words feel stuck in my throat. I have been holding in my anger for weeks, wrapping it around myself like a shield, with him standing in front of me, I don't even understand how to drop it. I had been crushed by the weight of the plan he set in motion, without even considering how it would affect me so deeply. The betrayal stings like the day I found out, the pain still raw beneath everything I have tried to push down.

Nevertheless, when I look at him now, something changes. It's subtle at first, like a crack in the wall I have built around my heart. His shoulder are hunched, his eyes are searching into mine with such depth of regret, it is almost too heavy to bear.

I have seen guilt in him before – when he tried to smooth things over, when he struggled to make it right with words – though this was different. This was real. There wasn't any defensiveness in his posture, no excuse ready to escape his lips. Just a consuming amount of remorse.

As much as I want to stay angry. To keep the wall between us, to let him feel the weight of the damage he has caused. I can't.

The authenticity in his eyes, the way he is standing – open, vulnerable, waiting for me to say something – pulls at the part of me that still cares. And I cannot ignore it, no matter how hard I could try.

The words I have been holding feel tremendously small, too petty in the face of his apology. It is as if everything that has been unsaid for too long has finally risen to the surface, brushing the anger aside and leaving the everlasting ache of everything we have been through.

"I never should've done it." Eli continues, taking a hesitant step closer. "I thought I was doing the right thing – I thought I was helping. But I see now... I clearly just make everything worse." Something passes in his eyes, though I don't have time to think much of it as he continues, "I shouldn't have pushed Cole into that. I shouldn't have thought that making the choice for you would fix things."

He pauses, his voice breaking ever so slightly. I can tell he is struggling, and something inside me softens at the vulnerability I am seeing. It clearly not easy to admit that he had done something wrong, but he is doing it, and I can't help but listen.

"I wanted to protect you, Blair. I wanted to keep this place safe. I thought I could do that by keeping it all together; by controlling the situation... but I should have been honest at the very start."

I take a deep breath letting his words sink in, feeling the weight of them press into my chest. For so long, I'd let my fury define my thoughts, wrapping myself in the belief that Eli's plan was nothing more than an attempt to take something important from me. I'd built walls around myself, convinced that the way he went about everything was pushed by some selfish desire to control what was never his to control. But now, as I stand here listening to him, I realise something. I'd been so caught up in my own pain, in the rush of emotions that came with losing control over something that had been my entire life, that I hadn't stopped to consider his side of it.

He never wanted to steal the ranch, not really. He wanted to fix a situation that was falling apart in ways he didn't know how to control. He was scared, more than he let on, and the way of him dealing with this fear – was taking charge, pushing forward with a plan that seemed like the only way out – it was flawed, but it was driven by the honest desire to help.

It's a humbling realisation. The anger I'd held onto for so long starts to unravel, and in its place, there was a mix of gloom and understanding. I can see the desperation in his eyes, the situation hanging heavy over his head. He didn't have all the answers, but his heart was in the right place – even if his actions didn't always reflect that. And somehow, that changes everything.

"I should've trusted you," I say quietly. "I should've known that it wasn't about the land to you. You were just trying to fix something that… wasn't yours to fix."

Eli's expression softens, for a moment, I can see the old Elijah – the one who'd be there when I need him. Though, that's when I think about everything that has happened. I think about Cole and what he's been through. I think about the way they have both been hurt by this situation.

"I can forgive you, Eli." My voice is thick with emotion. "I know you didn't mean to hurt me. But what you did – it's wasn't just about me. It was about

Cole too. And what you did to him... it's not something I could just forget, not yet."

He looks away like he wants to say something more, but the words don't come. I don't know what more he can say. There is a part of me that wants to reassure him that it will be okay, that we can go back to the way it used to be, yet I don't think that is possible.

"I can't fix what happened between you and Cole," I continue. "I can't fix the damage of what you had done to him. But I'm willing to try. I'm willing to forgive you, but it will need time. And maybe Cole won't forgive you. Not now, not ever.

Eli looks down and shoves his hands inside his pockets, and for a moment, it looks like the weight of the guilt is pressing down on him harder than ever before. He nods, accepting what I have just said, though I can see the regret still in his eyes.

"I understand." He mutters; eyes still cast down on the dirt. "I'll do whatever it takes, Blair. I will work for it. I just... I'm sorry. I *never* wanted to hurt either of you."

I don't know what more to say. I've forgiven him, but that doesn't mean everything will be fixed. It doesn't mean the scars are going to disappear, it doesn't mean that Cole and I are fully back on the same page. Though, I have to believe that we are all trying to make things right in our own ways.

Eli stands there for a moment longer, his eyes exploring mine as if he's waiting for some kind of sign, some signal that I'm ready to let him go. But there's nothing more for him to say. He's done what he came here to do – apologize, explain, own up to the mistakes that have remained between us like a shadow. And even though it hasn't fixed everything, even though there's still so much left unsaid, I can feel the weight of those unresolved weeks beginning to lift, just a little bit.

With a deep sigh, Eli takes a step back, his hand grazing over his forehead as he looks at me one last time. There's a helplessness there I've never seen before, a rawness in his expression that makes me ache in a way I didn't expect. It's the kind of look that says he knows this is it, that whatever bridge we had between us is fractured beyond repair, and all he can do now is walk away and hope I understand.

Finally, with a last, remorseful glance, Eli turns to leave. His boots crunch softly against the gravel as he walks back toward his truck, each step measured, like he's carrying more than just the weight of his own regret. The air between us feels charged, still thick with the tension of everything that's been said and unsaid.

As Eli climbs into his truck and drives away, I feel a strange sense of closure settle over me. It's not perfect, and I know that time is still going to be the thing that heals the wounds between us, but for the first time in a long while, I'm not weighed down by the past. The road ahead is still uncertain, but at least I don't feel so heavy walking it.

When I turn to go inside the house, the cool breeze stirs around me, though it does little to ease the heaviness on my shoulders. I can feel the weight of what is yet to come, the long road ahead. There is no straightforward way to undo what has already been done. No magic that can erase what happened between me, Eli and Cole.

The damage runs deeper than a conversation, deeper than an apology or a promise to change. Though, I know in my heart that Eli didn't intend for all of it to unravel like this, I can't pretend it doesn't hurt. That it hasn't changed things in a way I'm not sure we will ever get back.

However, even as I close the door behind me, I try hold onto that last slither of hope that, in time, Cole would eventually find a way to forgive Elijah. He isn't there yet, I can tell. I know how deeply betrayed he feels, how much he has internalized all of this, thinking that Eli's decisions were made without any consideration. But I also know Eli. I know he isn't malicious; he would never intend to hurt anyone – least of all Cole.

The problem is forgiveness isn't something to be rushed. It's not some checkbox that you can simply mark off. It's a process that is slow and painful and requires more than just words. It takes time, and right now time is something we all need.

I lean against the kitchen counter, my thoughts spinning. I hope Eli has the patience to wait for that time. To wait for Cole to process everything. To let the wounds heal before attempting to repair the bridges between them. I hope Cole can find his way back to the Eli he used to trust – the Eli who didn't have hidden motives, the Eli who was his friend. I know it won't be easy, but I believe it's possible.

As much as I wish I could fix everything, I can't. The only thing I can control right now is my own heart, and I know what it needs: patience. Patience with Eli, with Cole, with the past – and with myself. Because all of us are broken in diverse ways, but there's a chance, a small one, that we can heal together, if we give each other the space to do so.

I exhale slowly, letting the weight of the moment wash over me.

Time, I think. Time will tell. It always does.

Chapter 38

Cole

It was that peaceful time of day where everything seemed to slow down. The sun was starting to descent down the hills in the distance, casting Copper Creek in golden hues. For only a moment, the weight of the world felt a little less heavy.

I have been spending the last few hours cooped up in the barn alone, trying to escape the never-ending list of tasks waiting for me on the ranch. Still, with the light starting to fade and the silence stretching, my thought go to Blair's mom and the conversation I knew that would be coming.

I never expected it, the unexpected arrival. She was the last person I thought I would be seeing at the end of my day. Though when she pulled up in her fancy car, I wasn't surprised to see her at all. Always the one to make a grand entrance, no matter how much time had passed.

The sleek, black sedan pulled up with a soft hum, it's polished exterior glistening under the fading sunlight. She stepped out leisurely, her heels clicking sharply against the gravel drive as she walked toward me. Her posture was as rigid and controlled as ever, but there was something in her eyes that seemed... different. Less confident, maybe even uncertain.

I wiped my hands on my jeans, trying to shake the tension from my shoulders as I watched her approach. It had been years since we'd had a real conversation, and every time I'd seen her since, it had been tense – full of unsaid words and things we'd both been too afraid to confront.

Her figure was framed by the fading light, but it wasn't her sharp figure that made her stand out – there was something different about the way she was carrying herself. Something tentative, almost fragile.

"Hey, Cole," she said when she was close enough, her voice was softer, shaky compared to the usual bite I was accustomed to. I could tell she didn't know where to start. "Do you think we could talk?"

I fold my arms around my chest and give a small nod. "What about?"

I watch her eyes flicker, like she was assessing something heavy inside her before speaking again, her gaze shifting as if searching for the right words that had been buried for too long. I could see the conflict in her expression, the subtle squeezing of her jaw as she wrestled with herself, as though saying what she was about to say might somehow shatter something that had been held together for years. Her fingers twitched at her side, and for a moment, I wondered if she was going to turn around and walk away. But instead, she took a slow breath, her shoulders sagging slightly, and then she finally spoke, her voice quieter than before, as if she were opening a door, she wasn't sure she was ready to cross.

"About the ranch. About my daughter. About everything I have done, or rather, everything I should've done differently."

I couldn't keep my surprise from showing on my face. Admitting she had mistakes? That was something that I never thought I would hear, at least not from her. It was always everyone else's fault in her world, not hers. But now, standing in front of me, I realised that maybe she is finally ready to face the past.

My tone is guarded when I speak. "You've got my attention." I wasn't sure where this conversation was going, still, I'm not going to make this easy for her.

She takes a deep breath, steadying herself. "I know thing haven't been... easy between us. And I know I was never around when you needed me. I pushed Blair to sell the ranch. I thought it was the right decision at the time, yet now, looking back, I can only see how I made it worst." Her words hang in the air, each heavier than the last.

My jaw tightens. Hearing the words that *she* pushed Blair to sell the ranch... they hit a lot harder than I was expecting. I always knew she had it in her, still, hearing it directly from her feels like a punch to the gut. This place – this ranch that had been in her family for generations – was a lot more than soil and fences. It was history. And it was like she was ready to throw it away without a second thought.

"What are you trying to say?" My voice is steady, though it drips in frustration.

She sighs, "What I'm trying to say is that *I'm wrong*. And I should have known better than to put that pressure on Blair to let go of something she cares so much about, what cares to both of you." She hesitates before adding, "And I should've been there for you when your father... when things with him started to get worse."

I felt a bitter twist in my stomach at the mention of my father. His decline, his memory slowly slipping away from him, was something I'd been dealing with on my own for a while now. Every time I saw him struggle to remember things – faces, names, the smallest details of his life – it felt like another piece of him was fading, and with it, any hope I had of him ever being the man he once was. *She* had known about it, of course, but it was like she'd turned her back on everything – on the ranch, on her family. It hurt more than I cared to admit.

"Where were you when I need help with him?" The words come out harsher than I intended. "When my dad started to forget everything, when I had to do it all on my own, where were you?"

Her face pales, and I could see that I had hit a nerve. "I know." She mutters. "I failed you. Both of you. I was so wrapped up in my own fears and regrets that I couldn't see what was right in front of me. I let your father and Blair's grandfather carry everything, I stood back expecting it to... work out."

The silence was thick, each of us carrying the weight of our memories, our own guilt. I could hear the faint hum of crickets in the background, and for a moment, I wasn't sure what to say next.

When she finally spoke again, her voice was soft but also firm. "I was shocked when Blair's grandfather left the ranch to her. I can admit, I never saw it coming. I always thought he would leave it to someone else – someone who could handle it better. Yet, when he chose Blair… I was surprised, and *scared*, scared that she wouldn't know how to keep the screws in place to hold everything together."

I watched her cautiously, trying to decipher the woman standing before me. There was something different in the way she held herself – less certain, more vulnerable – but I couldn't tell if that vulnerability was real or just a carefully crafted mask. Was she apologizing because she truly felt remorse? Or was this just another attempt to regain some sense of control she'd lost over the years, a way to justify her actions without truly confronting the depth of the damage she had caused?

The years of distance, of her avoiding responsibility, made me wary of believing anything she said without question. Part of me wanted to see this as a genuine moment of considering, to finally get the closure I'd been needing for so long. But another part of me – one that had been hurt too many times – couldn't shake the suspicion that this was just another one of her calculated moves. A way to make herself feel better about the past without ever profoundly changing.

"It's hard to take something like this on, especially when it feels like everything is slipping away," I say quietly, my thoughts drift back to my dad. "It's not just buildings and land. It's history. And now, with my dad…" My voice faulters, though I force myself to keep going. "I'm trying to hold onto what I can, but

it's getting harder every single day. Watching him forget... watching everything slip away."
Her eyes soften, a look of sympathy strikes across her face for the first time. "I know, Cole. I see what you're carrying. And I *want* to help. I've made mistakes, but I *want* to make it right."
I shake my head with force, feeling a mix of emotions that I can't sort through. "I don't even know where to start with all of this."
"One step at a time." She expresses gently. "We can start by not giving up on this ranch. Not giving up on how much my daughter means to you... and to your father."
I stare at the women in front of me, unsure whether to believe the sincerity of her words. But for the first time in what felt like years, I felt like maybe, just maybe, there was finally room for things to change.
"Alright." I breathe after a long pause. "Let's take that step. Still, it is going to take more than words. We have to show up for each other. It isn't about the ranch. It is about *all* of us."
She nodded, her shoulders relaxing as if the heavy weight she has been carrying for years has lifted. "I will be here Cole. For Blair, for the ranch, everything."
And for the first time, I actually started to believe her.

Chapter 39

Blair

The sun had finally set, leaving behind a soft twilight over the ranch. The air was cool, carrying a faint scent of fresh earth and the lingering scent of hay from the barn. The crickets had begun to sing their evening symphony, and the ranch, which had always felt alive with the hum of activity, now finally felt like it was at rest.

I sit on the porch steps, my legs stretched out in front of me, feeling the cold timber beneath my bare feet. I let my hand rest on the worn wood, the slight roughness reminding me of the past few months I've spent here, how many memories the old house has witnessed.

The ranch has always been a place of chaos and hard work, where the days bled together in a never-ending rhythm of sunrise to sunset, filled with the clatter of hooves, the traces of hay, and the constant hum of labour. But tonight, as the sky turned a deep shade of indigo, and the air grew cooler with the promise of fall, it felt different.

There was a quiet tranquillity, a rare serene that seemed to settle over the land like a soft blanket. The usual noise – the whispering of the wind through the trees, the distant calls of animals – was there, but it felt peaceful now, familiar in the way the ranch had always meant to be.

It was as though everything that had been torn, broken, or forgotten in the past years, had finally found it's place. Tonight, the weight of all the struggles, the challenges, the moments of doubt, had fallen away, and I realised, for the first time in what felt like forever, that it was *home*. Like everything – *everything* – was finally... right.

The sound of boot crunching against the dirt pulls me away from my thoughts. I didn't need to look up to know who it was. I could feel him – the steadiness in his stride, the calm that he brought with him.

A beat later, Cole steps onto the porch beside me, exuding a quiet confidence. His worn jeans, the sleeves of his shirt rolled up to his elbows as always, and that effortless smile of his – one that never failed to make my chest tighten and my heart do a little flip.

"You're still out here?" His voice was warm, like he was genuinely curious, but there was an undertone of affection that I couldn't ignore.

I give him a half-smile, a tiny teasing. "Just enjoying the peace and quiet. What about you?"

He shifts to sit beside me, his knee brushing mine as he lowers himself onto the step. His hand rest casually on the edge of the porch, the warmth of his body transferring into mine. "I was hoping to find you out here." He says, voice dropping ever so slightly. "It's better when you're around."

I turned my head to look at him, my heart skipping a beat at the authenticity in his eyes. There was always a bit of a spark in them, a mischievous gleam that hinted at a roguish side, but tonight – tonight, it was different. The regular twinkle of humour was still there, but it was weaker, like it had been calmed by something deeper, more intense.

The heat in his gaze made me feel seen, as if, for once, I wasn't just another person passing through his life. No, tonight, his eyes were filled with something far more real – something tender and exposed. It was as if everything he had ever kept protected, hidden behind that rugged, steady exterior, was laid bare for me.

There was a quiet force there too, but it wasn't the usual violent fire I had come to know; it was a steady flame, one that held everything that mattered between us – trust, love, and a bond that had only deepened over time. The way he looked at me in that moment told me everything I needed to know. He was here, fully, without hesitation.

It made my chest tighten, and I couldn't look away, because I knew – without a doubt – that this wasn't just a passing moment. This was real. This was *us*.

"Are you saying *I'm* the quiet you are enjoying?" I raise a teasing brow, playfully nudging his shoulder with mine.

He chuckles, a rich sound that rumbles his chest. I feel it down to my toes. "Absolutely. You are the best kind of peace."

I couldn't help but smile. It felt effortless, like this moment was exactly what we needed. There was something about the way he made everything feel so simple, like all the noise and complications of life didn't exists when we were together.

"Do you ever think about how far we've come?" I asked softly, my voice almost tentative. It has been a question that has been rolling around in my head for a while, and now that it was out there, I wasn't sure if I wanted to know the answer.

Cole turns towards me, his rough hand brushes mine before he shifts into a comfortable position beside me. His eyes soften as if he has already thought of it. "Every day. It feels like it happened so fast, but then I look back, and it feels like we've been heading in this direction for months."

I could feel the truth in his words, each one sinking into my chest like a weight being slowly lifted. It was like everything that had brought us to this point – the mistakes, the missed opportunities, the pain, and the joy – had all been leading us here, to this very moment. I could feel the years of distance between us, the silence, and misunderstandings, fading away, like the night gently erasing the daylight. The arguments, the doubt, the struggles we'd faced – none of that seemed to matter anymore. What mattered now was the quiet connection we shared, something that had grown between us despite everything that could've torn us apart.

It was as though every hard decision, every tear shed, every step forward and back had been a necessary part of the journey, and now, in this peaceful silence, I understood. There were no more questions. There was no more hesitation. There was just us – two people who had weathered the storms of life and had come out on the other side stronger, bound together by a love that had been tempered by time.

Sitting together on the steps of the ranch, the one place that had always held both our pasts and our future, I felt it – a deep sense of belonging. The land, the life, the history – it all felt *right* again. The ranch, once a symbol of so much madness, now felt like *home*.

Though, it was more than just the house or the property; it was the people who had come to reclaim it, to breathe life back into it. And as I sat there beside Cole, I realised that *we* had come to love it all over again, just as we had come to love each other. And in that quiet moment, surrounded by nothing but the sound of the night and the warmth of his hand in mine, everything finally felt like it was exactly where it was meant to be.

"Yeah." My words come out slower now, like I was processing them as I spoke. "Like we were always supposed to end up here, with each other."

I peer over at him, my heart swelling with something that felt like both happiness and relief. For years, I had run from everything I was afraid of – the past, the responsibilities that had me tethered to the ranch, even my own feelings. But in this moment, with Cole by my side, fear didn't have a hold on me. I felt like I had finally found my place in this world.

"Well, who would've thought that this ranch would bring us back together?" I say, though my voice is teasing, there is a truth that is buried beneath my words. This place that had always been a constant

reminder of so much struggle, now it felt like a place with endless possibilities. The ranch was never about the land – it was about the people. About us.
"I think the ranch is a lot smarter than we think." Cole says, with a grin. He nudges me back playfully, the familiar twinkle in his eye. "We're just in it for the ride."
I roll my eyes, though I couldn't hide the smile that tugged on my lips. "You're ridiculous."
"But you love me anyways." He replied with a cheeky grin, eyes lighting up with mischief. "That's what counts."
I smile up at him, my heart feeling so full of affection that it makes it hard to breathe. "I do," I whisper, my voice almost like a sigh. "I really do."
His hand finds mine in the dim light, and as his finger thread through mine, it feels like nothing else matters. The world spinning around us – everything that had come before this moment – fades away. There is only us now. And that is more than enough.
"You know, I could stay out here all night with you." I murmur, leaning my head against his shoulder, the words slipping out my mouth before I had the chance to catch them.
"Me too." Cole's voice is low and comfortable, as though he had all the time in the world. He shifted slightly so his arm drapes around me. I melt into his side, my own arm winding around his waist. "But if we stay out here any longer, your mom is going to think we've disappeared."

I let out a soft laugh, the sound barely more than a breath. When my mom showed up unexpectedly, I was caught completely off guard. Sure, we had resolved some of the tension between us in New York, but I hadn't anticipated her showing up here, trying to make amends so soon. There was a part of me that had almost braced for her to keep her distance, for things to stay complicated. So, to see her stand there, clearly trying to bridge the gap between us, felt... surprising. I hadn't expected her to take that first step so quickly, but I guess life had a way of throwing curveballs when you least expected them.

"That's the least of my worries. I'm more concerned about how many barns I still need to paint *'flamingo'* pink." I giggle as I watch Cole roll his eyes.

"I can't believe I allowed this to happen." His lips curl into that crooked smile I adore. "I thought you were here to help the ranch, not turn it into a flamingo-coloured nightmare."

"I'm trying to bring some *colour* to the place, add some flair." I say, trying to hold back a laugh.

His grin widened. "Flair, huh? If that is what you call flair, then I am in a lot of trouble."

We both fall into a comfortable silence, the kind that only comes with knowing someone completely. I could feel the heaviness of the day slipping away, and for the first time in a long time, I wasn't carrying the world on my shoulders. It was never about the ranch, or cattle, or anything that had been feeling like a weight. It was about us, and that is what I needed.

"I think we are doing fine." Cole whispers in my hair, giving my hand a reassuring squeeze.

"I think so too." I hush, leaning up to kiss him on the cheek. "With the ranch, with everything."

The night stretched out before us, the stars above shining brightly, and as I sat there in his arms, I realised that this – this feeling – was exactly what I had been searching for.

We had both made it here, together. And no matter what came next, I knew that with Cole by my side, we could handle anything.

We had each other. And that was all I needed.

Chapter 40

Cole

One month later

The soft glow of golden light settled across the land, stretching far and wide in every direction, casting a warm, almost magical hue over the ranch. It was the kind of light that made everything look just a little more beautiful, a little more alive.

For as long as I could remember, this place had been more than just land to me. It had always felt like an extension of my family – it's soil had shaped me, just as it had shaped my father before me. Every field, every barn, every corner of this place held memories – some etched in joy, others in hardship. The ranch had been the constant in my life, the one thing that had never wavered.

My father had taught me everything I knew, and I had poured my heart into every inch of this land, just as he had. But there was something about tonight that made everything feel different.

The land seemed to hold its breath, as if waiting for something more to come. Maybe it was the years of demanding work, the battles fought both inside and outside these walls, or maybe it was the quiet hope that had begun to take root in me over the past few months. Whatever it was, I couldn't shake the feeling that everything was about to change.

And standing there, looking out over the place I had always called home, I realised it wasn't just the ranch that had shaped me. It was the people in my life, the ones who had come and gone, and especially the one standing beside me now – *Blair.*

The ranch wasn't just a piece of land – it was a place we had both fought for, worked hard for, and finally we can call it our own, our home. But tonight, it felt different – like everything had been building up to this moment, as if all the days before had been pushing us toward this one ultimate step.

I glance at Blair, the women who had not only became a part of the ranch, but also a part of me. She was standing next to me, her fingers delicately brushing mine, her gaze was soft as she looks at the horizon, as if she too, could feel the weight of this moment.

The air was thick with a quiet promise of something new, something deeper than I had ever known.

For an extraordinarily long time, I was content on who I was as a person. The man of the ranch, doing the work, carrying the burden, trying to keep the family legacy alive, and trying to hold everything together. Though, when Blair came crashing into my life, everything had changed. She came in like a whirlwind, disrupting everything I thought I knew about love, about family, and about what mattered the most.

I thought I had to build my life alone, thinking that solitude was the only way to truly thrive, to protect myself from the uncertainties that came along with relying on other people. For years I convinced myself that I didn't need anyone – that distance was the safest option in life. Yet, when Blair came along, everything I knew about strength and independence was turned upside down.

She didn't just slip into my world; she reshaped it. She had a way of breaking down the wall I never knew that I had built. Slowly, gently, she showed me that I didn't need to push anyone away to hold onto my own sense of self.

Blair had awakened a part of me that I never even knew existed – a side of me that wanted to share my burdens, to let someone else in without fear of being judged or rejected. She made me realise that being vulnerable didn't make me weak, it made me human. And more than that, she taught me how to genuinely love and, perhaps more importantly, how to allow myself to be loved in return. She didn't ask for perfection – she just wanted me, all of me, with all my flaws and scars. And in giving her that, I had found something I never even thought I was missing: the kind of love that was deep and real, the kind that was built on trust and understanding, not walls and distance.

My heart tightens in my chest as I look at her, heavy with the decision I am about to make. This wasn't about asking her, it was about giving her all of me – every part of my heart, every broken piece, every scar – and asking her to do the same.

I took a deep breath, trying to steady the racing thoughts in my head. My heart pounded in my chest, and my palms were clammy as I turned toward her, the words I had rehearsed in my mind over and over, now feeling so much harder to say in the quiet stillness of the moment. For the first time in years, I felt nervous – a tight knot in my stomach, a flutter in my chest that made it hard to breathe. It was a feeling I wasn't used to. I was the one who had always been steady, calm under pressure, the one who could handle anything this ranch – or life – threw at me. But this... this was different.

This wasn't just about the ranch, or the land we had built together. It was about something so much more. It was about Blair, the woman who had completely turned my world upside down, making me feel more alive than I had ever thought possible. I had always thought I knew what mattered – work, responsibility, the legacy of my family. But Blair had made me realise that love, real love, was what filled the gaps in all of that. It was the thing I hadn't even known I needed until she walked into my life.

But as I stood there, looking at her, everything I wanted to say felt like it was lodged in my throat. I wanted to tell her how much she meant to me, how she had changed everything, how I couldn't imagine a life without her. But more than that, I wanted her to understand just how deeply I felt, how the way she had opened up parts of me I never knew existed made me want to give her everything – my heart, my future, my forever. And that was what scared me. Because giving someone all of that was something I had never done before, something I wasn't sure I could do without losing a piece of myself.

But standing here, in this moment with her, I realised that maybe – just maybe – this was the one thing worth risking everything for. She was the one. And for once, I wasn't afraid to admit it.

"Blair." I say, my voice low and steady, though inside I felt anything but calm. "I've been thinking about this, about us. About everything.

She turns towards me, her eyes meeting mine, soft and understanding. But I could see a small glimmer hidden in her eyes, as if she knew that this moment is coming, that she felt it too.

I swallowed hard, trying to gather my thoughts, still, my mind keeps going back to the way she had entered my life. The first time I'd met her; I hadn't been looking for anything more. *Hell*, I never realised how *lonely* I was. Yet somehow, she had found her way into my heart without me even realising it.

She stayed when she seen me through at worst. She'd been there through rough days, quiet moments, and the most messy, complicated piece of my life. I couldn't imagine going through any of it without her by my side.

"You've been a part of this ranch, this family, in a way no one else has ever been." I continue, trying to steady my voice, though it is thick with emotion. "You have made me see what really mattered. And I know that this…" – I wave my hand around us, at the sprawling fields, the barn, the horses grazing in the distance – "doesn't mean anything without you. You're the one who makes this place a home. You're the one that makes me feel whole. And I want you to know that no matter what happens, I am always here for you."

I watch Blair's lips tremble ever so slightly; however, she doesn't speak. Her eyes, though, were filled with so much love, of understanding. It was like she knew exactly where I was going before, I got to finish speaking.

"Blair," My voice drops lower, thick with raw emotion. "You have taught me what it means to love. Not just words, but with actions. You've been here, through everything – the good, the bad, the messy, and I have come to realise that life is a hell of a lot better with you in it. I don't want to go another day without saying that you are truly mine. Without knowing that we are building something together.

"I want you by my side, not just for now, but for the rest of our lives. I want to be the one you wake up to every morning, the one I come home to every night. I want to face every storm and every sunrise with you. I want to give you all of me – every piece, every moment. I want to spend every day with you, fighting, loving, laughing, just being together. And I know – I know that there is nothing in the world I want more than that."

My hands shiver as I take a step closer, not being able to wait any longer. I drop onto one knee, my heart pounding so loudly in my chest I'm certain Blair could hear it. "Blair," I whisper softly. "Will you marry me? Can I be yours, for all the days of our lives?"

Her breath hitches, and for a spit second, time seemed to freeze. I watch her eyes widen in shock, but then I saw it – the realisation, the joy, something

else that I couldn't put into words – before she finally whispers, "*Yes.* Yes, Cole."
The words that come out her mouth feels like music, like everything I had been waiting for. It was a promise. And as soon as I pulled her into my arms, I could feel that weight of the promise settling between us, the knowledge that nothing could ever take this moment away from us.
When we kiss, the world around us fades away into the background. In that moment, it is just the two of us, our hearts beating as one, everything we had to fight for led us to this most beautiful, life-changing decision.
"Thank you." I whisper against her lips, my voice filled with emotion. "Thank you for choosing me, Blair. For letting me be a part of your life."
She looked at me with her big, bright eyes that had seen all of me. "Always." She hushes, her voice filled with certainty, "I will always choose you, Cole. *Always.*"
And with that, the ranch – this land, this life – finally felt complete. Because now, it wasn't just mine or hers. It was ours. And nothing was going to take that away from us.
This was our beginning.

Epilogue

Blair

Three months later

The atmosphere was electric with the cheers from the crowd, the harsh stomps of hooves against the earth, and the steady hum of adrenaline as the competition move forward. I could feel the vibration of the energy around me, the kind of charged buzz that came with watching a rodeo – a place with excitement and danger mingled in every moment.

Sitting next to Cole, my hand clasped in his, I couldn't help but noticed the tension radiating off his body. His muscles were ridged, eyes narrowed as he studies his brother from a distance, who is next in line for the bull riding event.

I had grown to know that Milo is a fearless rider, his talent undeniable. He had a natural connection with the bulls, a sort of unspoken understanding that seemed to make him invincible in the arena.

Though, as much as I admire his skills, I couldn't ignore the worry gnawing at my stomach every time I watch him climb into the chute. There was always that underlying fear, a small voice in the back of my head that reminded me how dangerous these kinds of sports are. How quickly it can change from ecstatic to terrifying. The bulls were unpredictable, no matter how much experience you have under your belt, anything can change in a blink of an eye.

I squeeze Cole's hand gently, trying to offer some reassurance, though I could feel the tension in his fingers as he grip tightens in response. His knuckles were white, his hand stiff in mine. I could hear his rapid breaths, and the faint tremor in his hands as he watches his brother prepare for the ride.

I can see how hard he is trying to hold it all together. The sharp, intense focus in his eyes told me everything I needed – this wasn't just another bull ride. This was his brother, flesh, and blood.

And that is what made everything feel so much more real. Danger wasn't something you can brush underneath the rug, especially if it involves someone you love.

"Don't worry, he's got this." I whisper, my voice a little shaky, though, I am trying to convince myself more than him. "Milo's got this."

His laser-like stare doesn't leave the chute. He didn't answer, but I saw the way his jaw tightens and the small beads of sweat drip down his forehead. His emotion were bursting underneath the surface, and I knew, no matter how hard Cole could try to hide it, this was hard for him.

He wanted to protect Milo, wanted to shield him from all the risks of this dangerous life, but he knew better than anyone that sometimes there is nothing you can do.

I squeezed Cole's hand again, silently offering my support. He finally glanced at me, his lips pulling into a tight smile that didn't quite reach his eyes. But it was enough. I knew he appreciated my presence, my quiet support, even if words weren't necessary. We were in this together, for better or for worse.

The gate swung open with a loud crack, and the bull surged forward, charging into the arena with power and fury. Milo was on him in an instant. He was fluid, an expert at his craft, moving with the bull as though they were one.

The crowd was going wild for their favourite cowboy, but my stomach twisted with every violent move of the bull, every buck sending dust in the air.

For a few moments, everything seemed perfect — Milo was riding with effortless grace, his body moving effortlessly with the bull's powerful, unpredictable jumps, every twist and buck in perfect sync with his own fluid motions.

The crowd's cheers intensified around us like a wave, an overwhelming roar of excitement that filled my ears and made the air feel thick with energy. Yet, despite the outward perfection of the moment, the gnawing fear never left me. It always lingered, like an invisible weight pressing down on my chest, reminding me of the fragility of it all. There was always that brief, terrifying moment when the illusion of control shattered, that split second of doubt when I wondered if this would be the time things went wrong.

That tight, aching knot in my stomach, the sudden breathlessness as I watched him soar through the air, could this be the one moment the bull took him off? Could this be the ride where everything changed in an instant? The fear always lingered, even in the midst of the excitement, lurking in the corners of my mind.

And then it happened.

The bull twisted violently, bucking to the side in a way that threw Milo off balance. I watched in horror as his grip slipped just enough for the bull to make a move that sent Milo crashing to the dirt.

My breath caught in my chest; my heart completely stopped.

"*NO!*" Cole shouts, his voice is raw, his body already moving to the edge of the arena, but I couldn't move. I couldn't tear my eyes away from Milo. He was laying there, unmoving, his body twisted in an awkward angle. The crowd went quiet, collective gasps ripple throughout the stands.

It felt like I couldn't breathe, my heart was hammering against my chest as I stood frozen in place.

Please be okay.
Please be okay.
Please be okay.

I repeat the words like a mantra, though the sickening feeling in my gut told me that something was awfully wrong.

I watch as the paramedic rush into the arena and towards Milo. Though, before I could even process what was happening, I saw something else moving amongst the chaos – *someone* running into the scene.

A girl.

She was fast, moving with urgency that stood out immensely. Her camera hung from her neck, swaying with each determined step she took as she weaved through the chaos toward Milo. It bobbed against her chest with a rhythmic clink, a constant reminder that she wasn't here for the same reason as the others. While the paramedics were moving with their usual urgency, clad in their standard uniforms, with medical kits and equipment in hand, she was different. She wasn't wearing scrubs or the usual protective gear that would mark her as part of the medical team. No, she was just... a photographer.

She was dressed in a simple, worn denim jacket over a graphic tee, with dark jeans and sturdy boots. The look screamed casual professionalism – a photographer who was used to being in the middle of things, capturing the raw moments. But in this moment, she stood out like a stark contrast to the sterile, clinical world of emergency response around her. She didn't belong in the way the others did. Her presence was both jarring and captivating, as though the camera was her only badge of identification, her lens a tool for something bigger than what any of us could fully understand.

Despite not being part of the paramedic team, she moved with an air of purpose and authority. There was no hesitation in her movements, no uncertainty as she approached Milo. She had an intensity in her gaze, a sharp focus that set her apart from the panic of the moment. It was as though she wasn't just watching the situation unfold – she was part of it, too.

Every step she took was measured, precise, as if she had been in this very scenario countless times before. Her camera may have been her tool for capturing moments, but there was something else about her that made it clear she wasn't just another onlooker – she was deeply involved in what was happening. And despite not being a medic, she had a way of fitting into the chaos like she belonged, moving seamlessly through it as if she knew exactly what needed to be done.

While the paramedics worked quickly to get Milo onto the stretcher, the girl stood by his side. She moved with them, one hand gripping onto his arm, her face a mixture of concern and determination. It was as though she had been a part of this all along, as if she had been waiting for something like this to happen.

The paramedics carefully wheeled Milo off the field, and the girl stayed close to him, never leaving his side. I could barely hear the conversation between them, but it was clear she was speaking to him, trying to comfort him as he stirred slightly on the stretcher.

As they start disappearing, I glance over towards Cole who gaze is locked onto the girl, expression unreadable.

"Who is she?" I mumble quietly.

Cole doesn't answer right away. He just shook his head, his jaw tight, "I don't know." He finally says, his voice distant, almost lost in the noise of the crowd. "But I'm going to find out."

I watched as he turned and walked toward the exit, the storm in his eyes unmistakable. I didn't know where he was going, but I had a feeling that whatever the answer was, it was going to change everything.

For now, all I could do was hope that Milo would be okay. And pray that whatever was happening, whatever secrets were tied to that girl, wouldn't come crashing down on all of us.

Rodeo Hearts

Be sure to check out the Rodeo Hearts playlist on Spotify!!!

Make sure to follow me on my socials for updates!

Instagram:

@natalietaylorauthor

TikTok

@natalie.booktokk

Acknowledgments

WOW!!! I'm literally screaming and kicking my feet right now. When I first started Rodeo Hearts it was a silly little dream that I thought I wouldn't show anyone. But now, as I stare at my word and page count, it all feels a little too real.
I would first like to thank my mum and dad for supporting me through everything that I do, whether it is something small, or large – like this book. You inspire me to chase my dream, and I will be forever thankful for you both.
I would also like to thank, my best friends, Sian, Naomi, and Chloe. You were my first ever supporters (who weren't family related). The excitement and encouragement that you showed me, pushing me into finishing my novel – I will forever be thankful for having friends like you.
I would love to lastly say, that this book is dedicated to my Nanna. I think about you every day, and I can see you with a proud smile on your face at the fact I have authored this book. I love you so much and we all miss you.

Printed in Great Britain
by Amazon